The Veil and the Crown

Book I

The Stolen Girl

The Stolen Girl

Zia Wesley

Copyright 2014, Zia Wesley
Print Edition published by Zia Wesley 2014
Cover design by Clark Walker
Print formatting by A Thirsty Mind Book Design

ISBN: 978-1499642209

For more information about the author please visit:
www.ZiaWesleyNovelist.com

This book is dedicated to my daughter, Ariane, who encouraged me to write it for more than thirty years,
through many false starts, rough drafts and
personal challenges;
and to all of my friends who read the many iterations:
Ciji, Mary, Carole, Margaret, Barb, Deb,
Rain and Roxanne.
If I've forgotten anyone it is simply due to the fact that
so many years have passed.

Author's Note

The legend of Aimée Dubucq de Rivery, the young French convent girl stolen by pirates and given to the Sultan of Turkey, has survived on three continents for more than two hundred years. There is no disputing the fact that such a girl was indeed born on the island of Martinique in the year 1763, along with one Marie-Josèphe-Rose Tascher de La Pagerie, who later became the Empress Josephine Bonaparte. The latter claimed Aimée as a cousin and told a bit of her story to Marie Le Normand, a noted French spiritualist of the time.

All of the other main characters lived during the eighteenth century, interacted together and participated in the events that are described. I took the liberty of creating some minor characters to help fill in parts of the story that had been lost, and chose the words they spoke.

The prediction of Euphemia David is documented in *Mémoires historiques et secrets de l'impératrice Joséphine* by Marie A. Le Normand, published in France in 1820 and in America as *Historical and Secret Memories of the Empress Josephine* by John Potter and Company in 1847.

When you have finished reading, I hope the story inspires you to do some research and detective work of your own about these two women, and that you let me know what you find.

I personally choose to believe that Aimée did in fact

live the life I have put down on these pages, and that her story, as well as that of Marie-Josèphe-Rose Tascher de La Pagerie, was more extraordinary than fiction.

Historical Characters

Aimée Dubucq de Rivery, who becomes Nakshidil

Marie-Joseph Rose Tascher de la Pagerie, Rose

Euphemia David, The Irish Pythoness, Obeah woman (seer) of Martinique

Vicomte Alexander de Beauharnais

Désirée Renaudin, Rose's aunt in Paris

Eugène de Beauharnais, Rose's son

Hortense de Beauharnais, Rose's daughter

Claire Vergus de Sannois, Rose's mother

Joseph Tascher, Rose's father

The Circassian Kadine, Mihrisah, mother of the heir, Selim

The Kizlar Agasi, chief black eunuch in the sultan's harem

Baba Mohammed Ben Osman, Dey of Algiers, Captain of all Barbary pirates

Nuket Seza, the Baskadine (mother of the first born son)

Mustapha, first born son of Sultan Abdul Hamid

Sultan Abdul Hamid I, Sultan of the Ottoman Empire from 1774 to 1789

Roxelana, Ukranian odalisque who was the first to ever legally   marry a Sultan in 1541

Sultan Suleiman I, Suleiman the Magnificent, the first Sultan to ever legally marry. Reigned from 1520 to 1566

Map of 18th Century Martinique

ISLE DE LA MARTINIQUE

ATLANTIC OCEAN

To Nantes, France

Pointe de la Caravelle

Basse Pointe

Islets des Salines

Saint Anne

Bourg du Vauclain

Bourg du Diamant

Trois Islets

Fort-ROYA

Saint Pierre

Le Carbet

Bourg et Par de la Trinité

Bourg du Prêcheur

Map of Aimée's Journey

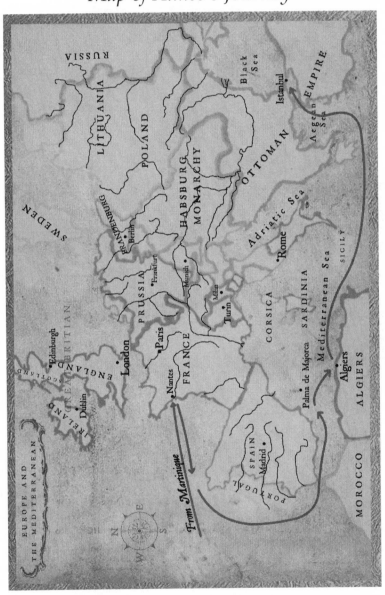

Chapter 1

Martinique, July 30, 1777

Aimée was fairly certain she would burn in hell for the sin she was about to commit. What fatal flaw did she possess, she wondered, that was going to make her do it anyway? How many times had Father Christophe told her that the path to damnation was paved with souls just like hers, born in sin and hoping for redemption? She crossed herself and silently prayed to God to intervene on her behalf; open the heavens, send thunder and rain, something, anything to postpone this evening's imminent clandestine encounter. Could one beg forgiveness in advance of committing a sin? She fervently hoped so, praying silently, "Forgive me Father, I know not what I do."

The sun had just begun to slip beneath the gentle, rolling hills at the western end of the island. As Martinique slid languidly into dusk, Aimée and her cousin Rose snuck cautiously out of Rose's bedroom in the main house of the family's sugar plantation, Trois Islets. Bending low to avoid being seen by yard slaves, they ran across the huge expanse of unkempt grass into the dense underbrush of the island's jungle. The humid heat of the day still hung in the air, making the girls' thin muslin night shifts cling to their naked bodies. They followed an overgrown path through fruit-laden banana and mango trees, their sandaled feet slipping on the remains of rotting fruit. Each step released a heady aroma, fecund and sweetly pungent, a Caribbean blend of island air, ripe fruit and jungle floor. Mynahs and macaws, whose evening rituals were disrupted by the unexpected passage of humans, screamed indignantly to one another from treetops in the canopy above.

Aimée, a fourteen-year-old blonde sprite, scrambled along behind her cousin, trying to calm the fear that caused her whole body to tremble. She bit her lower lip to keep from crying, fearing divine retribution, and fighting her sense of dread at every step. She had never been in the jungle at night, and the only thing more frightening was the fear of losing the approval of her closest friend, Rose. Despite a mere six-month difference in their ages, Rose was fearless.

Unwilling to show the depth of her fear and hoping that her cousin might reverse her resolve to proceed, Aimée asked in a small voice, "Rose, are you sure we should do this? It's getting darker and the jungle is a bit frightening."

Annoyed by the delay, Rose stopped abruptly to face her cousin. She jammed her fists hard onto her hips and leaned in close to whisper. "Why did you say you wanted to come? Hmmm?"

"You know why. I'm just not as brave as you, and Father Christophe says…"

Rose cut her off. "Oh, pooh to Father Christophe. I

don't know why you ever bother listening to him. He's not your real father. You don't have a father or a mother to tell you what to do."

Stung by her cousin's insensitive remark, Aimée's face crumpled and her eyes filled with tears. *It's not my fault that I'm an orphan,* she told herself, *and I'll never be as brave as Rose.*

Rose immediately regretted speaking so callously. "Why must you always do as others wish? Don't you hate it?"

Aimée sniffled in response. Rose took a deep, slow breath and softened her tone. "Try not to be such a baby, Maymay. Now, hold onto my hand. We are almost there." *Why did I insist Aimée accompany me tonight? Because I was too was frightened to make the trip by myself.* Her cousin's constant whining raised her own fears. As if ridding herself of pesky demons, Rose swept her mane of black, wavy hair away from her face and continued to lead the way through overgrown hanging vines with leaves larger than her head.

Aimée held her cousin's hand tightly and stumbled along behind her, bolstered by Rose's strength but still listening to the battle in her head. Another frightening thought popped into her mind, and she asked in a panicky voice, "Rose, what if Grand-mère Sannois finds us gone?"

Rose rolled her eyes in annoyance and continued to crash through the thick underbrush. "She drinks her laudanum and brandy right after supper and goes straight to bed. Hurricanes do not wake her once she is asleep."

Both girls stopped abruptly and gasped as a figure suddenly appeared in front of them.

"Is me," the shadow whispered, as a teenaged African girl moved towards them.

"Mimi, you gave me a terrible fright," Rose scolded. "No one saw you leave, did they?"

"No one see *me*, Yeyette," she replied, using the family's pet name for Rose. "My skin same as night." They all giggled nervously. "But you can't tell no one I take you to dis place or...*i pa bon*, it be very bad for me."

"I will never tell and neither will Aimée," Rose promised, glaring pointedly at her cousin.

Aimée nodded rapidly. She would not wish to put the young slave girl in danger, but *why*, she asked herself for the tenth time, *am I putting myself in danger? Why do I always go along with Rose's deceits?* The battle between her curiosity and her devout Catholicism constantly raged. *Why am I doing something that I know to be sinful? If I confess to Father Christophe, will he tell Aunt Lavinia?*

As they stumbled along, Aimée made one final attempt to discourage her cousin. "Rose, please let's not go. It's almost too dark to see, and I'm so afraid."

Before her impatient cousin could rebuke her again, a small shack appeared in a clearing before them. The three girls stopped, peeked through the heavy foliage and caught their breath as one. In the fading light of dusk, they saw a shabby little house, roughly covered in thatch and surrounded by huge hibiscus trees whose flaming red blossoms had fallen to cover the ground like a burning carpet. The soft, amber light of many candles glowed from within, and they heard the faint sound of a solo voice's singsong chant. Seeing the witch's house heightened their fear—as well as their excitement—and they stood frozen for a long moment before Mimi finally spoke.

"I goin' in first an' tell her you comin'." Before anyone could object, she ran across the clearing and disappeared into the little house.

Rose held her cousin's shoulders and looked into the frightened girl's eyes. "Come now, Aimée. Don't be such a goose. I am not the only one who is fourteen with no prospect of marriage. We made a pact and now we are going to know."

Rose opened a small sack of ground coffee and scooped out a handful. Taking hold of Aimée's right hand, she deposited the grounds into it and closed Aimée's fingers. "Hold that for your offering," she instructed.

Despite Aimée's wish to have her fortune told, she was not practiced in duplicity, and the fear of being discovered at something as forbidden as divination scared her more than the prospect of meeting the old witch. She had never lied to her aunt and uncle before, and could not imagine how they might respond or what punishment they might impose. And what might God do to her? The Bible spoke clearly and often of His wrath against sinners. Would he turn her into a pillar of salt or send frogs raining down upon her head? She crossed herself again and silently prayed, *Holy Mother, forgive me and protect us.*

"Stop that!" Rose hissed. She gave Aimée's arm a sturdy tug, pulling her towards the shack and dragging her up the rickety steps. Once on the porch, Rose pulled aside the tattered curtain that covered the door and the singing stopped. An ancient-sounding voice with the gravelly quality of an old person who'd smoked a lot of tobacco began speaking softly in the island's own *Créole martiniquais* dialect. It was a lilting, musical cadence; poetic and singsong.

"My mout' exhales no poisonous vapor; no flame surrounds my dwelling; no volcano vomits out a sulfurous cloud around me. Dare be no devils here."

Aimée's first thought was how odd it was to hear Creole spoken in such a formal manner. Then, she saw the infamous *obeah* woman: an old mulatto of indeterminate age squatting on her haunches in the center of the small room. This was Euphemia David, "the Irish Pythoness," a renowned fortune-teller both feared and respected throughout the Caribbean. The daughter of a wild redheaded Irish plantation owner and one of his young slave girls, she was revered because her predictions *always* came true. Although the white, largely Catholic population made a great show of denigrating her abilities, many of them secretly turned to her in their times of need. *She is a devil*, Aimée thought, crossing herself and lifting the tiny gold cross that hung around her neck to kiss it. Rose shot her a look of disapproval.

Without looking up from the pieces of white bone that occupied her attention on the floor, the old woman said. "No, *ma petites*, doan be afraid, doan be sorry you have come. Me t'inks you honor me wit' your visit."

She was dressed in Creole fashion, a large multicolored headscarf wound around her head several times, and dozens of shiny gold bracelets stacked up her skinny arms almost to her elbows. A tattered red silk skirt, the remainders of an old ball gown, spread around her in a circle and a worn-thin muslin blouse hung limply on her bony frame. Her wrinkled skin was the color of *café au lait,* her face sprinkled with dark brown freckles. Deeply ingrained laugh lines fanned out from her pale, sea green eyes, and wisps of wooly grey hair escaped the headdress to frame her face. A long, thin, white clay pipe protruded from the corner of her toothless mouth, producing puffs of fragrant smoke. Her gnarled hands moved rhythmically as she picked up and scattered small bits of bone on the earthen floor in front of her. In one corner of the small room, wooden shelves were stacked with hollowed gourds of dried herbs, bones and other necessities of her craft. Several small, empty cages made of woven sticks leaned against the walls, and candles of all sizes, colors and shapes burned everywhere.

"*Vini,*" she said. "Come here," and she motioned with one hand for the girls to sit opposite her.

Curiosity now outweighing their fear, the pair crept forward and knelt on the earthen floor, disturbing a layer of white chicken feathers that lifted into the air and floated around for several moments before resetting on and around them. Aimée wrinkled her nose as the distasteful odor of blood entered her nostrils. It smelled like the yard when the slaves slaughtered fowl for dinner — but she was too fascinated to feel frightened.

Mimi squatted silently by the old woman's side, her eyes wide and focused on the ancient hands manipulating the bones.

The seer paused to look up and honor them with a toothless smile, as her right hand removed the pipe from her mouth and her left palm extended towards Rose. Her green eyes fixed Rose with a steady gaze. "You holden somet'ing for me, *Doudou* [dear one], and I holden somet'ing for you…maybe be your destiny, hmmm?"

Rose placed a small sack of coffee into the woman's palm, and then quickly retracted her own hand to hold it against her heart. The old woman looked from one girl to the other, taking in their striking good looks. *Two beauties like night an' day,* she mused. *Night an' day in more dan jus' looks, me tinks.* She smiled broadly again.

The old woman saw it all. They were opposites in appearance as well as demeanor. *One a dark-skinned Creole: dis girl's nature lives in dose eyes, so passionate for one so young…an old soul too. But de fair one…pure and delicate as a frangipani blossom…silky blonde hair and creamy, white skin…pure French, an' de deepest blue eyes I ever see. Dis one still innocent. She de good girl. This one 'fraid of life 'cause she know death so young; parents maybe dead before she five. Yes, dey opposites and each want to be more like da other. Isn't it always dat way? Everybody want what dey doan have.* She considered all of this while puffing on her pipe and gently nodding her head.

Both girls sat perfectly still as the old woman turned her eerie eyes on Rose. She placed the coffee in a gourd to one side, laid the pipe next to it and scooped up the scattered bones with both hands. Muttering softly into her cupped hands, she closed her eyes, then raised her face skyward and exhaled all of the breath in her body at once. It made an unearthly whooshing sound that caused the girls to gasp and rock backwards. She flung the bones onto the floor in front of her, creating a small cloud of dirt, dust and feathers that rose and then settled as the bones came to rest. Her eyes widened as she deftly moved her fingers over the bones without touching them. "Oh, *chérie*," she whispered, and then studied the bones for another few seconds before looking up at Rose.

Her eyes sparkled as she crooked her index finger for the girl to move closer. When their faces were only inches apart, the old woman whispered, "You will marry."

Rose's hands flew to her open mouth. *I will marry! This is what I prayed to hear.* Excitedly, she grabbed Aimée's hands and giggled. The old woman's words had banished any remaining fears, and they sat transfixed, waiting to hear more.

"You will marry a man of fair complexion." Euphemia closed her eyes, cocked her head and frowned before continuing. "Dis man was meant to be da husban of another in your family."

The girls exchanged puzzled looks. *What does she mean?* Rose opened her mouth to ask for clarification but, as if reading her mind, the old woman continued matter-of-factly.

"Da young lady whose place you are called to fill will not live long."

The girls were shocked by the mention of death. A girl in their family? One of their cousins or one of Rose's two sisters? They did not dare to ask. Their breathing became shallow as they waited for the old woman to continue.

The seeress muttered to herself and shook her head slowly back and forth, poking at the bones and whispering to them in a strange dialect. Then she looked directly into Rose's eyes again and spoke softly. "A young Creole, who you love, does not cease to tink of you, but you will never marry dis boy."

Rose's face flushed deep red as she released Aimée's hands and moved back, widening the space between herself and the witch. *How could she know about William?* No one knew of her trysts with William, not even Aimée.

Aimée's brow furrowed and she shot her cousin a look that asked, *what boy?* But Rose shook her head, shrugged her shoulders and carefully removed a small white feather from her lap.

Euphemia David smiled slyly and nodded her head. "You will have two marriages, *chérie.*"

Both girls shifted their attention to the seeress. "Two?" Rose asked.

"Your first husban' will be a man born here on dis islan but who resides in Europe. Dis man will wear a sword and enjoy some moments of good fortune." The old woman paused.

"And?" Rose asked.

"A sad legal matter will separate you from him, and after many great troubles, which are to befall da kingdom of da Franks, he will perish tragically, an' leave you a widow wit' two children."

Two children. A bittersweet smile crossed Rose's face. *Marriage and children—but first the death of a girl in my family, and then my husband.* This prediction was proving to be far more complex and serious than she had imagined. The gravity of the woman's words subdued her initial excitement.

The old woman's bracelets jangled as she poked at the bones again. "Your secon' husban will be of an olive complexion, of European birt' and wit'out fortune." She paused, unsure of what she saw and then became excited. "Yet, he will become famous and will fill da world wit' his glory, subjecting many great nations to his power." Her voice rose. "Wit' him you will become an eminent woman an possess a supreme dignity." She paused again to let her words take effect as Rose imagined herself a grand lady, the wife of a powerful and important man. The old woman's voice brought them back to the present.

"Da country in which what I foretell must happen is part of Celtic Gaul. More dan once, in da midst of your prosperity, you will regret da loss of da happy an' peaceful life you had here, on dis islan'."

Aimée bit her bottom lip. *I knew I should have resisted Rose in this endeavor. It makes no sense. How can one be great and powerful and yet unhappy?*

The old woman laughed softly. "Lest you tink my words untrue, at da moment you shall leave dis islan', a flame of light will appear in da sky, da first sign of your astonishing destiny."

Euphemia David clapped her hands once in front of her face, then leaned forward to look directly into Rose's eyes and whispered, "You will be a queen, *Doudou*."

Mimi, who had not moved a muscle since the woman had begun to speak, suddenly came to life and screamed, "You gonna be a queen, Yeyette! She say you gonna be a queen!"

Rose and Aimée grinned at each other, then laughed.

With her last words, the withered old hands reached out almost too quickly to be seen and scooped up every bone on the floor in one deft motion. She deposited them into a hollow gourd by her side and fell into fits of laughter.

The three girls were stunned. In a matter of minutes, the old woman had painted a vivid picture of Rose's life to come, which included deaths of loved ones, travel to France, two marriages, children, fame, fortune and regret. The images swarmed in their heads.

The old woman wiped tears off her face, closed her eyes and spoke softly once again. "After having *astonished* da world, *ma chérie*, you will die miserable and alone."

Rose's brow furrowed momentarily, then she shrugged her shoulders. "I shall not care," she said in an imperious manner. "To be a queen in life shall be quite enough." She tilted her beautiful head, nose in the air, *la grande dame* posing for a portrait.

Euphemia David observed the pose and nodded slowly, as if her prediction had already been confirmed. "*Oui, ma chérie, oui.*" Then she turned her gaze towards Aimée.

Rose prodded her cousin to make her offering, but Aimée did not move. After hearing Rose's fate, she no longer wanted to know her own. *What if it was as sad as*

Rose's? She turned to her cousin with pleading eyes, but Rose sighed with exasperation and shook her head. Aimée took a deep breath and cautiously extended her closed right hand towards the old woman.

When their hands met, Euphemia David held Aimée's firmly with both of hers, and closed her eyes. The girls could see the woman's eyes move rapidly beneath closed lids. She turned Aimée's hand palm up and pried it open to reveal the coffee grounds. At the sight of it, the old woman uttered a sharp cry and held on tighter. Aimée tried to free her hand, but the woman held it fast. She moved her weathered face closer to the girl's open palm, and tilted her head slowly from side to side, as if listening. She bowed closer to Aimée's palm and began to speak.

"You will soon be sent to France, to perfect your education," she said quietly.

Paris, Aimée thought, as all her trepidation instantly disappeared. Her heart was pounding so loudly that she had to move closer to the woman to hear her words. Rose and Mimi also moved in closer.

The woman spoke the next words very rapidly. "When you leave dat place, your ship will be taken by Algerian Corsairs who will take you captive. From dare you will be conducted into a seraglio." She paused for a moment to look into Aimée's startled eyes, although she had comprehended only part of what was said, the word "captive." She tried in vain to free her hand from the seer's grasp.

Euphemia David looked back into the coffee grounds and continued, "Dare you will have a son who shall reign gloriously. But da steps to da throne will first have been sprinkled wit' da blood of his predecessor. As for you, you will never enjoy public honors of da court, but you will live in a vast and magnificent palace, in which you shall rule." Again the woman stopped, poking carefully at the coffee grounds and muttering to herself. All three of the girls were frozen by the old woman's words. No one moved or even seemed to breathe.

"At da moment when you t'ink yourself most happy, your happiness shall vanish like a dream, and a wasting disease will conduct you to da tomb."

She turned Aimée's hand over abruptly, dropping the coffee grounds into her own palm. Stunned and confused by the woman's words and not having understood them entirely, Aimée looked at her cousin, who simply stared at her with an open mouth and wide, frightened eyes. Both girls were still unable to speak.

Having said all she had to say, Euphemia David emptied the grounds into the gourd and picked up her pipe. She stuck it into the corner of her mouth and lit it, inhaling deeply. With a mischievous grin on her ancient face, she looked from one girl to the other then nodded her head and said quietly, "Two queens. Me t'inks I see *two* queens in my house today."

The witch's words broke the spell of speechlessness.

Two queens.

The cousins' startled expressions collapsed as they began to laugh nervously. Scooting backwards on their hands and knees, they moved away from the old woman, then stood and ran out of the house. Rose shrieked, "Two queens, Maymay, two queens!"

Mimi followed them out of the house and led the way through the jungle back to Trois Islets. All of their fears had dissolved with the impact of those final words; Rose and Aimée would both be queens. Aimée's fear of retribution, Rose's fear of remaining unwed and Mimi's fear of being sold for her part in the transgression—all disappeared. Who could think of anything bad when they were both going to be queens?

Before entering the darkened house, the three girls held hands in a tight circle and swore to keep their visit and its revelations secret.

"And do not even *think* of confessing this to Father Christophe," Rose admonished.

Aimée looked at the ground and remained silent.

"Aimée? You must agree or we will all be lost."

With the realization that she would be putting them all in jeopardy, she agreed. "Of course. For all of our sakes."

Mimi ran to her quarters and the cousins crept back into Rose's bedroom unobserved. They climbed into adjoining beds, letting down the mosquito netting to make one big gauze tent around them. Then they began to discuss every part of the predictions the old woman had made.

"We will both travel to France." Aimée squealed. "Paris, Rose, truly."

For more than a year, the girls had discussed little else. Nothing ever happened on the island outside of weddings, funerals and baptisms at the church. The annual governor's ball in Fort-Royal was the only social event of the year, and their single experience of that had been hugely disappointing because it was attended by the same people always present at church functions. New faces rarely ever appeared anywhere on Martinique, which explained Aimée and Rose's preoccupation with Paris. Their regular daylong discussions of a future filled with fancy balls, teas, operas and horse races accounted for much of their entertainment.

"Not only will I marry, I shall marry twice. I shall have two husbands...befitting a queen," Rose said grandly, "and dozens of lovers. Why did she not tell about my lovers?"

"Oh, Rose. How *can* you speak so blithely of such a thing?" Aimée replied, embarrassed by her cousin's open sensuality. They fell into fits of nervous laughter.

"And a flame from the sky will burn up my ship!" Rose declared dramatically.

"No, not burn it up, light it up," Aimée corrected. "It will light up the sky I think."

"Ooooh, I can't wait to go to France, but how stupid of her to say that one of my family will die so that I may marry. How perfectly awful to say such nonsense. Perhaps we should not have gone after all," she teased Aimée.

Aimée's fear of retribution suddenly resurfaced. "Do you really think it will come true? Is it the price of our sins for consorting with the Devil?"

Rose thought for a moment, then sagely replied, "Don't be a ninny. She is just an old woman, and only the good parts will come true."

Aimée wanted to believe Rose, but her mind was filled with conflicting thoughts. *Was the woman one of the*

Devil's minions, tempting her with tales of Paris and queens?

They listened to a nighttime cacophony of the island's frogs and crickets wafting through the open windows with the warm, heady scent of datura and frangipani. "Rose, what exactly is a corsair?" Aimée asked.

Rose rolled her eyes at her cousin's naiveté. "A pirate, silly."

Aimée bolted upright in her bed, her eyes wide with fear. "Pirates are going to abduct me and put me in a seraglio? Oh, Rose, what *is* a seraglio?"

Rose doubled over with laughter and smacked the bed repeatedly with her hands. "Aimée, how can you be so stupid?" she squealed. "Don't you know anything?" She flopped onto her back, and pulled the linen sheet up over the lower part of her face to cover everything up to her eyes. Still holding the sheet to her face, she sat up and moved towards Aimée. "A seraglio, my little cousin, is the Sultan's harem."

"Harem? Holy mother of God!" Aimée furiously crossed herself and whispered, "A fate worse than death. Rose, to be amongst barbarians? I knew it was a sin. God forgive me, Blessed Mother forgive me. Witchcraft is the Devil's tool, Rose. We consorted with the Devil and even if her predictions don't come true, we sinned just going there. Oh, why did I listen to you?" she wailed.

Rose climbed into her cousin's bed and wrapped her arms around her. "Don't be stupid, Maymay. No one is going to steal you away from us. And where does the Bible say that it's a sin to know the future?"

"Rose, witchcraft is blasphemy, a sin against God.

They burn witches. We have sinned and will surely be punished."

"Oh, that's what old Father Christophe tells you. *My* Papa says that it's just superstitious mumbo jumbo to scare ignorant slaves. So which is true?"

"I have always believed Father Christophe, but now," she paused and furrowed her brow, "I do not know what to believe and I certainly do not wish to have sinned."

Rose sighed heavily. "Well then, Aimée, maybe you should just become a nun."

"But I would much rather be a queen."

"Of course you would. So, believe what I tell you, silly. Only the good parts will come true."

Rose bounced back to her own bed and Aimée held onto the tiny gold cross at her throat, fervently wishing to believe her cousin's pronouncement. "I would so love to be a queen and wear fine silks and live in a palace with a king."

"More fun than being a nun." Rose teased.

Both girls squealed with delight. They continued to talk and giggle until they were too tired to stay awake.

Chapter 2

July 31, 1777

The following morning, Aimée opened her eyes to the familiar mosquito netting surrounding the beds in her cousin Rose's room. Soft morning sunlight filtered through the wooden shutters that had been left ajar to let in the cool night air. The morning coolness would soon be replaced by burning midsummer heat. She turned her head to the left, and saw that Rose was still asleep. *If I don't wake her I can have a few more minutes to myself,* she thought.

The tragedy and loss of her early life had given rise to a habit of introspection, a propensity not shared with her cousin, who seemed to breeze through life without ever needing to think about it. *I wish I could be more like Rose—so unconcerned with matters of conscience and morality. But, surely this attitude will eventually lead her into the fires of hell—if they haven't already. I must remember to ask what the old woman meant about Rose loving a boy. What boy and why don't I know about him?*

At the moment, Aimée needed time to sort through the events of the previous evening, to find some way to atone. *How am I going to make my weekly confession to Fa-*

ther Christophe without lying when omission is a lie as well? I promised to keep our secret but if I don't confess my sin, how will I ever be absolved? Rose had no understanding of it, but the priest was chosen by her dying mother as the guardian of her daughter's Catholic soul. She felt closer to him than to her uncle, who was seldom home and with whom she rarely spoke.

She crossed herself and clasped her hands in prayer beneath her chin. Squeezing her eyes shut, she focused all of her attention inwardly to the place where she hoped her prayers might gain enough strength to reach God's ears, an image Da Angelique had passed on to her when she was a child. First, she appealed to His willingness to give sinners a second chance. *Dear God,* she silently prayed, *forgive me for I have sinned.* She bit her lower lip to increase her concentration, but could not decide on the order to list her transgressions. *Why did I allow Rose to lead me into temptation in the first place? Why do I always?*

Before she could begin her prayers, Rose rolled over groggily. Masses of wavy black hair obscured her face, and she reached out a hand and gently poked Aimée's side. "Wake up, sleepy girl, or we'll be late for mass."

Aimée quickly unclasped her hands and rested them on her chest. "I am awake, cousin, awake and mortified at my behavior of last night."

Rose sat up abruptly and swept her hair off her face. "Don't be a ninny. It was just a lark."

"A lark you say? How can you? It was a sin, Rose. I know I should not have gone. Why did you make me?"

"No one *made* you do anything, Maymay. You know perfectly well that you were just as curious as I. And anyway, we were not discovered, so what harm can it possibly do?"

"What harm? I am to be abducted by Corsairs and put into a...a..." she sputtered in frustration, "a seraglio."

Rose laid her hand on her cousin's shoulder and lifted her chin to look into her eyes. "Aimée, you can't believe what that old witch said. Not a word of it is true. The woman is plainly a fake, telling us we will *both* be queens. Ridiculous, I tell you."

Aimée's brow furrowed momentarily, but her cousin's certainty always alleviated her fears. *Rose knows better than I,* she told herself. "It does sound rather preposterous. Have I exaggerated again?" she asked. She lowered her eyes in embarrassment. "If she had said just *you* were to be a queen I could believe it."

"Stop worrying, chérie," Rose said. "It's just *vodoun* rubbish...and you're probably right. We should not have wasted our time."

Aimée felt relieved. Despite the fact they were the same age, she always thought of Rose as older, wiser and worldlier than herself. "Truly silly. Of course, you're right, as usual, but I wish I had never heard of such things as corsairs and seraglios. And Rose, do you think she may not be a minion of the devil if she can't really see the future?"

Rose hugged her. "Oh, hush, Maymay. Remember what my Papa says." She neglected to add that her Creole mother believed wholeheartedly in divination and that, on occasion, she herself relied upon the power of the *vodoun* charms her kitchen servants brought from the *vodouisant*, the old herbalist. Catholic mysticism and West African *vodoun* had become so enmeshed by the island's population that they could no longer be separated. Catholic saints and West African spirit gods, or *loas*, had coexisted peacefully in the Caribbean for more than one hundred years, ever since Catholics had decided it was their mission to save the "heathen African" souls.

"I wish I knew what to believe this morning," Aimée said.

"Then believe what I tell you and put this silliness from your mind. You think far too much and those worry lines," she said pressing her finger between Aimée's brows, "make you look like an old woman." Rose bounced off the bed and stood before the open window, stretching her arms over her head in the sunlight. "Isn't it glorious?" She was secretly thrilled to know she would soon be married.

Aimée smiled wanly and nodded agreement, wishing more than ever to be worthy in her cousin's eyes. She adored Rose, and if her wise cousin put no store in the fortune-teller's words, than neither would she.

"Promise me you will say no more of this nonsense," Rose said, hoping Aimée would follow her advice as she always did and forget about the devastating prophecy.

"I promise," Aimée said. She would put the encounter with Euphemia David away like a vivid nightmare and remind herself it was not real.

Aimée continued, "But Rose, what did the old woman mean about you loving a boy?"

Without the slightest hesitation she replied, "Oh, just poppycock like all the rest."

As they dressed for Sunday mass, Aimée wondered about divergent ideas of goodness. Rose thought they had done nothing wrong, but what would Aunt Lavinia and Father Christophe think? Something altogether different she was sure. So, how was she to know for herself? How was it possible to be a good girl in her cousin's eyes *and* in Father Christophe's, when their ideas of goodness were so different?

"And what of the slaves?" Aimée asked aloud.

"What of them? What are you talking about?"

"Well, if we will burn in hell for consorting with witches, why don't they?"

"Because they are not Catholic, silly. They don't believe in hell—not in Catholic hell anyway. Now braid my hair."

Aimée reached out the bedroom window and plucked two gardenias from the bush growing there. She tucked one behind her right ear and handed the other to Rose, who settled herself on a small chair. Aimée asked, "But if they don't believe in it, does that mean it won't happen to them? *We* believe they will burn in hell *because* they are not Catholic."

"Oh stop. It's too confusing and makes my head hurt. What does it matter anyway?"

"Because I know that Mother would wish me to be a good Catholic and to obey the rules of the church," Aimée said.

"Your mother is no longer here to tell you what to

do," Rose replied, frustrated by her cousin's constant whining about goodness and Catholicism.

"Aunt Lavinia *is*, and she always reminds me, 'Your mother would wish you to do this or that,' or 'How would your mother feel if she knew you had disobeyed?' It's just the same as if she were here." *Except something was missing*, she thought to herself. *It really was not the same at all.*

"Aunt Lavinia is so much stricter than my mother," Rose said. "Probably because mine was not born Catholic, but she surely wants *me* to be."

Aimée finished braiding Rose's hair, secured the gardenia behind her ear, and sat down to let Rose reciprocate.

As Rose plaited her cousin's flaxen strands, she silently wished, as she always did, that she were as beautiful as Aimée. *She looks like a living cameo, with her perfect, heart-shaped face, ivory skin, Cupid's bow mouth and that little nose that tilts up slightly at the tip. I wish I had her silky blonde hair. Too bad she doesn't know how beautiful she is. But, who might she impress here anyway? All the important boys are sent abroad to school.*

Rose sighed audibly. She wanted to say how much she hoped the witches' prophecy would come true for her, but could not do so without bringing up the same possibility for Aimée.

"There," she said, fixing the gardenia behind Aimée's ear. "Perfectly beautiful as ever."

Once they were dressed, the girls checked each other's appearance, straightened waists and sashes, smoothed skirts, and made sure they looked their best.

The social highlight of their week was Sunday mass at the local church that served the plantation families. It gave them occasion to wear their best clothes and ride in the buggy, even if there were no young men for them to impress.

As they left the room to join the rest of Rose's family at breakfast, Aimée clasped her cousin's hand and said, "I wish we could live together all the time."

"Me too. I like you ever so much better than my sisters."

"At least you *have* sisters," Aimée said reproachfully. "But Aunt Lavinia and Uncle Jean-Luc could not manage without me."

"Humph, pompous old Uncle Jean-Luc has a hundred slaves to look after them. I don't know why they need you."

"That's unfair, Rose. Had they not adopted me when mother died, they would be childless, and it is a daughter's filial duty to look after her parents in their old age."

Rose rolled her eyes. "Honestly, Aimée, must you believe everything you are told?"

"I suppose I try to. Do you think that sins cause some people to be childless?"

"What an odd question. I'm sure I have no idea."

"Aunt Lavinia thinks so, but hasn't told me her sin."

Chapter 3

Martinique,
August 13, 1777

Two weeks passed following her visit to Euphemia David, and Rose blithely went about her daily routine, secure in the belief that her mother was unaware of the incident—until the afternoon a visitor arrived from Fort-Royal. The woman, a dressmaker, was stepping into her carriage as Rose returned home. Rose entered the house, and saw her mother sitting on the edge of a small wooden chair. *She is waiting to pounce,* Rose thought, as she paused just inside the doorway.

"Have you taken leave of your senses?" her mother asked in a low, angry voice.

"To what specifically might you be referring?" Rose replied.

"Well, I could begin by asking how you enjoyed your little visit to the old *obeah* woman."

Rose held her breath.

"And if that were the only indiscretion that had been brought to my attention, I would probably allow you to explain why you chose to do something so utterly foolish." She raised her index finger, signaling the girl to keep quiet. "But you are not simply foolish, are you?"

She paused dramatically, rising from her chair and walking towards Rose. "No," she growled between clenched teeth. "You are a stupid, stupid girl, Marie-Josèphe," she said as she slapped her sharply across the face.

Rose held her stinging face and tried to speak, but her mother cut her off. "Go and sit," she commanded.

Still holding her smarting cheek, Rose sat in the little wooden chair.

"Do you have any idea how difficult it is to carve a cultured, civilized life out of this jungle island we live on? How your father and I strive to insure the good reputations and social standings of our daughters so they may marry well and, God willing, leave this place? And you choose to carry on with the son of a tradesman?"

"He is of no consequence." Rose blurted out.

"I gave you no permission to speak." her mother fumed. "I assume you refer to his station, in which case, you are quite correct. He is of no consequence...unless of course, someone should learn of the affair and then, you wretched girl, you are ruined. Ruined by a boy of absolutely no consequence." She began to pace back and forth. "I will not tell your father of this...of this boy...because he might kill him, creating an even larger scandal and *insuring* your ruin. I will inform your father *only* of your visit to the obeah woman and no one shall hear another word of your disgraceful behavior. I am confining you to the cellar of the *soucherie* for two weeks and then sending you away to the Jesuit school in Fort-Royal, where you will remain until we may secure an appropriate betrothal on your behalf. Rest assured that I will not burden poor Lavinia with the knowledge that you brought Aimée along on your little adventure. It would send her into a fit of apoplexy from which I fear she might never recover."

Rose kept silent and offered no apology, wishing she could tell her mother how excited she was about the *obe-ah* woman's prediction for her. She wisely held her tongue, knowing her mother was not open to hearing good news at that moment.

~ ~ ~

The cold, dark cellar of the *soucherie*, the plantation's sugar refinery, was Rose's home for the next two weeks. A kitchen slave, forbidden to speak with her under threat of the lash, brought her food. Only two visitors were allowed: the local midwife, who subjected her to a humiliating examination to insure no child occupied her womb, and Father Christophe. The priest received her confession and preached about celibacy as if he didn't already know her soul was damned. Mimi crept over to visit on the nights she was able to, but Rose thought it better to not send any messages to Aimée. It was Mimi who revealed that the information had been leaked by Euphemia David herself, who had been astounded by the revelation of two future queens on her very own island. She proudly bragged of the discovery to everyone she came in contact with, and would continue to do so for the remainder of her life.

The time alone forced Rose to reflect, something she rarely did. The old *vodouisant* had been wrong about one thing. Rose did not love the young Creole boy, William. His low station simply made him safe for experimentation. What she loved was his strong muscular body and his hardness. She also loved his need for her, and his unquenchable passion. It was a delicious pleasure she might gladly have shared with others like him were more to be found on Martinique. In fact, her reflections focused more on her *enjoyment* of the forbidden encounters than remorse, of which she felt none.

Her first intimate experience had been with an old family friend when she was no more than a child. Rather than frightening her, the abuser had been gentle and clever, making the improprieties a sensual game that Rose grew to enjoy. She willingly kept it a secret on the condition that it would continue, which it had until she was twelve and the man left Martinique. The early promiscuity, coupled with her natural curiosity and fearlessness, made her bold in a way that was uncommon amongst her class. It was a boldness that would both serve and undo her in the future.

She also thought about other choices she had made, some more dangerous than the affair, like the herbs she got from one of the family's cooks, a lesser *vodouisant* from the African Gold Coast. Not just the usual herbs to protect her from evil and ward off illness, but the other ones she used to avert pregnancy. *Thank the saints and* loa *they work*, she thought. She took great comfort in the predictions of Euphemia David as well, and spent many uninterrupted hours imagining what her future life would be like in France, with her husband and children.

Despite Rose's silence, it did not take long for the

news of her punishment to reach Aimée through the slave grapevine. The slaves may have been prevented from talking to Rose, but that did not stop them from talking with each other. This method of communication was the fastest on Martinique.

Aimée prayed the news would not reach Aunt Lavinia, taking comfort in the fact that her aunt rarely socialized with anyone because of her "delicate condition" and predilection towards hysteria. Still unaware of the true reason for Rose's punishment, Aimée blamed herself for what her cousin had now to endure. Had she dissuaded Rose, stood her ground, and refused to participate, maybe Rose would not have gone alone. *It was my fault for not following the precepts of the church and for not making Rose follow them too.* Although she could think of no time that Rose had ever heeded her council.

Now that her transgression weighed heavily on her conscience, she prayed harder and more often than usual, making bargains with God with promises of future fealty. She also laid offerings of sweets and flowers on her mother's grave, beseeching her spirit to protect her. Making offerings to her mother in times of need had been a regular practice since the age of five, when Da Angelique taught her how to honor the *loa,* spirits of her dead parents. Many other graves in the churchyard were similarly adorned with flowers, candles, fruits, banana beer and rum, and she never saw this for what it actually was—the *vodoun* practice of feeding departed souls. She did not identify any of the small acts she regularly performed as such—pouring flower-infused water over herself after bathing, wearing a secret *gris-gris* bag of roots and herbs around her neck for protection, or burning the hair she collected from her hairbrush to prevent anyone wishing her harm to use it against her. These small daily rituals were no different to her than her nightly prayers.

The persistent ministrations of Aunt Lavinia and Father Christophe also made her a devout Catholic, fully accepting of the precepts of the Church. After Aimée contracted a dangerous fever at the age of twelve, Aunt Lavinia had kept a prayer vigil by her bed for three days. When the fever broke, her aunt explained that Jesus in his mercy had saved her mortal soul. Later, Da Angelique told her a different story. The offerings made on her behalf by many of the slaves and the charms placed beneath her sick bed had "sent dos evil spirits back where dey belong" and made her well. At the time, Aimée had believed both explanations but now she began to wonder which might be stronger, God or spirits.

She wished to please everyone, but found it increasingly difficult to continue to blindly accept beliefs she had previously not challenged. Consequently, the things in which she normally took comfort no longer soothed her.

She longed to discuss these things with Rose, despite her cousin's lack of interest in such matters. Unfortunately, her only friend was gone, and she blamed herself and felt more alone than ever. She vowed to be more pious, to try harder to be good, because once again, someone she loved had been taken away from her—first her father, then her mother and now Rose. *It must be my fault*, she thought.

~ ~ ~

That evening at dinner, she asked her aunt and uncle if she might join Rose in Fort-Royal. Her uncle's reply was swift. "Absolutely not. I am relieved that she is gone. The girl has become a willful heathen, a terrible influence whom you will be the better without. And you are needed here, *Mademoiselle*. Your aunt is neither well nor strong and you are finally of an age to be of real service to her."

The words chilled Aimée's heart. *Service? Is that all I am? Will I be bound to them forever? If Aunt Lavinia is unwilling to spare me to attend school in Fort-Royal, will she ever allow me to marry?* The last thought gave her a knot in her stomach. Pleading a stomachache, she excused herself, and went to her room to think.

Alone in her room, the importance of leaving Martinique and going abroad to Paris suddenly became clear. *I will be fifteen soon,* she thought, *already too old for marriage in some minds, and what will happen if I remain on Martinique? Even if I were not forced to stay at home to care for Aunt and Uncle, what else might I do? Nothing ever happens here, and I would die of boredom. I suppose I might be a governess to someone else's children. But, I want my own children and a handsome husband who will escort me to grand balls where I shall wear beautiful gowns and dance and dance.* She imagined her presentation at court as she held the edges of her muslin skirt, executed a clumsy curtsey, lost her balance and almost toppled over. *What does it matter if I lack grace, or do not know the latest dances? If I could travel abroad I would master everything. I must convince*

Aunt and Uncle to send me. It is my only hope. But, how?

Aimée had always been an obedient, well-behaved child, out of fear that her aunt and uncle would put her in an orphanage if she were difficult or less than perfect. She never begged or pleaded to get her way. She had no right to argue or to show displeasure in their decisions on her behalf. In truth, she would not have had these rights even if she were their own child. *Therefore, the decision to send me abroad must appear to be their idea. What might induce them to put my wishes before their own?*

She needed to discuss this with Rose, who was so much cleverer than she, but Rose was unavailable. So she asked herself what Rose might do and pondered the question for several weeks, until the solution hit her like a coconut falling from a tree. The only problem was that it required some duplicity. In fact, it would be a huge lie. She struggled with this for another week before deciding to proceed. If she did nothing, she would certainly die an unmarried woman, probably caring for strangers on an isolated, tropical island.

~ ~ ~

The following Friday she made her weekly confession to Father Christophe, as usual.

"Forgive me, Father, for I have sinned," she confessed.

"What is your sin, my child?" the priest asked automatically, with no genuine expectation. Aimée had never confessed anything of the slightest interest to him.

"I am not certain."

"Not certain, eh? Well, what have you done?"

"I have done nothing. It is just thoughts of a sort."

"Ah, pernicious thoughts."

"No, no, Father. Nothing like that."

"Well, thoughts of what nature, my child? There are many types of sinful thoughts." He absently picked at some errant threads hanging off the end of his belt.

"As you are aware, I have a rather large dowry as a result of the sale of our family plantation upon my mother's death." She paused.

He lifted his head attentively. "Yes?"

"Well, my aunt and uncle, out of nothing more than kindness towards me, wish to keep me with them — while I wish for something else."

"Do you presume to know better than your elders?"

"Oh, no, Father, but I would like very much to attend a convent abroad." *At least that much was true,* she thought.

The priest sighed heavily. "And in what way is this a sin?"

"Well, I feel rather ungrateful. Is it not a sin to repay their kindness with my own selfish desire to enter the Church?" She crossed her fingers, legs and ankles, hoping she wouldn't topple over where she knelt.

"Enter the Church? Do you mean to become a nun?"

"Yes, Father, I would like to." *God forgive me,* she thought. *Mon dieu, can I ask God to forgive me when I am lying to his priest?*

"Oh, my. I had no idea. Become a nun," he mused. "And thus relinquish all your earthly goods to the Church instead of to your aunt and uncle? Yes, now I see your quandary." In fact, he understood it very well. He thought of the generous amount of Aimée's dowry, and began to calculate the percentage that would stay with him for sending a child in his ward to a convent.

Aimée knelt quietly, her hands clasped together beneath her chin, squeezing them so tightly that her knuckles went white. She hoped the priest could not hear the wild pounding of her heart in her chest. *Please don't let him see I am lying,* she prayed.

After what seemed like hours of silence he said, "But surely Aunt and Uncle would wish you to be closer to God, would they not?"

She exhaled gratefully, her whole body relaxing. "One would think so, Father. They are such devoted Catholics."

"You have not sinned, my child. It is not a sin to wish to serve God. It is the highest calling. In any case, say five Hail Mary's and one Our Father for the salvation of your soul, and I will think on this matter and speak with your family as I see fit. Go with God."

Aimée left the confessional in a state of elation. *My plan is working. I told a lie to Father Christophe and he did not know.* Her aunt and uncle would never refuse a request that came from him...from her spiritual guardian.

Before leaving the church, Aimée lit a candle and said a special prayer of thanks to the Blessed Virgin. Nevertheless, she suspected it to be the offerings to her mother that had helped her wish come true, for surely her mother would want her to have a family. For the second time she wondered if the spirits of the dead might be as powerful as God. *Is it heresy to even think so?*

How can I be sure which actions tipped the scales on my behalf? Lately, she seemed to be plagued by questions she had never before entertained about God and spirits and morality. She wondered why she suddenly cared so much and if it was because she was almost fifteen.

As she fairly skipped home, she planned and plotted the next steps. Once she was ensconced in a French convent, common decency would require her to pay a visit to her relatives in Paris. Her sophisticated French relatives would instantly surmise that becoming a nun was neither to her taste nor best interest, and present her to all of the most eligible bachelors. *I will pray harder, and tomorrow morning, before sunrise, I will lay more flowers and sweets on Mother's grave. I will not stop until Father Christophe has convinced Aunt and Uncle to send me away.*

She walked home watching the heavens for a sign of God's disapproval, but nothing happened. *Please let it be all right*, she silently prayed, *and let me go to Paris.*

Chapter 4

Even with the help of Father Christophe, it took Aimée six months to sway her aunt and uncle's resolve to keep her with them. She had not needed to tell any more lies as such. She simply imagined a bleak future of familial servitude, rather than her romantic dream of wealth and opulence. This charade transformed her into an unhappy, moping young woman whom Lavinia found intolerably unpleasant.

"Surely, there is something you can say to stop her fits of uncontrollable sobbing," Jean-Luc told Lavinia. "The girl mopes or cries and complains of stomach pains, headaches, and God knows what else. She has become unbearably tiresome, and I find her behavior unacceptable. You must put a stop to it, *Madame*." He saw his future with *two* hysterical women in his house—and that would simply not do. "Please remember," he added, "that she is not our own daughter. But if she were, I would most likely feel exactly the same. So, if you cannot reverse this tide of sentiment, I shall send her abroad and thereby restore some modicum of peace to this house."

"I am not sure I know how to reverse this particular tide, *Monsieur*. But I shall try."

"That is all I ask of you."

But Lavinia was powerless against Aimée's de-
spondence, and the histrionics finally caused her uncle
to make good his word, which turned the tide in her favor.

One night as her uncle retired for the evening, he
announced to Lavinia, "I have decided that Aimée shall
set sail for France sometime in June. I will leave it to Father Christophe to arrange for her attendance in a convent school of his choosing. At an appropriate time, she
will travel to Paris to meet my brother and his family
with the purpose of 'investigating' the possibility of es-
tablishing herself amongst the Parisian gentry."

"Yes, of course," she replied. But her heart sank at
the thought of Aimée in Paris. The girl would no doubt
be dazzled, and quickly abandon her plan to take vows.
She would be lost to Lavinia as well as to the church. She
was unable to express this sentiment to her husband, so
simply said, "You are quite right, *Monsieur*. It is proper
for her to meet her only other relatives."

"Once she has had a taste of Paris, I doubt the convent will still suit her," he mused. "And she surely will
not want to return here. Perhaps they might find an appropriate husband for her. Sophie is at the pinnacle of
Parisian society, and Aimée desirable in many ways. She
is a tenth-generation aristocrat, after all, despite having
been raised in this colonial backwash. And her dowry is
substantial enough to be attractive to suitors lacking
money. She may even do well."

Lavinia thought *I could have told you that*, and then
said aloud, "But Parisians are so treacherous towards
outsiders; even to their own, for that matter. As lovely as

Aimée appears, she is still a country girl with no social graces or idea of how to comport herself in polite society. She may feel awkward and out of place."

"Yes, quite true. Well, sink or swim, she must meet them anyway. It would not do for her to be on the continent without contacting them. They might think they were being overlooked. I'll post a letter to Antoine next week."

There goes any chance of her ever coming home, thought Lavinia. *Who will be my companion now?*

~ ~ ~

Aimée was ecstatic with the news, and now that her departure was imminent, Lavinia began to wish the best for her, albeit for selfish reasons. If the girl made a fool of herself amongst her husband's family, whom would they blame for her lack? Lavinia, of course. She did not wish to be blamed for the girls' shortcomings.

Lavinia explained, "You know so little of society, Aimée, but I think you may find it more stimulating than you can possibly imagine. Uncle feels it would be a mistake to choose to devote your life to God without first experiencing a bit more of life."

Aimée was thrilled by these words, and smiled broadly at her aunt. Yes, she craved exactly that. She had been praying for this conclusion, and now that their goals were aligned, perhaps she might feel less guilty about her pretense to become a nun.

"Oh, yes Aunt," Aimée enthusiastically replied. "Having known so few of my family, I look forward to meeting my father's other brother and his wife. I shall welcome the opportunity to meet them and to visit Paris."

"Your Aunt Sophie will arrange introductions for you to all the best people in Paris. She is quite the social butterfly, and such introductions are the only way to assure any social success. Parisians are meticulous in their social hierarchy and customs. But if properly managed, these should yield an ample number of potential suitors."

Aimée heard the word "suitors" and her heart soared.

~ ~ ~

Weeks of preparations followed. Two of the island's best seamstresses artfully created an entire new wardrobe: six day dresses for travel and the convent, with two pairs of sturdy shoes for negotiating country grounds and the cobbled streets of Paris, gloves, hats, waistcoats and purses to match the day wear and six fully accessorized evening ensembles for formal dinners and social gatherings. Two formal gowns, with matching satin slippers and shawls, were fashioned for balls and the opera, which was currently all the rage. Aimée felt like a princess. She was enchanted by the finery, and thrilled to think of wearing them all in Paris. Secretly, she considered them her trousseau.

Father Christophe enrolled her in the *Couvent de la Visitation* in Nantes, in southern France. As it was unacceptable for a young lady of her stature to travel alone,

Da Angelique would accompany her on the journey and serve as her personal maid in France. She was no longer a child. She was a young French aristocrat, a young lady of substance and worth.

When all was finally ready on the day of her departure from Fort-Royal, her trunks were loaded onto the ship that would take her to France. "I shall miss you every day, Aunt Lavinia, and I pray for your continued good health. Thank you so very much for all you have given me and for this gift." They embraced, and Lavinia wiped a small tear from one eye.

Jean-Luc extended his hand to her as he would a son, tipped his hat and said, "Safe journey."

Tears poured from her eyes as she hugged her cousin Rose. "Promise you will write me with all the news, Yeyette," she implored. "I will miss you so very much."

"I promise I shall. And remember," Rose whispered into her ear as she kissed her damp cheek, "I will be there one day soon also." It was the first time in more than a year that a reference to Euphemia David's predictions had been made, and Aimée was so excited by the prospect of her voyage it did not disturb her.

"Yes, dear cousin," she whispered back, "we shall be in Paris together."

Chapter 5

Le Couvent de la Visitation,
Nantes, France
August 1779

Eight weeks later, after an uneventful voyage on a French passenger ship that also carried sugar, Aimée and her companion arrived at the *Couvent de la Visitation* in Nantes. The short carriage ride from the docks passed through the most beautiful countryside Aimée had ever seen, and both were surprised that the slave had been permitted to ride in the carriage rather than on the seat with the driver. They drove through rolling green hills, the tallest of which were crowned by towns with extraordinarily high stonewalls. On the fertile flatlands, small thatched houses sat in the midst of orderly fields of wheat and barley, or orchards and vineyards heavy with fruit. The sky was deep blue with only a few small, puffy white clouds, and the air felt comfortably dry and warm.

Aimée and Da Angelique were the only passengers in the open carriage, and in less than an hour's time, they passed through the cloistered walls of the convent and rolled to a stop. As the footman helped her to step down, Aimée closed her eyes and took the first deep breath she had taken in months. She drank in the warm, fragrant air and felt immediately welcomed. Then she giggled. *How funny it is to arrive in a convent, filled with the hope of meeting a husband,* she thought.

It was mid-summer, and the well-kept grounds were a verdant green. She looked up at the church's bell tower rising majestically into the sky, and thought it might be high enough to send her prayers even closer to God's ears. All of the buildings were constructed of dark gray granite blocks with small, deeply set windows imbedded high in the walls. The church was the tallest structure in the complex, with two long, single-story buildings stretching out from either side. Wisteria vines shaded walkways between the buildings, their sweetly scented purple flowers drooping down like a floral veil. The heady scent of the blossoms reminded her of home, and she thought, *I am going to be happy here.*

Turning to Da Angelique she said, "Isn't it lovely?"

The sturdy slave surveyed the landscape and frowned. "Dis look like da prison in Fort-Royal," she said. She was a short woman, almost as wide as she was tall. The darkness of her ebony skin was enhanced by the riot of color she wore on her head—a traditional headscarf, wound around her head several times and knotted on the side. She shook her head imperceptibly, unable to find any beauty in the bleak, foreign place. Her feet, enclosed in full leather shoes for the first time in her life, pained her terribly, and she hoped the climate would remain warm enough to not have to wear them at all. "Where everybody?" she asked. "Why nobody here t'meet you?"

"Hush now," Aimée said. "Make sure they unload all of my trunks."

Aimée liked the look of the manicured grounds, neatly laid paths, geometric buildings and, mostly, the neat and tidy rows of trees and flowerbeds. No jungle vines encroached and entangled the buildings or would reach out to grab one's ankles as one walked. No screaming mynahs or macaws disturbed the carefully managed silence. Instead, a soft, yawning quietness seemed to envelop her, making her feel safe. All of these thoughts and impressions flooded her mind at once, and her outward response was a wide, spontaneous smile. However, she was not prepared to feel the ground rocking beneath her feet. Da Angelique took hold of her arm to steady her, but found herself off balance as well. After an eight-week voyage, their bodies still rocked to the rhythm of the ship on the water.

They stood swaying on solid ground as the coachman unloaded Aimée's trunks and drove away. The Mother Superior approached, her hands folded inside the sleeves of her habit. Her long, milky-white face looked painfully squeezed by her starched wimple, and the thin lips of her hard mouth seemed to press together in disapproval. She removed her hands from the sleeves and extended them forward to greet Aimée. When their hands clasped, Aimée was surprised to find that on this warm, sunny day, the nun's hands were icy cold.

The Mother Superior arranged her face into what she hoped might resemble a smile, and said, "Welcome to the *Couvent de la Visitation*, Mademoiselle de Rivery."

Aimée observed that the woman spoke without

seeming to move her lips. "Thank you, Mother."

The Mother Superior immediately turned and began walking briskly.

Aimée walked unsteadily beside the nun as they spoke. "I am afraid that I feel rather unsteady on my feet," she said.

Without slowing her pace the nun replied, "Yes, it will take several days for you to adjust to being on land after such a long voyage. You may feel quite nauseated when lying down as well."

"Oh," was all Aimée could think to say.

"You are not the first girl from Martinique to stay with us, you know. Several years ago Margot de la Sort came to us for a period of two years. A fine young lady from an excellent family. You must know them."

"I know of the de la Sort family, but did not know Margot, as she was much older than me."

The Mother Superior stopped abruptly and faced Aimée. "'Than I,' child. 'She was much older than I...*was*,' you see?" she corrected. *Mon dieu, her accent is deplorable; this girl is here to stay,* she thought. From as far away as twenty paces she had seen that Aimée would never attract a sophisticated suitor. She was beautiful but without grace, and those clothes. The Parisians would devour her, and then spit her out, after which she would make a *perfect* novice. *Her sizeable dowry will help me to build the new rectory,* she thought—and almost smiled.

Aimée flushed bright red. She was not accustomed to being corrected. Hoping to make a good impression, she hid her embarrassment and simply replied, "Yes, thank you, Mother."

"Remember, you are here to learn. It is our goal to improve all aspects of your demeanor."

"Yes, Mother." *So that I will make a good wife*, she reminded herself. She had already decided that she would endure anything (even criticism from an ice-cold nun) to achieve her goal. Then she silently chastised herself for thinking ill of the woman. *She is a servant of God, and I need all of his help I can get.*

The convent was much larger than Aimée had imagined. Besides the hundred pupils, the Mother Superior explained, it housed an additional thirty widows, along with forty nuns and novices who ran the convent and taught the classes.

As a young nun approached them, the Mother Superior said, "This is Sister Constance. She will show you to your quarters and then take your maid to hers. Constance, this is Mademoiselle de Rivery. I will leave you now and see you at vespers."

Constance was a chubby young woman with so many freckles that at first her skin appeared to be rusty brown. Her bright, cinnamon-colored eyebrows told Aimée she was a redhead. "Welcome, *Mademoiselle*," she said with a genuine smile, taking Aimée's elbow to help steady her as they walked. "I am sure you will like it here," she assured. "I came here four years ago to study, like you, then last year decided to stay and take vows. The food is wonderful."

Aimée smiled at the thought that cuisine may have been the deciding factor in the girl's choice to serve God. However, she was sincerely pleasant, almost jovial, and talked nonstop. "You must tell me all about Martinique. I have never met anyone from anywhere off the continent. How exciting it must be to have grown up on an island. Are there jungles and wild animals?"

Aimée tried to answer, but the girl barely left space between her questions, which made Aimée giggle.

Constance gave her arm a squeeze, and said, "I know we are going to be such good friends." With a bouncing step and a slower pace than the Mother Superior's, she led Aimée to one of the tiny rooms in a long two-story building. Aimée looked up at the window set high in the wall. "Why are the windows so high?" Aimée asked.

"Well," Constance recited the reply by rote, "the purpose of the window is to allow light *in*, but our focus here is inner contemplation, so one has no need to look *out*." She paused, and then said with a wink, "It also prevents *anyone* from looking in."

Surprised by the young nun's wink and inference, Aimée opened then closed her mouth and smiled. She supposed that one could follow a holy calling and still be humorous, although this was her first experience of such a person, and she liked her immediately.

~ ~ ~

Aimée quickly settled in to convent life and agreed with Constance that the food was indeed exceptionally good. Her days began and ended with a long mass, filled in between with lessons in Latin, French, history, literature, art and music as well as the more practical arts of sewing and embroidery. She even learned to weave on a small handloom. The classes that prepared the girls for marriage were the most enjoyable. However, being a convent, the preparations did not include the "private" aspects of marriage, which were never mentioned. Had she not been raised in the country, she would have remained ignorant of their existence.

Unlike her cousin Rose, Aimée had subverted all of her sensual adolescent urges, confessed all sinful thoughts regularly and tried to follow the dictates of the Catholic Church in all matters regarding chastity of thought and deed. The task had been a difficult one on Martinique, where she had been surrounded by the "wanton" leanings of the Creole and slave populations. In the convent, she felt comforted being in the company of other girls who felt the same way as she. Or so she believed.

Aimée sang in the choir, her full, alto voice seeming incongruous with her petite frame. She often accompanied herself on the harpsichord. Sometimes, widows who resided there gave her sheets of their favorite music, and in this way, Aimée became familiar with a variety of musical styles, as well as songs in German and Italian. She was surprised to discover that she had an excellent ear for languages, picking up inflections and intonations very quickly. She was even more surprised to learn that the *Créole martiniquais*, the French Creole dialect she had grown up speaking, was quite different from the way French was spoken in France. It seemed that every time she spoke, someone corrected her, and for the first time in her life, she began to feel that she might be wanting as a person. On Martinique, she had rarely been corrected in anything—it now seemed that everything she did was wrong. This new insecurity made her feel shyer than ever and she began to doubt her own value. *What if prospective suitors find me wanting?* She tried harder than ever to learn what anyone said she must and to please those around her, the fear of not being good enough driving her while it chipped away at her self-esteem.

The only men ever present in the convent were visiting priests or grown sons making relatively rare visits to aging mothers. The thought that one of the latter might be an eligible widower had crossed Aimée's mind, but most were too old for serious consideration. She still dreamed of a dashing young man who would introduce her to the pleasures of Parisian society and romantic love, two things about which she actually knew almost nothing.

As a young girl, Aimée's romantic notions had been gleaned from old French newspapers that had survived the long voyage to Martinique. She was fascinated by the illustrations of fine ladies bedecked in the latest fashions. They helped her to imagine herself similarly dressed at sumptuous balls, dancing the latest dances with dozens of handsome young men. Such fantasies had occupied many hours of boring days at sea, and she was already planning her first trip to Paris, where she imagined being the belle of the ball, charming and dazzling everyone she met.

Chapter 6

Three months after her arrival in France, Aimée's fondest dream was about to come true. She was going to Paris to visit the uncle and aunt in whom she placed so much hope but had known only through letters. Antoine Dubucq de Rivery was her father's younger brother, and Aimée believed that his wife, Sophie, held the key to her future happiness. She felt sure that through Sophie's introductions she would meet her future husband.

Aimée fussed and fretted to choose her most fashionable wardrobe for the trip. She would take only her newest frocks, hats and shoes that had been made in Fort-Royal, with Aunt Lavinia's promise that they "echoed" current Parisian fashion. She assured Aimée that the seamstress, shoemaker and haberdasher had done marvelously well with the caveat, "Parisian fashion is so capricious that by the time you arrive, it may well have changed."

Now, in the confines of her tiny room, Aimée tried on each ensemble, feeling certain of their magnificence, despite the lack of a proper looking glass. In fact, they were more stylish and sophisticated than anything she had ever worn and made her feel like a princess.

Da Angelique packed each article of clothing with reverent care. "You gonna be *tres, tres belle, Doudou.*

Mmm mmm. No more islan' gull in dese. You a fine, propah lady now. "

"One hopes," Aimée replied studying herself in the tiny mirror that Da Angelique held for her. She pulled in the corner of her lower lip, biting it with her upper teeth, an unconscious gesture she resorted to when nervous. Her longing for a husband and family had grown even stronger within the confines of the cold convent walls. *Please let me meet him in Paris*, she silently prayed.

~ ~ ~

On the following day, Aimée and Da Angelique boarded a coach for the two-day trip to Paris that stopped in Nantes, where Aimée's ship had docked. There they picked up three other passengers: a middle aged man and his wife who were returning to Paris from their summer home nearby, and an older gentleman going to visit his ailing sister. As they headed north, the coach bounced uncomfortably through gloriously lush French countryside, fields of barley, flax, sunflowers and lavender, vineyards and chateaux. Aimée had never seen such fine, large homes and marveled at the fact they were all made of stone. The married couple was friendly towards her and offered a wealth of information about each area they passed through. The conversation and scenery were almost enough to distract her from the discomfort of the ride, but on the second day, as the coach approached the outskirts of the city, the view began to change drastically. Green fields gave way to muddy enclaves of makeshift shacks overrun with shabbily dressed people, mangy livestock and piles of garbage.

"Surely, this can't be Paris," Aimée said. "Who are these people and why are they here?"

"Millers, butchers, tradesmen and the like," the husband explained.

The road became narrower and rougher, strewn with garbage, urine and dung from the rickety carts that traveled to and from the city. As the progress of the coach slowed, people with filthy clothing and faces watched its passage, sometimes calling out crude greetings to the passengers.

"*Salut, mon ami,*" a toothless woman dressed in rags called out as she lifted the front of her filthy skirts. "*Je t'aime beaucoup,* I love you a lot. Anyone tired will find some peace here. For a very small price too."

Embarrassed, Aimée caught the eye of the wife, who raised her brows and shrugged her shoulders as though the woman's behavior was commonplace. The other passengers turned their faces away from the open windows and lifted scented handkerchiefs to their noses. Da Angelique retrieved two of the same from her large travel bag and doused them with lavender scent before handing one to Aimée and then pressing the other to her own offended nose.

As they entered the city, the streets became even narrower and more crowded. Aimée glanced up at a shabby two-story tenement just as a woman flung the contents of a chamber pot onto the street before them. Dozens of grime-covered children ran alongside the coach in the sewage and muck, their hands extended, begging for coins to be thrown to them. Shabby crowds mingled at open butcher stalls displaying fly-covered hanging carcasses of pigs, lambs, chickens and goats, some in advanced stages of decay, while the butchers slaughtered and skinned animals right in the street. Acrid smoke from cooking fires rose to blacken the air and bring tears to the eyes.

Aimée pressed her scented handkerchief more tightly to her face, her stomach beginning to rise in her throat. "Oh, the stench." she exclaimed. "Why are they so poor and dirty?"

"The king has sent our armies and all our money to the colonies in the New World to fight the British," the older man replied contemptuously. "And doing that not more than ten years after losing the Seven Years War. The fool is bankrupting us to save the colonials, damn his soul. Ridiculous, if you ask me," he added. "And for what? No one will ever travel that far abroad to an empty land full of hostiles. Stupid waste, just like everything else he does."

"It's that queen's fault," his wife added. "Damn foreigner."

Aimée could see the man's point, despite having grown up in what most people thought was a colony. Martinique was technically "an overseas region" of France, and all its inhabitants' full French citizens. Very few French ever visited Martinique, and fewer still relocated there.

"Is this truly Paris?" she asked.

"A good part of it," he replied. "It's not all like this, and one becomes accustomed to it after a while. You're going to one of the most fashionable sections, which is quite lovely."

It was difficult for Aimée to imagine a "lovely" area anywhere within the landscape she observed. In the near distance the tall smokestacks of a large factory—a tannery perhaps—belched clouds of dark brown smoke, giving the air an ochre pallor. Aimée's mythical dream of Paris was crumbling before her eyes. The poverty and filth seemed to go on forever, with ramshackle buildings of rotting wood, chimneys spewing coal smoke and beggars of all ages. Nothing looked as though it might be able to stand very much longer...neither buildings nor people. The site hurt not only Aimée's eyes, stomach and nostrils; it broke her heart.

But true to the passenger's word, as the coach moved on the street gradually became wider and smoother, bordered on the right by the River Seine. A long avenue of beautiful homes appeared behind tall, graceful wrought-iron fences, and well-dressed pedestrians replaced the ragged throngs on the streets. Within moments, everything had acquired a stately orderliness.

Aimée felt a flood of relief. "Oh, look, Angelique. Here is the Paris I dreamed of."

She drank in the beauty of the stately houses and fine carriages traversing the street, quickly forgetting the squalor through which they had just passed. However, the stench was not barred from permeating even the best neighborhoods. In fact, the smell of Paris seemed to follow them everywhere.

The coach came to a stop in the center of a block in the eighth *arrondissement* on the fashionable *Rive Droite*.

It was a three-story house elegantly designed of granite block. Copper gutters and ornate wrought-iron trim bordered the steep mansard roof. Six unusual windows that looked more like covered doorways marched proudly across the topmost floor.

Aimée had never seen anything like it. Her eyes opened wide as she made to step from the carriage. With the help of the footman, she descended the steps and looked up at the house again to see a liveried servant open the elaborately carved black front door. In the following moment, two people who must be her aunt and uncle filled the doorway. Posed gracefully in a studied stance, his left arm raised waist height with hers resting lightly upon it, they were the most magnificent human beings Aimée had ever seen. Their clothes were a compilation of soft pastel satins, silks and lace, their hair (actually wigs) masses of platinum curls piled high and cascading past their shoulders. Sophie's coiffure was adorned with ribbons, silk flowers and pearls. Their faces were the purest white, each with a black beauty mark beneath the left cheekbone, and perfect little cupid's bow mouths painted the color of deep, claret wine.

There the young girl stood, mouth open and gaping at the splendor of her relatives and their elegant home, thinking them every bit as glorious as the King and Queen. *They are more beautiful than I ever imagined*, she thought, as she ascended the marble steps where her aunt and uncle greeted her formally with a curtsey and bow. Had anyone asked her at a later time to describe their faces, she would have been unable to do so, as she had been so thoroughly enchanted by their costumes.

Aimée's uncle kissed the air on either side of her cheeks without actually touching them, welcomed her to his home with a few formal words and then retreated to the interior of his house. She would see him only occasionally during the next month.

"Welcome, niece," Aunt Sophie cooed, hiding her shock at the girl's appalling appearance, and guiding her through the rococo foyer into the formal drawing room. Aimée continued to openly gape at the opulent surroundings: silk covered walls and gilded furnishings, crystal chandeliers, marble fireplaces and satin brocade drapes. She was unaware that Sophie had taken an instant accounting of her and had audibly sighed.

Well, Sophie thought, *what could one expect from a girl raised in the wilds of a pagan island colony?* Her own youngest son, Henri, a commissioned officer serving in the King's army, was at that moment in the American colonies fighting that ridiculous war, and his letters home told tales of savages and the rough life one was forced to abide in the New World. *Well, at least the girl has a natural beauty. With that and her substantial dowry, I* might *be able to transform her into an acceptable young lady worthy of introduction, if not at court, certainly to my well-chosen clique of personal friends. Mon dieu, this is going to require an enormous effort.*

"I trust your trip went well," Sophie said aloud. "No untoward occurrences or mishaps along the way?"

Before Aimée could pull herself together enough to answer, Sophie continued. "The first thing we must do is make arrangements to have some proper gowns fashioned for you. You are too lovely for words, but that ensemble you are wearing, *tsk, tsk, tsk,*" she intoned, shaking her head slowly from side to side. "It will never do in Paris."

Aimée was tongue-tied. She would readily admit that her dress could not compare to the magnificent one worn by her aunt. Moreover, the woman's matching satin slippers with silver buckles were the finest she had ever seen. Her aunt even carried an ebony walking stick with an intricately carved silver head. *This* was what Aimée dreamed of in her fantasies of Paris. For all she cared, her fashionable relatives could burn every piece of clothing she owned.

"As you wish, Aunt," she was finally able to reply.

Sophie seated herself on a tiny gilded chair with a dark green velvet cushion, and indicated a similar chair opposite to Aimée. Hanging on her aunt's every word and paying no attention to where she was about to sit, she plopped her bottom down and tipped dangerously to the left, almost falling. She righted herself by flailing her arms and then grasping the seat of the chair to steady it. Sophie gasped audibly and clutched her breast.

Aimée flushed. "Oh my goodness," she giggled. "I did not realize how small it was."

Sophie did not smile in response. She regained her composure by speaking in a measured tone that signaled her displeasure at her niece's gauche behavior. "Imagine," her aunt said slowly, "perching—like a tiny bird on a branch. Softly… gracefully… now, up, up." She indicated with one hand that Aimée should rise. "Please, try again."

Wanting very much to please her exquisite aunt, Aimée rose, and then looked back over her shoulder to assess the size and placement of the small chair.

"No, no, no!" Sophie commanded, knocking her stick on the floor sharply. "Never look behind yourself. Walk away a few steps and approach the seat again as if you are entering the room for the first time."

Aimée did as she was told and began to sit down.

"Your skirt, child," Sophie barked. "You must first lift and fan out your skirt."

Aimée bent forward and awkwardly clutched her skirt with both hands.

"No, no, child," Sophie scolded, and then stood up to demonstrate. "Place the toe of your left foot slightly forward for balance, then bend only your right knee, like so. Gather your skirts gently and lift them. One must *alight* upon a seat, rather than," she searched for the word, "plop. You see?"

Aimée nodded, then copied her aunt's example and found herself indeed "perched" upon the little chair. She smiled broadly at her own accomplishment.

"Better," her aunt said, "but please make an effort to smile less broadly, and never with an open mouth. To smile or laugh with one's mouth open is coarse. It also distorts the contours of the face and conveys far too much emotion."

Too much emotion? Aimée thought. *This is going to take an enormous amount of effort.*

Sophie continued. "I cannot stress enough the utter importance of proper comportment. When amongst polite society, one never knows *whom* one may meet, and one does not wish to convey the wrong impression."

Long before Aimée's arrival, Sophie had spent many hours arranging for her to meet an appropriate assortment of suitors and to attend countless numbers of social events. Now, having actually seen the girl, her mind reeled with everything she would need to do to make her presentable. It would not do to have Aimée cast as a "country bumpkin," which reflected poorly on her sponsor. The girl's appalling manners must be dealt with immediately and, clearly, an entirely new wardrobe would need to be ordered. That would take a week or more. Sophie's mind whirled with plans. While the clothing was being made, she would need lessons in social graces, manners and elocution. *Mon dieu, there was so much to do.* She was going to need several weeks.

However, Sophie's facial expression did not reveal her mental machinations. She was well past her prime, but still considered beautiful. She gracefully extended her right arm to the wall behind her and gently pulled the tasseled end of a thick, woven cord. Before she had replaced her hand in her lap, a liveried servant entered the room and stood just inside the doorway.

"Yes, Madam?" he said without looking directly at Sophie.

"Summon my dressmaker and tell her to come *immediatly*."

"Yes, Madam," the servant bowed and left the room.

As he did so, another man entered. He was probably no more than five years older than Aimée, and dressed in a very casual manner with heavy tan leggings, soft black leather boots that rose just over his knees, and a roughly woven white cotton blouse, open at his throat to reveal the smooth, olive skin of his hairless chest. His long, black, wavy hair was loosely tied at the back, and his handsome, dark face made Sophie's pale complexion appear ghostly in contrast. Standing just inside the doorway, he executed a bow.

"My lady," he said with an accent unfamiliar to Aimée, who automatically rose from her seat.

"*Please*, do sit down, child," Sophie scolded. "Allow me to introduce Signore Cavalieri. Signore Cavalieri, may I present my niece, Marie-Marthé Aimée Dubucq de Rivery, who has just arrived for a visit from Nantes."

The dashing young man approached Aimée with a languid gait. He bowed, fixing her in his devilish smile, his dark eyes with their long, black lashes seeming to sparkle. Taking her hand in his, he gently touched it with his lips. "*Salve, Mademoiselle.*"

It was the first time anyone had ever kissed her hand. She flushed scarlet, unable to respond, while thinking him the most beautiful young man she had ever seen. Her hand felt as if it were melting in his light grasp, and she could still feel the touch of his lips on her skin. "How do you do?" she whispered.

"Signore Cavalieri is my protégé from Rome. His portraits are quite the rage in Paris at the moment, and I have given him a studio in which to paint, on the top-most floor."

"Perhaps your aunt will allow me to paint your portrait while you are here, *Mademoiselle*," he said, his eyes never leaving hers.

Speechless, Aimée stared into the exotic eyes and

made a small mewing sound in her throat.

"Right now I am sure that my niece would like to refresh herself after her long journey," Sophie said, pulling the cord that summoned the servant, who once again materialized in the doorway. "Show *Mademoiselle* to her rooms, and close the doors behind you," she added.

Aimée rose and attempted two awkward curtsies, one to Sophie and one to Signore Cavalieri, who had completely unnerved her.

The young man smiled broadly and bowed in response, while Sophie snapped open her fan and brought it to her face to conceal her annoyance.

Blushing, unsteady and aware that she had again somehow displeased her aunt, Aimée received another bow and stellar smile from Signore Cavalieri, then followed the servant out of the room. Her heart was beating faster than usual and her knees were shaking. She was thrilled by the thought that he might be a potential suitor, but why had her Aunt referred to him as her "protégé?" *Whatever was that?* She had been so mesmerized by his bold stare that she had barely heard her aunt's words. *Oh, Paris is wonderful.*

When they were alone, Sophie crossed the room to the young man and cocked her head to the side. "Do not even think of it, Carlo. She is a virgin and needs to remain so. Also, she could never afford you."

"*Bella* Sophia," he said, wrapping an arm around her waist and drawing her close to him. "How could you think so of me? She is a child and *you* are the woman who makes my dreams come true, no?"

"I am the woman who scooped you out of the gutters of Rome and purchased that fine linen shirt you are wearing, not to mention a new raft of oil paintings."

"Ah, *bella* Sophia," he murmured.

Had Aimée witnessed this scene, she would have been surprised to see her cold, imposing aunt melting into the arms of her young Italian lover.

"I will paint the last moments of her innocence, before you sell her to the highest bidder, no?" Carlo said softly. Then he drew her even closer to his body and buried his face in the nape of her neck to gently bite her.

"If you wish, my love," she replied with a low laugh. "If it makes you happy, Carlo."

Chapter 7

Aimée proved to be a willing student, who quickly adopted every gesture and physical nuance imparted by her aunt. To Sophie, Aimée's ability to mimic and assimilate so much so fast was a hopeful sign. She had learned to rein in many of her natural impulses, and no longer grinned like a monkey or laughed aloud. She was able to sit correctly and understood the intricacies of managing her skirts and other aspects of her complex wardrobe. With the help of a dance master, she had quickly learned all of the latest dances quite perfectly. She was light on her feet, with a flawless sense of rhythm and timing, and it was plain to see her enjoyment, which was perfectly acceptable when one danced.

Her walk, no doubt the result of being raised in the wild by natives, remained a problem. To Sophie's eyes, the walk betrayed an intimate aspect of the girl's nature that was inappropriate for one so young. It was a languid, fluid movement led by her hips swinging easily from side to side, with her back slightly arched and chest lifted. The undulating movement was a blatant display of innate sensuality that Sophie failed to comprehend in one who was still a virgin; a fact she had been surprised to learn when the ruse she had used to dissuade Carlo's attentions turned out to be true. Voluminous skirts helped to conceal it, but a four-sided box that began at her throat and reached down to her ankles would be the only costume that could completely disguise it. *Or a nun's habit*, Sophie thought.

As presentable as she may have become, the girl was persistent in her inability to master the most important attribute of all, the lack of which would surely prevent her from entering the choice echelons of society. Aimée was unable to grasp the art of wit.

In Parisian society, wit was *everything*. Anyone, male or female, who possessed the ability to fling a quip, *bon mot* or sly comment ruled the uppermost tiers of the city's social set, often capturing the favor of the King himself. Those who excelled in this art were elevated so quickly for the sheer distraction they provided the bored monarch he often conferred titles of nobility upon them. Absolutely all social discourse was based upon the issuance and enjoyment of clever repartee, often at the cost of someone's reputation. Verbal battles could silence a crowded drawing room and bring a party to a halt as a pair of the city's cleverest personages, fencing with words, cut each other to shreds with their tongues. To Parisians, the only thing more exhilarating and dangerous was an actual duel. The repartee was applauded, and then discussed at gatherings for days or weeks to follow. The results were in no way benign. Such exchanges elevated or ruined one's reputation, gained or lost favor with the King, and determined one's standing, virtually one's station in society.

Unfortunately, wit was almost impossible to teach.

Certainly, it could be cultivated and honed in those who *understood* its nature, but it eluded those who could not first comprehend it. Regardless of how Sophie explained or demonstrated, the biting exchanges evaded Aimée's grasp. Her kind nature and strict Catholic upbringing had taught her to respect others rather than ridicule them, and the entire concept of wit to her seemed no more than verbal cruelty. Try as she might, her mind could not comprehend its nuances. Consequently, the more dull-witted she appeared, the more lavishly Sophie dressed her. If the girl's scintillating conversational skill would not attract a husband, her attractiveness and hefty dowry might.

Aimée approached the weeks of grueling lessons as if she were playing a serious game, one that would, if mastered, reward her with her heart's desire—a husband to provide a family and a lofty place in Parisian society. This was her life's goal, and nothing had ever been more important to her. She memorized every instruction, practiced sitting and walking in voluminous gowns supported by hoops, fitting the edge of her bottom onto the edge of a chair, just so, snapping her fan and turning her face in profile to one seated to her side to show it to best advantage. She was terribly frustrated by her inability to grasp the concept of wit, but she continued to try, despite how unfair and unkind it seemed. *But, how important could that actually be?* she thought. From Aimée's perspective, the hardest thing she had had to learn was keeping her hands still while she spoke.

"It is vulgar to use one's hands while conversing,"

Aunt Sophie instructed. "Only peasants gesticulate thusly. We shall practice conversing whilst you sit upon them."

Aimée tucked her hands beneath her and found it difficult to think clearly. *I hate her,* popped into her mind and made her laugh. *I suppose I am thinking clearly after all.*

Finally, after fifteen days of arduous practice, Sophie's pupil was able to think and speak without moving her hands. She could also hide almost any feeling beneath either a placid gaze or a flick of her fan. The one she practiced hiding most was her dislike of her aunt. It seemed that all the woman cared about was appearance. She was, in Aimée's estimation, the vainest being she had ever met. In all the time they had spent together Aimée had never once seen her aunt laugh. Her every movement and comment were carefully thought out and planned to evoke a specific response. No joy emitted in her conversation, or apparently in her life, and Aimée began to wonder if everyone in Paris acted this way. If that was true, their lives were not possibly as wonderful as she had always imagined. It was her first hint that something might be missing from the plan she had conceived of as her life's dream.

Aimée enjoyed herself most during the hours spent sitting for her portrait in Signore Cavalieri's atelier. He was neither an aristocrat nor a gentleman but he was the most perfectly beautiful and interesting man she had ever met. She wondered if the strength of her attraction was due to his being a foreigner or if she would find any Frenchman to be equally fascinating. What she did not know about him was that he had not actually been rescued from the gutters of Rome, as Sophie maintained. The rescue had been, more accurately, from the balcony of a bedchamber.

Giancarlo Vincenzo Cavalieri's father had been a master plaster mason in Venice, where the boy was born. He began teaching young Giancarlo his trade when the boy was ten years old. His talent proved so exceptional that, two years later, his father sent him to Florence as apprentice to a friend, an artist who would teach him the art of painting frescos. By the time Giancarlo turned fifteen, he was receiving his own commissions. His exceptional talent, fueled by ambitious drive, insured a meteoric rise for three more years, until it was abruptly interrupted. The young artist was discovered in flagrante with the wife of a prominent Venetian.

He fled to Rome and with a recommendation from his old tutor, secured a position painting images for a famous *commedia dell'arte* troupe. Unfortunately, he soon found himself in another unsuitable position with another wayward wife. Following that debacle, it was suggested he ply his trade abroad, where a more modern attitude towards marriage and fidelity prevailed. It was common knowledge that French husbands were more accepting of their wives' indiscretions—because they, too, were discretely juggling mistresses and paramours. When the opportunity to travel to Paris with the *commedia* presented itself, he eagerly accepted, and that is how he met Sophie de Rivery. Of course, he did not share all of the details of his journey with Aimée.

While he sketched and painted, he entertained her with fascinating stories of the glories of Rome, the wonders of Venice and the centuries of magnificent art in Florence.

"Of course you know Leonardo da Vinci?" he asked.

"I am sorry to say, I do not."

"*È vero?* Truly? *Era un uomo molto coraggioso.* He was a very brave man with extraordinary vision and a great artist, not just a painter and sculptor. He was a thinker, *un filosofo*! I saw many of his drawings and some of his writings when I was a student in Firenze. He was able to imagine and make things, like the things we only dream of—flying machines and such."

"Flying machines?" she asked, incredulously. "*È vero?*"

"*Brava, signorina,*" he laughed. "You speak to me in Italian now. *Sì, è vero.* Ah, I wish I could show you Italy."

Aimée wondered, *does the signore find* me *attractive?* She imagined how exciting it would be to be courted by such a man. He was vivacious and so full of life that she marveled at the contrast between him and her aunt, whose every word and gesture was carefully orchestrated. She loved it when he sang Italian songs at the top of his voice. And he cared nothing for protocol or manners, so she was not afraid of saying or doing anything wrong in his presence. She could be herself with him. The stillness required of her portrait sessions was welcome because she could stare at the triangular patch of bare skin on his chest. Sometimes she would become so engrossed she would completely miss whatever he was saying. His eyes, which at first appeared to be dark brown, were in fact a deep jade green with a starburst of gold in the iris. She secretly wished that he were an appropriate suitor rather than a poor painter with no station or social standing. It never occurred to her that her pompous aunt was equally attracted to the *signore*'s charms, or that he traded sexual favors for introductions to members of the king's court and an elegant roof over his head.

When her portrait was finished, he led her into the atelier with her eyes shut. "Keep them closed until I say to open," he instructed. "All right, now you may open."

"Oh, *signore*, am I truly that lovely?" she asked without artifice.

"*No, signorina, ma grazie.* My brushes and paint could not capture your true beauty. It is only the best a poor artist may do."

"*Non è vero,*" she said. "*È molto bella.* I must be the luckiest young woman in all of Paris." Aimée considered the beautiful image a good omen. Painted on a six-inch oval of porcelain and enclosed in an intricately carved, gilded oval frame, her deep blue eyes gazed out directly, drawing the viewer in, and her creamy skin looked so realistic that Aimée fully expected it would feel warm to the touch. He had insisted on posing her in a simple, ecru silk gown, with a rose-colored satin sash. The only adornment was a small gold tiara with a six-pointed star atop her head, tied with an almost transparent silk scarf, which he wound once around her neck. Then he painted the scarf as if it were blowing in the wind. As an afterthought, he had draped an ermine cape over her shoulders but did not like the way it looked until he allowed it to slip almost completely off her right shoulder. In doing so, he had captured her essence—sensual innocence that was oddly regal.

"*Grazie tanto, signore.* I shall treasure it always," she said.

"*Prego, signorina.* It is a souvenir of this small moment in your life. A moment that can, sadly, never last."

She wanted to throw her arms around him and kiss him. Instead, she extended her hand for him to kiss and whispered, "*Mille grazie.*"

~ ~ ~

In the late morning of the same day, sixteen days after her arrival in Paris, Aimée heard the sound of the huge brass doorknocker echo through the house, and tiptoed to the upper stair landing to see who had arrived. Looking down onto the grand entry hall, she watched the houseman open the front door. In swept the dressmaker and her three assistants, weighed down with stacks of boxes surely filled with her new clothes. The entourage paraded up the stairs, peeking around the sides of the tall stacks of boxes to avoid tripping. They filed into Aimée's suite of rooms, followed by Aimée herself, bouncing up and down on her toes and clapping her hands with excitement.

Sophie entered the suite to oversee the presentation, as she had overseen the entire design and fitting processes. Exasperated as usual by the girl's open display of emotion she banged the floor several times with her walking stick and commanded, "Please! Control your-self, child."

Aimée attempted to remain calm, but as each box was opened to display its contents, she found it impos-sible not to gasp or squeal with pleasure. Each dress, jacket, hat, pair of shoes and pair of gloves was a work of art. Even the whalebone corsets looked beautiful to her eyes. It took Sophie three hours to inspect and ap-prove each piece of clothing while Aimée tried them on. When the dressmaker and her staff had gone, she gave Aimée the first and only compliment she would ever receive.

Aimée stood regarding her reflection in a large oval mirror. She wore an elegant, pale pink silk day gown sewn with vertical rows of dark green ribbons. A single flounce, draped with a garland of freshwater pearl clus-ters, graced the bottom of the skirt. The low cut bodice displayed her firm, round breasts, greatly enhanced by a tightly laced corset.

"Do you see how the proper accoutrements improve your natural assets?" Sophie asked.

Aimée was surprised to hear that Sophie thought she possessed any assets at all. "Oh yes, Madame. Thank you so much. Thank you a thousand times for my beau-tiful clothes." The ensemble showed off her creamy white shoulders and bosom, and she thought she looked almost as lovely as her portrait.

"We must use your beauty to its full advantage, child, to compensate for the…" she paused, appearing to search for the appropriate words, "…the attributes in which you do *not* excel."

Staring at her reflection, Aimée felt certain she would captivate everyone who gazed upon her, regardless of Sophie's reservations. She made a small curtsey to her reflection and thought, *"How do you do, my future husband?"*

Sophie interrupted her fantasy. "Tomorrow I shall present you to a select assemblage of very important people at the home of my dear friend, the Countess de la Roche."

Aimée's hands flew to her mouth to stifle another gasp.

"Please refrain from making that horrid sound and gesture." Sophie said irritably. "It will be a small reception for Madame de Polignac, who has recently returned from a visit to Austria."

When Aimée made no response to the woman's name, Sophie said, "I assume by your lack of response you are not familiar with Madame de Polignac."

"No, Aunt, I am sorry. I am not."

"Mon dieu. Does no important news ever reach that horrid jungle island? Madame de Polignac is the very *closest* friend and confidant of the Queen. You have heard of Queen Marie-Antoinette, have you not?"

Aimée began to gasp and caught herself. She cleared her throat delicately instead and smiled slightly with her mouth closed. "Yes, of course, Aunt, and I shall be happy to make her acquaintance."

"Better," Sophie said, pleased with the girl's sedate response. "I think we had best devote the remainder of the day to lessons. We must be certain you have learned to control your emotions and comport yourself as a proper young lady. I will *not* present a heathen, *Mademoiselle*." She rapped her silver-headed cane once on the wooden floor. "*You* may care nothing for your own reputation, but you will consider *mine*."

"I promise I will not fail you or myself, Aunt. It is just difficult to hide my pleasure when I am so very happy. I do so appreciate your efforts on my behalf. I will not embarrass you, Aunt Sophie. I will succeed. I promise."

"One hopes," Sophie replied under her breath as she left the room.

Chapter 8

That night, Aimée was too excited about her forth-coming introduction to Paris society to sleep. She imagined herself making a grand entrance, as everyone fell silent at the sight of her, stunned by the magnificence of her ensemble, beauty and grace. Tomorrow would be the most important day of her life. How could she possibly sleep? She tossed and turned, imagining the crowd of women plying her with calling cards each hoping to be the first to introduce her to their sons. She envisioned dozens of invitations to elegant balls, surrounded by handsome young men wishing to court her. She could hear the music playing as she danced beneath crystal chandeliers. *I shall never stop dancing. I must write to Rose,* she thought. *Or maybe I should wait until after tomorrow so I can tell her about meeting the queen's dearest friend.* She finally dozed off, dreaming of waltzing with a handsome young prince.

The next morning Da Angelique dressed Aimée's long, wavy blonde hair, as she had been taught, weaving in green satin ribbons and arranging it atop her head with curtains of curls spilling down the sides onto her shoulders. She affixed three tiny glass vials, each holding three drops of water and one fresh pink rose, just above and in front of Aimée's left ear. "Don' you let dat auntie spoil your fun t'day, *Doudou*," she said, nervously looking behind herself after using the Creole familiar term for "dear." Sophie had sharply reprimanded her for the gross impropriety when she'd overheard it. "*Oui*, m'a'm," Angelique had said aloud, but under her breath had muttered, "I call dis li'l gull '*Doudou*' alla her life an no ol' *pitin* gone make me stop now."

"This is going to be the most wonderful day of my life, Angelique. I can feel it."

"Dat's right, *Doudou*. You da *tres* pretty gull dey ever see. An dos' yellow culls, mmm, mmm. Dey never see notin' like dat."

She applied a very light dusting of white face powder to Aimée's face, chest and shoulders, and a smidgen of lip rouge, the only enhancements her aunt would allow. The girl's complexion was the exact ivory shade that many Parisian women literally killed themselves for, by taking arsenic to whiten their skins. "We must emphasize the natural attributes you *do* possess," Sophie had said.

At precisely two o'clock Aimée and Sophie stepped into the carriage that would take them to the afternoon tea hosted by Sophie's old friend, Comtesse Laure Valontin Richard de la Roche. It was only a few blocks away, but ladies were always conveyed to events and social gatherings by carriage, regardless of distance. The nature of one's conveyance announced the passenger's worth well before they were ever seen. Sophie's elegant aubergine and black enameled carriage, with driver and footman in matching livery, proclaimed symbols of status as well as taste. Sophie de Rivery may have lacked any substance of real value, but she was a master of presentation.

The carriage arrived at the de la Roche mansion that occupied a prominent position on a wide avenue off the Bois de Boulogne. It was similar to the de Rivery's house in that it was also a three-story granite building, only larger and its roof, upper story and entrance were more ornately decorated. Like most Parisian homes of stature, it was flanked closely on both sides by other houses, each with one slender tree gracing the avenue before it. There were no lawns, flowers or other trees anywhere in sight, just hard-packed earth and cobbles. The distinguishing feature of this row of homes was the granite block walkway leading from the street to the bottom-most stair of each entrance. The walkways made the access from the street easier for delicate women's slippers and saved the hems of gowns from ruin in the dirt.

Aimée followed her aunt's descent from the carriage and looked up at the ornate façade, picturing herself as the mistress of such a house. She imagined descending from her own fine carriage, greeted by her own servants while her handsome husband eagerly awaited within. Her heart beat wildly at the prospect, and she carefully suppressed a grin so as not to displease her aunt. She knew without doubt that her new life was about to begin.

Sophie interrupted her fantasy. "Remain calm," she instructed firmly through tight lips as they ascended the steps. "Pretend that you have been here many times before."

Two liveried servants stood on either side of the

wide, black-enameled front door. One of them gave a perfunctory bow and opened it wide to admit them. Inside, the vast foyer, with its huge crystal chandelier, marble floor and columns, reminded Aimée of the Governor's palace in Fort-Royal, only grander. *Isn't it odd,* she thought, *that there was only one house such as this on Martinique and here they are row upon row.* She craned her neck slightly in an attempt to peek into one of the rooms off the foyer, but Sophie shot her a stern look. She had been warned not to show her ignorance of polite society by appearing unfamiliar or impressed with surroundings or customs. "If you are uncertain about *anything,*" Sophie had instructed, "watch me and do as I do."

Aimée composed herself, standing as tall as her five-foot height would allow, and stole cautious glances at the décor. Moments later their hostess, Comtesse Laure Valontin Richard de la Roche, swept out of double doors on their left and moved towards them in the most outrageous ensemble Aimée had ever seen. The chartreuse satin gown appeared to have almost no bodice, just enormous breasts sitting atop a tiny satin board. Below the waist, flounce upon flounce of fabric poured down to the floor, the skirt extending out six feet in either direction from her body. Four tiny, white, fluffy dogs with huge satin bows the same color as the Countess's gown, suddenly appeared from beneath the gown, running in circles and yapping at their mistress's feet, their sharp nails clicking madly on the marble floor. The Countess's long, aged face, naked shoulders and bosoms were covered in a thick coating of greasy white paste and crowned by a towering powdered wig, festooned with birds and flowers. Aimée's jaw dropped and she audibly gasped.

In an attempt to conceal her niece's faux pas, Sophie snapped open her fan in front of the girl's face as she took a step towards her old friend and cooed, "Comtesse, *ma chérie*, how marvelous you look. We are so pleased to join your little tête-à-tête this afternoon. May I present my niece, Marie-Aimée Dubucq de Rivery?"

But Aimée's reaction had not been lost on her hostess. Her painted vermillion mouth involuntarily pinched into a pucker, as if she had tasted a sour grape.

Aimée curtsied and rose smiling sweetly, her face flushed to a bright red.

The Countess narrowed her eyes and took a step towards her. She was taller than Aimée and looked down her hawk's nose as she extended her folded fan and used the end of it to lift Aimée's chin slightly.

Aimée thought she meant to slap her with the fan. When this didn't happen, she realized she was holding her breath, and slowly released it. All the while, her practiced smile was frozen on her face.

A long silence followed, during which the Countess blatantly evaluated every aspect of Aimée's face, dress and bosom before removing her fan. She cocked her head to one side and relaxed her pursed lips, which simulated the barest trace of a smile. She had seen through the carefully crafted façade, and it was clear she did not like what she saw.

"From whence have you come to visit Paris, Mademoiselle de Rivery?" she asked, and with the question, all of Sophie's hopes for her niece vanished.

"From Martinique, your grace." The remains of Aimée's Creole accent drove the final nails into her coffin.

The entire exchange had taken less than a minute, but had most likely sealed Aimée's fate. If she did not meet with the Countess's approval, she would not be introduced to Madame de Polignac. Nor would she be sponsored in any of the city's fashionable social cliques, and if she were not sponsored, she would not be introduced to any worthwhile sons of Parisian aristocrats. She might as well be dead.

"My niece is in Paris for a short visit from the *Couvent de la Visitation* in Nantes," Sophie quickly interjected. "She is here only to visit with her family and to attend the new opera by Monsieur Mozart," she added to deflect any embarrassment the Countess might feel by not extending further social invitations.

Aimée held her breath, as seconds that seemed like hours passed before the Countess made her reply. "Of course. What a pity she will not have time to attend any other festivities."

The young girl stared blankly. She understood the meaning of what had been said, but found it difficult to believe that one small faux pas could have had such a disastrous result. *Have I truly been shut out? Perhaps I misunderstood?* Filled with fear and mortification, she bit her lower lip to keep from crying. Her aunt shot her a look, and Aimée quickly snapped her fan open to cover her face and made a polite curtsy as the Countess flounced away, a wave of little dogs yapping loudly around her skirt.

Sophie almost felt badly for Aimée. Mostly, she regretted having spent so much of her precious time, money and effort for nothing. She should have known that the girl's shortcomings were simply too great to overcome. *Well, I have fulfilled my duty to my husband's family. What more could I have done?* "Let us join the other guests in the music room," she said, then added from behind her fan, "We shall discuss this matter later. Now compose yourself."

Aimée was in shock. She fluttered her fan in front of her face as she walked behind Sophie, her eyes downcast to avoid meeting the gaze of other guests. Her striking beauty caused a buzz of gossip amongst the women, but Aimée remained quiet, lest she alienate anyone else or embarrass herself further. Along with about twenty other guests, they entered a small, ornate music room, but Aimée was too upset to notice the opulent surroundings. The guests took seats on gilded chairs, as liveried servants passed amongst them, offering crystal glasses of sherry. Aimée took a tiny sip of the sweet amber liqueur, as she has been taught, then finished the entire glass in two large gulps.

A string quartet began to play. She tried to pay attention to the music but could think only of the foolish mistake she made in offending the powerful Countess. *How could I have been so stupid? How could I have forgotten everything I tried so hard to learn? It wasn't fair.* The small room was stiflingly hot and she fanned herself rapidly to no avail. Then the close quarters began to yield the unpleasant odors of unwashed bodies drenched in too much perfume, along with the stench of sewage that wafted in through the open windows. Aimée brought her perfumed handkerchief to her nose, but within moments, it no longer had the power to prevent the offensive odors from penetrating her nostrils. The sherry was making her head swim, and her tightly laced corset made it difficult to breathe. She did not want to insult her hostess further by leaving the room during the performance. The distance between chairs, which allowed for the voluminous hoop skirts, prevented her from reaching out to touch the arm of her aunt. She did not feel at all well, and her panicked eyes sought her aunt's over her fan, but before she could attract her attention, she felt the room begin to spin. She slumped sideways and slid off her chair, hitting the floor with a thud and sprawling inelegantly on her back in a dead faint. The music stopped as her hoop skirt sprang up and propelled her dress back over her face, exposing her pantalets.

The next thing she was conscious of was her aunt's face close to hers. Smelling salts passed beneath her nose, and she looked up into a sea of white, painted faces gazing down at her disapprovingly. Sophie shook her head sadly from side to side, making a tsk-ing sound with her tongue against her teeth.

Dizzy and disoriented, Aimée whispered to Sophie, "What happened? What have I done?"

"I am afraid you have ruined yourself, child...simply ruined yourself."

"*Couyon pitin!*" Aimée screamed, the popular Creole curse she had heard throughout her childhood, *idiot bitch*. Then she began to wail, loudly, with no concern for who would hear or what they would think. She was finished caring about what anyone might think of her now. All was lost. She had spoiled her only chance for happiness and could no longer control her emotions. "I shall never be married! Never, never." she sobbed aloud.

"Not in Paris," Sophie replied.

The news of Aimée's disastrous presentation at the Comtesse de la Roche's became a choice piece of gossip that spread through Parisian society like lice. Everyone secretly enjoyed the girl's unfettered reaction to the site of the dreaded Countess, a reaction they shared but could never express. Furthermore, few instances of public drunkenness ever involved a beautiful young girl, so that made it a real gem. As a result, the only invitations to arrive came from those who were curious to see firsthand the little country girl who had made such a fool of herself in public. No important invitations arrived, and no serious suitors presented themselves. All previously made engagements were cancelled. Sophie did what she could.

After two weeks of informal afternoon teas, evenings at the opera, and uncomfortable formal dinners with pock-faced, unmarriageable sons from the lower echelons of Parisian society, Aimée was more than happy to return to the comfortable and anonymous security of the convent.

Although her aunt politely invited her to return to Paris for visits, Aimée had no hope of finding a husband there. In fact, she had little hope of finding one anywhere. She now believed that God was punishing her for lying to her Aunt Lavinia and Father Christophe, for saying that she wanted to give her life to God. As a consequence, He made sure that He would be the only one who would have her.

Chapter 9

Following her return to the convent, Aimée was afraid that even if she made good on her lie and became a nun, God would not forgive her so easily. *If I am going to burn in hell for eternity because of one lie, how much worse might my punishment be if I commit another sin by becoming a nun without a true calling? Are there different levels of hell for those who commit one or two sins and those who sin throughout their lives?* She thought about her Aunt Lavinia and wondered how great a sin she must have committed to live such a pious life. *Must I now resign myself to live an equally repentant life?* Her feelings of guilt and doubt led to a serious bout of insomnia. She considered writing to Rose, but Rose did not think about such things and she still felt too embarrassed by her failure in Paris. She wished she could confide in the Mother Superior, for surely she would have the answers, but how could she ask without revealing her sin?

Questions like these kept her awake at night and one night, following evening prayers, she confided her insomnia—without revealing its cause—to Sister Constance, with whom she had become friendly.

"I know just the thing," Constance remarked. "A small glass of sherry will help you to sleep. Come with me." She took Aimée's hand and led her to a sitting room off the rectory.

Aimée remembered her Parisian debacle. "I do not think that sherry agrees with me."

"A small glass for medicinal purposes never hurt anyone," Constance assured her. "Father Sebastian always takes a glass here in the evening when he's visiting." She retrieved a partially filled crystal decanter and two small glasses from the sideboard cupboard. "Under the circumstances, I am sure he would be pleased to share a drop with you." She offered Aimée a filled glass and poured one for herself. "And me."

They sat on two high-backed chairs next to each other and Aimée took a small sip. The sweet wine burned slightly as it slid down the back of her throat. "My, but that is delicious."

"It warms one's innards," the nun said, taking a sip from her own glass. "Have you been unwell?"

"Oh, no," Aimée replied, without noticing how easily she now lied. "Only a bit homesick perhaps." She finished her sherry and patted her lips delicately with her lace handkerchief. The sudden warmth made her giddy and the realization made her laugh. She quickly covered her mouth with her handkerchief and peered sheepishly at Sister Constance, then hiccupped loudly.

Sister Constance clicked her tongue against her upper teeth in mock reprimand, then filled both of their glasses again. "The best way to cure the hiccups," she proclaimed, raising her glass to Aimée. "But you must drink it all at once." They drained their glasses empty in one draft.

Enjoying the feeling of relaxation, Aimée asked, "Constance, are you happy here?"

"Yes, very. I sometimes wonder what other kind of life I might have had, but can think of nothing I would *rather* have. When I think of my mother's life, with nine children and hardly enough food to go round, and my father...well meaning, I suppose, but drunk most nights and some days. I raised my four younger sisters and, had I remained, would have soon been raising children of my own alongside them. I did not want my Mother's life."

Emboldened by the wine, Aimée asked, "But do you never long for...a husband?" She had not intended to reveal any of her true feelings to Constance and here she was saying something that she might have only voiced to Rose.

"For what reason?"

"Why, for marriage and love...and for children."

"You forget, dear girl, I am married to our Lord, Jesus Christ," Constance replied.

"Oh, of course. I am deeply sorry. I did not mean to offend. I only meant marriage to—a *man*."

Constance reached for the crystal decanter on the side table and leaned over to refill their glasses for a third time. Her cherubic lips curled up slowly in a teasing smile. "And what could marriage to a *man* provide that I do not already have?"

"Children, for one. I have always wanted children," Aimée said wistfully. "If I had children I would never let anything bad happen to them, and I would never leave them." She took a sip of her sherry and then said the most forthright thing she had ever said aloud to anyone. "It seems that the closer I get to deciding to be a nun, the more I doubt the correctness of that decision. Also..." She paused to take another sip of sherry to fortify herself for what she was about to say. "Also, I have of late begun to yearn for the *companionship* of a man." She had admitted the same in her last confession and had been told that impure thoughts were equally sinful to deeds and that acting upon her desires fed the devil's hunger for her soul. This caused great confusion in her mind, as she had always planned to marry and had never been told that it was bad or wrong. So, why, exactly, was it wrong to *desire* such a thing?

"Oh," Constance replied, feigning surprise and moving to sit at Aimée's feet. Her brown eyes smiled up at Aimée. "It is *companionship* you desire."

Aimée looked down at Constance and became aware of her heart's rapid beating. She thought the sherry must be affecting her and nodded her head. "Yes, companionship and love."

Constance placed her glass down on the little table and took one of Aimée's hands into her own, turning it over to stroke the smooth inside of her palm. "Companionship and love may be achieved in many ways, Aimée," she said softly, then gently kissed her palm.

Shocked, Aimée retracted her hand and stood up too quickly, dropping her half-filled glass of sherry as she did. "Oh, no. I'm so sorry. I..."

Without looking back at the nun sitting on the floor, she ran from the room to her quarters, threw herself onto her bed and wept into her pillow. Now she was more confused than ever.

The only good to come as a result of her encounter with Constance was that despite being upset, the sherry brought her a good night's sleep. The next morning she sent Da Angelique into the village to purchase a bottle of the same from the local vintner.

"Spirits?" Da Angelique asked incredulously. "What you want wid dat? No young gulls got need of spirits, no lady either, mmm, mmmm, you don' need no spirits, *Doudou.*"

"I forbid you to treat me like a child," Aimée said, sharply stamping her foot. "*Es ou tandé sa mwen di ou?* [Did you hear what I said?] I am a young lady, and you'd do best to remember that. I am sending you to fetch something for me and have no need to explain myself to my maid." She felt badly speaking to Angelique this way, but had no choice.

"*I pa bon* [it's bad]," she replied, sadly shaking her head. "An' you in dis god's house too. Mmm, mmmm. What gonna be now dis young gull got no respec' no more?"

"And you will address me as '*mademoiselle*' from this day forward, and stop addressing me in any familiar manner," Aimée scolded. "And say 'please' when telling me what must be done."

Angelique glared at her mistress, took the coin and cursed quietly under her breath as she walked off muttering to herself.

The loss of Constance's friendship left Aimée no one with whom she could discuss the thoughts that plagued her, and she felt more alone than ever. One thing was certain; she no longer wished to encourage friendship with the young nun, or any others who might have similar notions about "companionship." Her loneliness led her to write to Rose.

23 January, 1780

My dearest Rose,

I have hesitated too long in writing this letter and do not wish you to misinterpret my silence for lack of interest, because I miss you terribly. It is lovely here at the convent, but there is no one with whom I can speak freely about personal matters, which makes me miss you even more. In truth, I do not miss anything or anyone other than you.

It pains me to tell you that my sojourn in Paris was an unhappy one. I embarked upon the journey with the highest of hopes, some of which were extinguished almost immediately by the city itself, which is the strangest combination of horrid and beautiful. Of course, I have no other city to which I might compare it, as you know, but it stank and everything is made of stone. The only green areas, called parks, with grass, trees and flowers, are in the middle of the city. Unfortunately, the stench from the slums and factories reaches everywhere and in the warm months (when I visited) is almost unbearable. Everyone carries scent and handkerchiefs to hold to their noses at all times.

Upon my arrival, Aunt Sophie pronounced my entire traveling wardrobe to be unsatisfactory (not fashionable enough) and ordered a new one to be fashioned for me, with two of the most exquisite ball gowns, too beautiful to even describe. And Rose, there was a young Italian gentleman, Si-

gnore Cavalieri, an artist, ensconced on the upper floor of Aunt's house in a painting studio, and he painted my portrait. He is the handsomest and most interesting young man I have ever met, and sadly, too far beneath my station to be considered. Which brings me to the terrible news I feel ashamed to tell—even to you my dearest friend.

Parisian society is so very complicated and unlike anything we have ever known. Through Aunt's tutelage I thought I had mastered everything so well, what was permitted and not permitted. Do you know Parisians frown upon smiling? I believe in saying that I have displayed what they call wit. If only Aunt Sophie had warned me of what to expect in the manner of the appearance of the Comtesse de la Roche I might not have been so shocked. But the woman was nothing short of a specter, her haggard old face and body painted white. Actually painted, Rose! And the huge skirt of the afternoon gown she wore harbored a bevy of tiny yapping dogs beneath it. Can you imagine such a site, Rose? I tell you, you cannot.

In actual fact, as I describe her to you now she becomes quite comical. I am laughing at the memory and only wish I could have done so at the time. I gasped at the sight of her— what a terrible gaff, and all my hopes were dashed. I was so unnerved by my faux pas that moments later, I drank an entire glass of sherry and fainted dead away, falling off my chair as I did so. It was truly terrible, Rose. I quite literally fell from whatever grace I had possessed. When I recovered my senses enough to realize what I had wrought, I shouted Angelique's favorite curse (which I have never uttered aloud before and cannot even bring myself to write now). Then, I cried publicly and uncontrollably like an injured child. Thus, I was judged unworthy of polite society and will never be introduced to any *prospective suitors...ever. My fondest dream of marriage and family will never be fulfilled, and I do not understand how I can find anything funny about the events that led to this debacle.*

What chance of happiness is there for me now, Rose? I will be eighteen on my next birthday and am unsure of what course to pursue. It appears the only path open to me is the Church, and the irony of that choice is more than I can presently bear.

Please respond quickly, as I anxiously await your council.

Your devoted cousin,

Aimée

Writing the letter to Rose brought some interesting questions to light. Aunt Lavinia used to tell her that "time and distance heal all wounds." Was this why she could now laugh at the memory of Comtesse de la Roche? She still pondered how something so miniscule could yield such an enormous result, and asked herself how she might have felt if she had succeeded in securing the approval of the Comtesse and her important guests. Would she have enjoyed their company? They seemed possessed by the goal of succeeding at court, as if that were the only aspect of their lives that mattered. *What about other things*, she thought, *like those Signore Cavalieri loved to discuss and ponder? What if I had to follow those stupid rules and ridiculous protocols for the rest of my life? If I did, where might I find pleasure in such a life?*

She quickly scanned through her memories of her month in Paris, and realized that the only times she truly enjoyed were those spent in the company of Signore

Cavalieri. *I felt happy then*, she thought, *because I was able to laugh freely, and the world he showed me was so different and interesting. He did not require me to act any way other than as myself.* It was an astounding realization to see everything she thought she had wanted crumble in an instant. Her long-held dream of the future life she had cherished was, in fact, nothing more than a dream with no resemblance to the reality of Parisian society. In truth, the only person she had genuinely liked was also an outcast of that society.

Flabbergasted by the realization, she sat at the tiny writing table in her room in a mild state of shock. She remembered every detail of seeing Signore Cavalieri for the first time, the way he had sauntered into Aunt Sophie's drawing room in his soft black leather boots and calfskin leggings, the open shirt revealing his smooth dark skin. The way he looked at her with those exotic dark eyes had made her heart thump in her throat. She had never felt anything like it before. Despite her nervous palpitations, he made her feel at ease when she posed for her portrait. She watched him, thinking about how it might feel to lay her cheek against his bare chest and breathe in his scent. *He may have been beneath my station, but he is the kind of man I want to marry, and that is how I want to feel.*

During the days that followed, Aimée kept to herself, praying earnestly, studying her lessons and taking solitary walks whenever she could. As a child, she had always relied on the beauty of nature to bring her solace, which it still did. The nights were made more bearable by sherry.

Less than a week after posting her letter to Rose, Aimée received her first letter. That could only mean their letters had crossed paths, for it was much too soon to be receiving a response. She tore the letter open and was shocked to read of the sudden, unexpected death of Rose's younger sister, Catherine, who had contracted a fever and died.

"And dear cousin, you will not believe what I am going to tell you, but the terrible loss of my dearest little sister was followed by a miracle. The Vicomte Alexandre de Beauharnais, to whom Catherine had recently been betrothed, has asked for my hand in her stead. The old witch was right. I sail for France in early February to marry the Vicomte!"

Aimée put the letter down, unable to read further. This was the first time in almost two years that she remembered the prediction. Now the first part of the old woman's prediction for Rose had come true, and she suddenly realized that so had the first part of her own. She had indeed been sent abroad to the convent school to "further her education." A shudder passed down her spine as she sat gazing out at the vineyards that spread down the gently sloping hill away from the convent. Parts of both predictions had come true. *How could anyone look at a handful of coffee grounds and bones and see the future? It was not possible.*

She read the rest of Rose's letter that told what little she knew of the Vicomte: he was from an aristocratic old family, handsome and dashing and a lieutenant in the army. Her Aunt Désirée Renaudin, her father's sister in

France, had arranged the marriage. Also, a hurricane had destroyed their house and her family was now living in the *soucherie*.

"Everyone still grieves the loss of sweet Catherine, especially poor mother, but with the end of her life a new one has begun for me. Isn't life a terrible mystery?"

Aimée read the words almost without recognition, unable to think of anything but the prophecy. She remembered the night in the old *obeah* woman's shack and the feel of the crone's leathery hands holding her own. Closing her eyes, she tried to recall everything the woman had said: two children for Rose, widowhood and a second marriage, while Aimée would have a son. *Would he be a king?* Then she remembered hearing about the pirates kidnapping her and taking her to a strange land. Instantly she clamped her hands over her ears in an effort to halt any further memories. She did not want to remember. No good would ever come of it, and look what had happened to poor Catherine.

With shaking hands, she folded the letter and put it down. Despite the early hour of the day, she drank two glasses of sherry and laid down for a nap.

Chapter 10

On the following day, Aimée took her morning walk to a stand of beautiful old willow trees that bordered a small pond on the convent grounds. She sat on the soft grass and tried to organize her thoughts. Rose would be coming to France and they would see each other. She was going to marry, to be the Vicomtesse de Beauharnais and live in Paris. Aimée imagined visiting her cousin, who would live in a house just like her aunt's. How exciting to think of her as the wife of a prominent young man. Then she realized that Rose, her dearest cousin, would soon be in a position to introduce her to eligible young men—men of *their* choice. Perhaps they might be country gentlemen, perfectly acceptable yet unfettered by the restraints of the higher echelons of society. *I might truly find happiness with such a man*, she thought *and if I marry and remain in France, the rest of the prediction couldn't possibly come to pass. Yes*, she told herself, *that is exactly what I must do.* Excited by her new plan, she quickly returned to her room to write another letter.

My dearest, dearest Rose,
Our letters crossed paths in transit, as yours arrived just one week after I posted mine. I am deeply saddened to learn of

sweet Catherine's passing, and hope that you and your family will find a way to bear the grief I know you feel. I am relieved to learn she did not suffer long, and know she is with the angels now. Please make an offering of sweets to her on my behalf when next you visit, and know that I include her in my prayers.

I cannot imagine how difficult it must be for you to grieve your dear sister's passing while being grateful for your own good fortune. I hope you take no blame upon yourself for this most unusual outcome, as I am sure Catherine would not wish it.

I am thrilled that we will be in France together! Where will your marriage take place and might it be possible for me to attend? If not, let us plan a visit to follow soon after. Do you know where you will be residing, and have you corresponded directly with your betrothed yet? I have so many questions, as I am sure do you.

Please respond soon as I am excited to learn more.

Your loving cousin,

Aimée

Aimée sealed the letter and felt a surge of hope. If Rose could succeed in finding a suitable husband without having had the benefit of Aunt Sophie's tutoring, so might she. Her hopes of marriage were suddenly rekindled.

But five months passed before another letter arrived from Rose. It was very short, but quite extraordinary.

Dearest Aimée,

I write to you from aboard the ship that carries me to my

destiny. Although this will not post until I arrive in France, I wish to describe an extraordinary event while it is fresh in my mind. And you, my dear cousin, are the only one with whom I may share it. Yesterday, as I boarded the ship in Fort-Royal Harbor a giant arc of blue and yellow light came down from the sky and made the mast and mainsail look as if they were afire! All of the people on the deck and the docks stopped to stare, and women screamed while the deck hands made efforts to calm everyone on board. The illumination lingered for several minutes. When it faded from the sky, the Captain addressed us, saying that the ship would not burn and that the flame was a natural occurrence, a kind of lightning called "Saint Elmo's Fire." Can you imagine? Once again, Euphemia David was right.

By the time you read this, I will have already met my betrothed. I promise to write very soon.

Your cousin,

Marie-Josèphe Rose Tascher de la Pagerie (almost Beauharnais).

Aimée stared at Rose's letter, stunned. *If this extraordinary occurrence came to pass, what might actually happen to me? I never made confession to Father Christophe, but it can harm no one now if I confess here.*

She ran to the Mother Superior's quarters to confide the incident with the fortuneteller and its frightening "results." In her heart, she hoped that confession would absolve her of the sin, and somehow halt the remaining prediction as well.

"Did you confess your sin and do penance immediately following your visit to the devil's servant?" the Mother Superior asked.

"No, Mother. I did not."

"Do you wish to burn in hell, child?" she asked sharply.

"No, Mother." She envisioned burning bodies writhing in pain, and began to cry. "Truly, I do not."

"You will do penance now, and I will grant you absolution, my child, but you must also repent within your heart. You must purge yourself of fear, as the fear of these things is in itself the work of the devil. This 'prediction' of which you speak is nothing more than coincidence. I bid you strike it from your mind."

That last instruction sounded familiar. Hadn't Rose said something like that to her? "Thank you, Mother. I will do anything you say, and I will sweep the memory from my mind. I will." *Yes, Rose had said exactly that.*

"What a pity we are no longer able to burn witches. Such women should be severely punished for consorting with the Devil as well as frightening young girls."

Aimée was almost as frightened by the Mother Superior's words as she had been by the prediction. *If fear itself was bad,* she wondered, *how was fear of the devil different from fear of God?* She did not dwell on this because she was desperate to believe the nun's rebuttal of the power embedded in the old woman's prophecies, and thus went immediately to chapel, where she knelt for the next hour in prayer. As she left, she resolved to follow the Mother Superior's instructions to the letter. She had said to "strike the memory" from her mind. *How exactly shall I do that? I simply will not allow myself to think of it, and if I do, I will think of something else instead.*

Comforted by the Mother Superior's absolution and confident that God would now forgive her, she vowed to pray daily, both longer and harder than she ever had before.

The mother superior watched as Aimée walked out of the chapel and thought to herself that despite the young lady's well-bred demeanor, her walk betrayed a surprisingly sensual nature.

She smiled to herself.

Chapter 11

Rose

Rose had never thought of herself as a child. Perhaps early maturity was innate, or it may have been the result of her unusual childhood experiences. Whatever its source, she willingly took chances, and often chose the unaccepted path. She did not openly disobey—she just did as she pleased whenever she could. Unlike Aimée, who strove to be the good girl, Rose cared nothing for following rules. Neither did she stand as much to lose. Aimée, being an orphan, wished to remain in the good graces of her relatives upon whose mercy and kindness she depended. No one ever thought of Rose as a bad girl so much as one whose high spirits would hopefully mellow with age. If girls might be compared to weather, Rose would be an unpredictable tropical storm while Aimée personified the essence of spring, filled with promise. In their early years, each fervently wished to be more like the other.

When, at the age of seventeen, the death of her youngest sister brought Rose a proposal of marriage, she quickly adapted to the idea. It was an event she had hoped and feared for almost three years, and the circumstances of her betrothal would haunt her for the rest of her life.

Now Rose's dreams were being shattered, although more slowly and insidiously than Aimée's. To her great disappointment, she had married Vicomte Alexandre de Beauharnais not in the Cathedral in Paris, but in a civil ceremony at her Aunt Désirée's country home in Noisy-le-grand, half a day's journey from Paris. The ceremony was attended solely by officers of the Vicomte's regiment, with no family members on either side present. Although Rose's father had made the long journey with her to France, he had become ill and unable to attend.

Rose tried to tell herself that her husband's choice showed nothing more than his disregard for church and ceremony, but in her heart, she feared it showed his disregard for her, a fact that was confirmed on their wedding night when Alexandre quickly performed his nuptial duty without affection or care for Rose, and promptly fell asleep. She forgave his lack of attention, attributing it to the fact they hardly knew one another. In fact, they had yet to spend more than a few hours together, having only met for the first time a few weeks earlier. But she could not help comparing him to her William, whose open adoration and romantic behavior always made her feel safe. A conversation with her Aunt Désirée began to breed more doubt.

"When Monsieur de Beauharnais rejoins his regiment next week," Aunt Désirée said, "I think it would be prudent to use the six months of his absence to begin your studies."

"Studies?" Rose asked incredulously. This was the first mention of such a thing. "What studies, Aunt?"

"Elocution, for one. If you have any hope of joining your husband at court, you must not embarrass him in any way."

"My husband finds the way I speak embarrassing?" Her face flushed, and she found it difficult to breathe.

"You must try to understand, my dear. Your husband is quite the figure at court. All the ladies vie for his attention—as a dance partner, of course. He is equally well liked by the men—an admirable position, I assure you. His title is older than most, more than eight generations, my dear, and you of course have only just inherited yours by virtue of your very recent marriage. Do you see my meaning?"

"It is with much trepidation that I fear I do. You are saying that the fact of my position as wife of a Vicomte does not ensure my position at court, and that my husband intends to attend without me?"

"Yes, of course. *Mon dieu*, you don't expect him to discontinue his attendance at court because of you?"

"No, Aunt, *au contraire*. I expected to *accompany* him to court."

"Well, shouting will not bring that about, I can assure you. You must study very hard and please him upon his return."

"Please him? When he cares nothing for me?" Rose fumed. "Why should I bother pleasing him?" she continued angrily.

"Because it is your place to please him, my dear. You are his wife, and that is what a wife does…pleases her husband. What did you think your purpose would be?"

"I suppose I believed we would please each other."

"And who gave you that foolish notion?" she asked with open disdain. "Your mother?"

"Yes, Aunt, my *Creole* mother. The one to whom your brother is married."

"That fact, my dear, is one I have attempted to forget. Had he remained here, where he belonged, he would still enjoy his rightful place at court. Instead, he ran off to that godless island and brought three girls into the world who must now somehow manage to find their places among society. I hope you realize that despite any affection you may feel towards your mother, her lack of station has given you a great obstacle that you must now overcome."

"And why, pray tell, did Monsieur de Beauharnais chose to marry into my less-than-desirable family, Aunt?"

"Surely you know the answer to that question."

"If I did, I would not ask. I am curious because if he is as desirable as you say, he might have had any woman of good birth in Paris."

"The wars and famines have drained the country of its wealth. France is quite bankrupt, my dear. Very few French girls any longer possess dowries, and Monsieur de Beauharnais, despite his impeccable social standing, is quite insolvent. So, no solvent family would consider him a candidate for marriage."

Rose was stunned. Neither of her parents had ever mentioned this. "Well, Aunt, I take comfort in knowing

that my *money* is good enough for Monsieur de Beauharnais. Now, if you will excuse me," she said, leaving
the room.

It was a collision of two worlds, the one Rose
thought she was entering as the mistress of a grand es-
tate, with a loving husband to introduce her to Parisian
society and the King and Queen, and the one she actually had entered. She felt both angry and sad. All she
cared about, hoped for and prayed for were those
things. It never occurred to her that she might not be
worthy of them. Now the man she depended upon to
give her these things, the man she was prepared to obey
and eventually learn to love, found her lacking. What
was worse, he had no money other than her dowry. He
was not going to provide any of the things she wanted,
and she could not get them herself. She had been correct
in her wedding night assumption of Alexandre's disposition and wrong about everything else in regard to her
new life. The only option left to her would be to spend
the six months of her husband's absence transforming
herself into the most desirable woman he had ever
known. When he returned, she must captivate him—and
he would do everything in his power to make her
dreams come true.

Chapter 12

Much to Aimée's great disappointment, she did not receive another letter from Rose for almost a year. During that time, she continued to take comfort in the hope of meeting a husband through her cousin. When the missive finally arrived, she was disheartened to learn that the reason for Rose's silence lay in the deep unhappiness caused by her husband's displeasure. He had married Rose not for love, but for her dowry. What was worse, he openly disapproved of her "country ways" and unsophisticated manner. He even went so far as to hire an elocution tutor to rid her of her "deplorable colonial accent." Rose had not written sooner because he forbade her any contact with "colonial riff-raff," which included all her family and friends from Martinique. He spent most of his time at court, to which she had not yet been admitted, and two weeks after their wedding he left to rejoin his regiment for a period of six months. During that time, she had dutifully followed his instructions to "better herself," but sadly, fell short of his expectations upon his return.

Rose had become pregnant on her wedding night and one month before writing the letter, on September third of 1781, had given birth to a boy, whom she named Eugène.

"Consider yourself fortunate, dear cousin, that you do not know the pain of loving a man who spurns you and, I fear, must prefer another, because he shows no interest in his marital rights. Is it not interesting that a man has marital 'rights' while a woman has marital 'duties?'

However, little Eugène is the light of my life and worth whatever consequences I must endure. I have hope that, eventually, mutual love for our son may bring us closer. Meanwhile, I still strive to perfect myself in the ways my husband prefers, and Aunt Désirée provides some little comfort. I wish my husband would allow you to visit, but alas that is not yet possible."

7 November 1781

My dearest Rose,

I am saddened by your unhappiness, and yet overjoyed by the news of your son. How wonderful for you to have a little baby of your own. I am sure he is an angel, and hope to meet him one day should your husband's heart soften towards me and other family members.

It appears that we have both suffered great disappointment. Are we not meant to be happy? Is it our sins that keep us from our life's dreams? The women here seem content with their lots, while I am never quite pleased with mine, always secretly wishing for something more: a husband and family, a place in society and all the finery that goes along with it. Perhaps I am undeserving, and the lies I told in order to gain such things were my undoing. Are we meant to pay for our transgressions by forfeiting the things we wish to have? Oh, how I wish you were here, dear cousin.

It appears the only option God has left me is to serve Him and to resign myself to a life of piety and renunciation. I wish I could tell you this with more lightness and joy in my heart, but I cannot. I have decided to take my vows.

What Aimée did not say in her letter was that she now drank two glasses of wine each night with her dinner, and several glasses of sherry in order to sleep. Sometimes she wished to drink much earlier in the day. Her life was not unhappy, it just did not feel full, and there was nothing for which she cared a great deal. In fact, she cared less than a little about almost everything. Perhaps she was just too young to accept quietude and piety as a way of life, although there were many novices of her exact age who appeared content in the convent. After her experience with Constance, she suspected that some of them had found furtive romantic love with one another. She wondered if such an assignation would satisfy her own emptiness, but had no desire to test it. Her strongest yearning was for motherhood. As an orphan, a loving family was the one thing she never had. And in her deepest, most guilty thoughts, she longed for the opulence and luxuries of Paris.

At other times she wondered what life might be like if she were a married woman living in any large city. There would certainly be more to do than reading, playing music, weaving and praying. She even wondered whether she would be happy if she were married and living on Martinique. However, all of this was mere daydreaming, for she had no means of meeting a husband. Her prospects in Paris had been exhausted, and she had no other relatives anywhere, except Rose, who, like herself, had not been welcomed into the bosom of society. Her Aunt Lavinia wrote from Martinique, but made no mention of any prospects there, although she would welcome Aimée back at any time.

Rose's reply to Aimée's letter arrived very quickly.

My dear cousin,

I fear I have no answers to your questions about God and sins. Everything I was sure I knew about such things has slipped from my grasp in the wake of my severe unhappiness. I miss the loas of our home, and perhaps their absence is the cause of our grief. We surely depended upon them in our youth and were indeed happy.

I am sorry to hear that you have decided to take vows without the passion of spirit it must take to do so. Have you no desire to return home? I would if I were able. My husband is gone again, and the only comfort that brings is my ability to correspond freely with you. I await his return with the hope that one day he will find me pleasing and allow me to join him in his life at court.

I remain, your loving cousin,
Rose

She read the letter with great sadness for Rose and herself. If any man could shun her beautiful, vivacious cousin Rose, what fate may have awaited her if she had also married? Why might her fate have been any different than her cousin's? Once again, Rose's predicament solidified her decision to take her vows, and she immediately set out to inform the Mother Superior of her decision.

"I would like to visit my family in Martinique first," Aimée said. "Once I become a nun, I might never see them again."

"Of course. The voyage will do you good, my child. You look a bit peaked of late, and the sea air will be invigorating."

"I will post a letter to my aunt today and secure passage for June, I think."

"God be with you, my child."

The Mother superior graced her with a rare smile, the source of which Aimée knew to be her own dowry.

Chapter 13

Nantes, France
June 1781

Shortly before embarking on her voyage home, Aimée received a brief letter from Rose, who wrote to share the news that she was pregnant once again.

"It is my greatest hope that the birth of this child will bring my husband home to me. If it should not, Aunt Désirée and her solicitor have advised me to take legal measures against him, for he not only denies me of himself (except to use me in the most cruel manner), but is not forthcoming with any means of sustenance. Were it not for Aunt Désirée's generosity, I know not how my children and I would survive."

Rose was in a desperate state, and Aimée felt helpless to ease her cousin's pain. She wished to help her in some way, but what could she do? An uninvited visit was out of the question, and she would be sailing in just three days.

She immediately sat down to write a letter that she would post on the day she set sail for Martinique.

My dearest Rose,
I pray that your situation improves with the birth of your

second child. Surely, Monsieur de Beauharnais cannot con-
tinue to be so hard of heart as father to two beautiful children.
One day soon, I know I will look upon the faces of my new
little cousins. We shall have many opportunities to do so, as I
have made the decision to dedicate my life to Our Lord and
Savior, and remain at the Couvent de la Visitation permanent-
ly, following a final visit to Martinique. Today I embark upon
that voyage. Upon my return to Nantes I shall be a novice and
one day take vows to become God's servant here on earth.

Please know that I continue to hold you in my heart and
in my prayers and I pray the day comes soon when we may
smile upon each other again. Until then, may God bless you
and your family and the Blessed Virgin bring compassion to
the heart of he who spurns you. I shall always remain your
loving cousin,
Aimée

~ ~ ~

The three-masted trading ship, with a crew of one
hundred and twenty, left the dock at Nantes on a bright
June morning, as soft white clouds scudded across the
azure sky and a brisk wind promised a swift journey.
The ship was fitted out for thirty passengers and regularly made the trip between France and the French Caribbean Islands, bringing mail and necessities and returning with cargoes of sugar and coffee. No flames leapt
from the heavens as they had on Rose's departure from
Martinique, for which Aimée was grateful.

Accompanying Aimée on her journey was Da Angelique, now elevated to the status of lady's maid, but

still unaccustomed to enclosed shoes. The cold French winters had made her bones brittle, and now that Aimée was going to be a nun, there would be no need for Angelique to remain with her. Aimée had granted her freedom and Da Angelique was returning to Martinique a free woman with a pension, enough to spend her days as she wished either in Fort-Royal or on the family's plantation. Her new position did not change her dogged protectiveness of Aimée, despite her verbal show of respect.

From the ship's deck, the old woman loudly warned the deck hands to be careful with Aimée's trunks, as she absently straightened the fitted waist of Aimée's silk brocade jacket. "Mam'zel', I gonna go down t' see t' your t'ings now...make sure all your trunks be dere. I don' trust dees sayla men—dey jus' t'row dees trunks aroun'." She shook her wrapped head emphatically. "An' you needin' to change out your travel dress before dinnah. I lay dem out for you. An don' stay out here long if de wind gets cold, *si ou plé*? No need for a propah young lady t'be standin about here wid dees sayla men all aroun'."

Aimée stood at the rail and answered without moving her gaze from the bustling dock.

"All right. I am going to remain on deck to watch the shore disappear." Then she smiled and turned to face her maid. "I am so happy to be going home."

"You an' me too," Angelique said, grinning broadly. "Why you wanna come back to dis place I never understan'. Maybe you change your mind once your home again an smell dose sweet, sweet flowers, dat nice warm breeze. Mmmm mmmmm." She patted Aimée's gloved hand affectionately.

Angelique waddled away, shifting her appreciable weight from one foot to the other to compensate for the discomfort of her shoes.

Aimée clutched her silk parasol with one white-gloved hand and held the ship's railing with the other. Deck hands scurried about making the ship ready to sail, as she watched the crew pull in the gangplank and unfasten the heavy ropes that held the ship fast to the dock. Two long pilot boats, each manned by twenty sailors, pulled the small ship out of the harbor toward the open sea.

A few of the other passengers remained at the rail with Aimée and watched as the coast of Southern France slipped farther and farther away. Once the harbor had been cleared, the pilots unfastened their ropes and rowed out of the ship's path. The foresail flapped noisily as it was hoisted and sprang to life with a burst of vibrato, wide open and ready to catch the wind. As soon as the mainsail filled, the small ship picked up speed and headed due west. With good winds, they would reach Martinique in seven to eight weeks.

Aimée inhaled a deep breath of salty ocean air and smiled to herself. *It feels good to be going home*, she thought. *I had not realized how much until now. Angelique might be right about the possibility of changing my mind.*

"You'll be glad to be home again I'll wager, won't you miss?" a man's voice said in the strangest sounding accent she had ever heard.

Unaccustomed to being addressed by strangers, she

knit her brows together, and turned her head to look up at him. A handsome young man with a strong, square jaw, thick, black, wavy hair and pale blue eyes smiled down at her. She held her breath.

He politely doffed his hat and made a small bow. "Angus Braugham's the name, and I'm to be the new white officer on your uncle's plantation."

She found it difficult to remove her gaze from the deep dimples in his cheeks. "I am Marie-Marthé Aimée Dubucq de Rivery." She blushed and averted her eyes to gaze back at the disappearing shoreline.

"I know, Miss. Not meaning to be rude, but your uncle wrote that you'd be making this trip and, I must say, described you quite correctly. There be no other such beautiful young fair-haired misses on this ship, I'm afraid, so you'll be standing right out."

Unfamiliar as she was to the company of men, she felt awkward, and stiffened at his forwardness and familiar manner, as thoughts crowded her mind. *He is probably no more than a few years older than I—and what terrible manners. We have not been properly introduced. I should not be seen talking with him. What must the other passengers think?*

Sensing her discomfort, he quickly explained, "Begging your pardon Miss, your uncle instructed me to put myself at your disposal during our voyage, and I just wanted to introduce myself to you to that purpose. So, if any needs there be, I'm your man." He grinned and nervously twisted his hat in his hands, embarrassed he had blurted out his intentions so crudely.

His frankness and uncommonly good looks completely unnerved her. "Thank you, Mr. Braugham. I will bear that in mind. And now, if you will excuse me I must go below to ready myself for dinner." *Why do my words sound so formal and stilted? Why do I feel so uncomfortable?* She was too flustered to do anything other than move away from the disconcerting young man as quickly as possible. Nothing in any of her convent classes had prepared her for the uncomfortably excited feelings this man incited in her. She hoped that no one would notice her burning cheeks. Her heart pounded in her chest as she briskly walked away.

Mr. Braugham doffed his hat and bowed as Aimée walked off. His smiling gaze remained for several minutes after she had disappeared, and anyone watching would have seen that he, too, was plainly smitten.

~ ~ ~

That night, after dinner, the women retired to the ship's small drawing room as the men remained at the table, smoking cigars and drinking port. Aimée eyed the port hungrily, but could not think of a way to obtain a glass without shocking her fellow passengers. Luckily, she had secreted two bottles of sherry in her trunk.

There were thirty passengers on board, ten of whom were women, with Aimée being the youngest. Seven of the others were traveling with their husbands, and two widows were traveling to Martinique to teach at the mission school.

Madame Leveaux, one of the widows, inquired, "Were you born on Martinique, dear?"

"Yes, Madame."

"You must be so happy to be going home to your mother and father."

Aimée paused for a moment. "Actually, Madame Leveaux, my father died shortly after I was born, and my mother when I was six."

"Oh, I am so sorry, dear." She clasped her hand to her mouth. The other women made cooing and clucking noises, muttering, "oh, so sorry, dear'" and "poor child" to each other.

"No, it is quite all right. My uncle and aunt adopted me right after my mother passed, and have always treated me as their own daughter. I have quite a few cousins on the island also."

"Oh, that's lovely then, dear." Madame Leveaux seemed relieved. "How long have you been away?"

"I resided at the *Couvent de la Visitation* for two years. I would have returned home sooner but for the war. My uncle thought it too unsafe to travel, so we waited."

"Oh yes, a very wise choice I am sure. One simply cannot be too careful when traveling about in the world." She shook her head and made a tsk-ing sound. "Conflict raging everywhere."

The passengers made sounds of agreement, and the evening passed with light conversation, mostly regarding explanations for making the journey.

~ ~ ~

When Aimée returned to her cabin that night, she

poured two fingers of sherry into her water glass and drank it down. The earlier conversation had brought thoughts of her mother, and she tried to remember her face. She could sense her more as a feeling than as a visual recollection. After the death of Aimée's father, her mother had taken over the management of the family's coffee plantation and had spent very little time with Aimée, who was raised mostly by Da Angelique and other house slaves. She was a young child when her mother died of a fever, leaving her in the care of her aunt and uncle and Father Christophe. Aimée never truly recovered from her fear of being alone. As she matured, she tended to distance herself from those she cared about, in the event that they too might leave her. Da Angelique had been the only constant person in her life.

~ ~ ~

For the next few days, as the passengers settled in to life on a ship at sea, Aimée spent most afternoons on deck with the young Scotsman, Mr. Braugham. The ever-watchful Da Angelique was never more than ten steps away, muttering to herself about what either young person had best not do. Aimée had come to understand that the young man's rudeness was actually the result of his deplorable lack of command of the French language, combined with his thick Scottish brogue. In a circumstance such as this, it was perfectly acceptable for her to tutor him. Consequently, they spent every afternoon seated at a small table in the salon, with one or more of the other women and Da Angelique present for propriety's sake. At the end of the lessons, Mr. Braugham would reciprocate by teaching the ladies the game of whist. As a result, Aimée became more comfortable in his presence, although she still blushed deeply whenever their eyes met.

Alone in her cabin, she spent most of her time basking in the giddy, warm feelings he elicited in her. He reminded her of Signore Cavalieri not just in looks but also in his thirst for life and life's experiences, and in how he made her feel. *Could this be love, I wonder? Could it be anything else? Isn't it wonderful?*

Angus Braugham had been born and raised on his family's large and very prosperous farm outside of Aberdeen. As the youngest of six strapping boys, young Angus had learned every task required on a farm, from milking the cows and goats to plowing furrows, planting crops, mowing hay and staying out of the way of his rambunctious older brothers when they were on a tear. He was born curious and asked unending questions from the very moment he began to speak, which might explain why he knew how to do just about everything. His curiosity extended far beyond the countryside he could see and roam over, which is how he became the first Braugham to ever leave Scotland.

"But, do you not miss your family?" Aimée asked.

"Ay, I miss them very much and when I've done seeing the world, I'll return home to them and start my own family there. 'Tis a glorious place, with the deepest and brightest colors everywhere—the bluest skies and greenest rolling hills and valleys—and the mighty rivers. There's nothing like it anywhere."

"Why then did you leave?"

"Well, I wouldna known that if I hadna left, would I?" he asked with a wink.

All Aimée could do was shake her head and laugh.

~ ~ ~

On the sixth day at sea, a storm suddenly came in from the east and began throwing the ship around as if it were a flimsy toy. The high winds and rain made it impossible for the passengers to venture above deck, so they huddled in their cabins, many of them too sick to rise from their bunks. Meals and tea were brought on trays to those still able to eat. Despite her delicate appearance, Aimée was unaffected by the ship's pitching and swaying, and attended to the bed-ridden Angelique, bringing her teas and broth and holding her head when she retched into the chamber pot.

The storm gathered momentum, with forty-foot waves and gale force winds mercilessly battering the little ship and making it almost impossible to navigate. At the onset, three men were lost over the sides in the wave's backwash, and another was hit by a swinging block-and-tackle and lifted out into the raging sea. The nose of the ship rose perilously high out of the water, and then crashed down repeatedly until a halyard gave way with a loud crack that echoed like lightning. When the next huge wave crashed over the deck, the forward mast snapped, freeing the rigging and sail to thrash wildly around the foredeck, catching four men and sweeping them overboard.

The passengers rode out the storm in their cabins, holding fast to whatever they could, and praying for it to end soon. Aimée tied Da Angelique securely to her bunk bed with a sheet, and held fast to an upright beam, praying aloud to the Blessed Virgin to spare them in Her mercy. The storm raged for several hours and then, in the late afternoon, began to subside.

When the captain assessed the extent of the damage he found the ship to be irreparable. The vessel had already begun to take on water, and the first mate hurriedly assembled the passengers on deck to prepare to abandon ship. Thirty people huddled in a frightened mass in the ship's raised bow, clutching whatever valuables and possessions they were able to gather. Aimée held on to Da Angelique, whose illness had turned her face an ashen shade. Both women carried bulging carpetbags.

As the crew began to lower the first of three large wooden rowboats, a Spanish galleon hove into view. Seeing the smaller ship's peril, the captain of the galleon quickly dispatched three sturdy lifeboats to their rescue. Rope ladders were lowered over the ship's heaving side, and one by one the petrified passengers made their way to the safety of the waiting rowboats. The churning sea made negotiating the ladders very difficult, and many sacrificed their possessions in order to make the descent, giving up their worldly goods in exchange for their lives. Aimée and Da Angelique threw their bags down to the waiting boat, where they miraculously landed safely, as did both women.

Mr. Braugham and the other male passengers helped deliver all of the women to safety before making the climb themselves. The dying ship heaved so roughly that it took almost two hours to safely complete the transfer of passengers. The first two boats rowed back to the Spanish ship, and sailors helped the women climb aboard, where a few of them stood at the rail to watch their men make the same climb down to the waiting boat. Still seasick, Da Angelique went below to find a place to lie down.

Mr. Braugham was the last passenger to make his climb to safety. Halfway down the ladder, the ship heaved to starboard, causing him to lose his footing and swing out precariously from the ladder. He swung from side to side, holding on with just one hand, forty feet above the water and the waiting boat.

Aimée watched in horror as his life literally hung before her eyes. Seeing him in death's grip, her knees buckled beneath her and she began to sob, "Dear God, please spare him. Please, don't take him, please." She crossed herself but could not look away from the horrifying sight.

"Please help us bring her below," Madame Leveaux requested of two of the men. Aimée struggled against their strong arms but lacked the strength to resist, and they carried her below deck.

"Oh, dear God, save him, I beg you! Mother Mary, have mercy on him and do not let him die!" She clutched the tiny gold cross that she wore at her neck and prayed fervently to Mary and Jesus. She had not known the depth of her feelings until seeing him in peril, and only now realized how deeply she cared for him. "Please do not take him from me. Dear God, please."

Moments later, Mr. Braugham regained his foothold and made his way down the ladder to the waiting boat.

"He is safe," a male passenger reported to Aimée, who instantly ran to the deck to see for herself. As the shaken young man climbed safely aboard the galleon, they shared their first embrace, holding onto each other tightly. Their words of affection and gratitude were lost to all ears but their own.

"I thought you were lost," she cried in his ear. "I begged God to spare you, pleaded with all my heart, and He did."

"Ay lass, He spared me for your sake, I've no doubt of that."

"I am sorry to be so overcome," she said, embarrassed by her show of feelings. "I should not have spoken so freely."

He lifted her chin to look into her eyes. "There be no shame in your words or your feelings, lass, for I feel the same in my heart."

"You do?" He was so beautiful she could not bear to look at him, but neither could she avert her eyes.

"Ay, *oui*, I do—however you'd like me to say it."

She felt love for the very first time, and instantly recognized it as what she had been missing. *This is the "more" I have craved, the new life that awaits me. God has answered my prayers in a man whom I love and who loves me in return. I will be safe in his arms forever, and I will serve God by being a good wife and mother. I had lost all hope, but here we are together.*

An ungodly loud noise from the sea commanded their attention, and everyone on deck watched as the abandoned ship upended completely and slipped beneath the choppy water.

A short while later the rescued passengers gathered in a cramped salon to learn that the ship now headed east, away from their destination, towards the island of Palma de Majorca off the coast of Spain. They would need to share quarters and make do with small rations of food, but, they would all survive. In a few days they would pass through the Straits of Gibraltar and turn north. After that, it should not be more than a week to their new destination, where they would be able to book passage on another ship to carry them to Martinique.

That night, in a tiny stateroom she now shared with five other women, each snuggled in a rope hammock, Aimée reflected on the near disaster of the foundering ship. Fate had taken a different turn from the one predicted for her; the sailors on the galleon were not pirates after all. They had rescued her, not abducted her. *The old witch had been wrong.* Certain that her fate had changed, she suddenly felt free of the fear that had haunted her for the past three years. Picturing the face of her new love, Aimée felt safe. Her dream of romance had finally come true.

Chapter 14

Da Angelique did not share Aimée's happiness. "I know what you tinkin', *chérie*," she said. "Dat young man is no gent'man, no, m'a'm. He got no binness pretendin' to be good enough for Monsieur de Rivery t'ever give for his lil gull. He not up high enough for dat, *chérie*. You know dis true. It's a good t'ing I got my freedom, or I 'spect he whip me when we get t'home. It don' matter he never whip me before'. Mmmmmm, mmmmm. He might jus' kill dat boy for t'inkin dat way 'bout you. An your auntie gonna be apaletic! She maybe never leave dat bed a hers again."

Aimée would hear none of it. "Angelique, as a free woman, you may think what you wish, but I forbid you to speak of Mr. Braugham in this manner to me or anyone else. He is a good man, and it is for my uncle to decide."

But Da Angelique considered Mr. Braugham someone who might easily damage Aimée's reputation, so she continued to watch over them diligently whenever they were together.

For Aimée, the first blush of love was intoxicating. She looked upon his worldliness with a kind of reverence, utterly charmed by his ability to enjoy life to its fullest. Although he always treated her with the utmost respect, as Signore Cavalieri had, he had escaped capture by society's dictates. Unlike her protected life, he had traveled the world alone for ten years, and was now embarking on a new adventure in Martinique, one she was beginning to hope they might enjoy as husband and wife.

During the next six days, Aimée and Mr. Braugham spent most hours of the day together, strolling the deck, in the salon for his French lessons and at all three meals. Neither ever seemed to be short of questions to ask the other. Nor were they the least bit put off by Da Angelique's constant presence—always close by with a disapproving scowl on her round, brooding face, muttering under her breath.

She learned that Angus Braugham's farm had been in the family for six generations, during which time no one had ever moved farther than a few miles away. She had not been too far off in guessing his age, as he was just twenty-eight.

"Why did you want to leave?" Aimée asked.

"A good question, that. My father said I had something called wanderlust. I always wanted to know what life was like in other places. When I was thirteen, I convinced him to sign me on a trader as a cabin boy. We sailed between all the countries that border the North Sea: Scotland, England, France, Germany, Denmark and Holland. It was amazing. When my two-year contract ended I dinna want to stop traveling, so I left the ship in Amsterdam and found work on a sheep farm. You must have wanted to see the world too, to travel all the way to France."

"Not really. I just wanted to see Paris. I thought I wanted to live there—until I actually went there and found it to be not at all the way I had imagined it to be."

"Yes, some places are so different from what we know that I could never have imagined them a'tal," he said. "Like Holland, where everyone wears wooden shoes."

"Shoes made of wood? Truly?" she laughed.

He spoke in an animated way, very excited about everything. "Yes, and everywhere people eat different kinds of food. I'd had no idea anyone ate anything other than fish, mutton and potatoes. Do you eat snails?"

"Snails? Do you mean the little worms inside shells...the ones that crawl?"

"The very same. People eat them in France, and I must say that with enough garlic and butter they're quite tasty."

"No, no, I cannot imagine! What did you like best?"

"Oh, that's easy. I liked the sweet hot-chocolate drinks in Holland." He smiled. "Sometimes I close my eyes and try to remember the taste."

"And are you able to?"

He shook his head. "Not really. It was sweet and bitter at the same time, but so delicious. Nothing else tastes anything like it. I've heard it might be possible to grow the cacao plants that are used to make the chocolate on Martinique, and hope to give it a try some day."

"How exciting. What city did you like the best?"

"I dinna like cities much a'tal. Too noisy and dirty, and not like farm dirt, it's filth really—sewage and factories and the like."

"I agree. As beautiful as parts of Paris were, there was a stench that followed one everywhere, even inside the most beautiful homes."

"Aye, that's why I prefer the country."

"And what made you choose Martinique?"

"Besides growing the chocolate, you mean?" They both laughed. "I've never been anywhere where it's warm all the time. I find it hard to imagine what it must be like to be warm day and night and be able to wear so few clothes."

She blushed deeply and looked away.

"Is it true one can bathe in the sea there?" he asked.

"Of course. The Creole do all the time."

"Do you?"

"Mr. Braugham!" she sputtered, as her face turned crimson.

Da Angelique saw the exchange without hearing the words and immediately strode to Aimée's side and planted herself firmly. "Ma'm'zell, you bes' take some tea now. It too col' t'be standin' out heah, mmmmm, mmmmm."

"I believe you are correct. It is a bit chilly. Good day, Mr. Braugham," she smiled sweetly.

~ ~ ~

Late the next morning, the shore of Spain came into view. They were still a half-day's sail away, but the excited passengers gathered on deck to mark the moment.

Aimée stood at the rail next to Mr. Braugham. Their mutual fondness was common knowledge among the other passengers, and an ease of relationship had developed following the leisurely days in each other's company. In fact, most of the other passengers had come to think of them as "a couple."

"Well, it'll be another long journey for the two of us, then," he said, raising his eyebrows and smiling down at her.

"Yes. Sometimes it seems as if I'll never reach home," she mused.

"Well, I canna speak for you, but for myself, I've quite enjoyed our little detour."

Blushing, Aimée lowered her eyes to stare at her hands holding her parasol, but did not reply.

"Mademoiselle de Rivery," he began and then nervously cleared his throat. "If you will permit me, when we arrive on Martinique, I would like to ask your uncle for your hand in marriage."

Aimée bit her lower lip to keep from gasping, then looked up into his eyes and smiled. "I would like that very much, Mr. Braugham," she replied.

"Well then, it's settled," he said, smiling broadly and squeezing both of her hands in his own. "Well then," he said again, not quite knowing what else to say.

Just then, a female passenger approached, and they quickly dropped hands. Aimée looked down and smoothed the skirt of her dress nervously.

"Mademoiselle de Rivery, will you come to the parlor and play a few last lovely tunes for us?" she asked.

"Of course, Madame, I'd be delighted." She smiled and nodded to Mr. Braugham, who doffed his hat and grinned from ear to ear. As she and the woman walked away, Aimée resolved to convince her uncle to allow her marriage to the captivating Mr. Braugham. He was not of her class, lacking both title and property, but he had helped to save her life, and that should account for something. He was honest and hardworking, with the promise of a good future and (most importantly) he had already captured her heart. Of course, she could not tell her uncle that. Her uncle was getting on in years, and if she married Mr. Braugham, he could take on management of the plantation. Since she was the only heir and would eventually inherit it, what better man to run the plantation than her husband?

Aimée looked back over her shoulder and smiled again at the handsome young man she now considered her betrothed, before going below.

The two women entered the salon, where passengers sat discussing their imminent arrival in port. Aimée made herself comfortable on the little stool before the harpsichord and began to play a lively tune by the young, popular composer named Mozart that she had learned from an Austrian woman at the convent. The women sipped tea and nibbled biscuits as they listened. Two men sat at the opposite end of the parlor playing cards. Aimée smiled as she played, excited beyond words by the declaration of Mr. Braugham's intentions.

Suddenly, everyone's attention was drawn to a commotion overhead—loud thumps, running feet and muffled shouts. Startled, the men stood and dropped their smoking pipes onto the tabletop to ready themselves for they knew not what. The women carefully put down their teacups and looked up at the ceiling. Aimée stopped playing but remained seated on the bench, also looking up. Fear registered on everyone's faces as the noises increased, punctuated by men's screams. Small explosions and popping sounds joined the cacophony of noise, as the women rose and moved instinctively towards the men. No one left the room. Heavy footsteps could be heard running up the ladder outside the salon. More shouts and screams followed.

Aimée watched one of the men close the salon door and cross the room to look out the porthole. There he saw another ship alongside their own, held close by long ropes with grappling hooks. It was a large galleon with black sails…the symbol of the dreaded Turkish corsairs. The color drained out of his face as he turned towards the others and whispered the word *pirates*! Aimée backed into a corner, terrified. She remembered Rose saying, "a pirate, silly" when she had asked what a corsair was.

One of the women fainted, as two others caught her. The men carefully laid her down on a settee as the women surrounded her, fanning her face with their handkerchiefs and loosening her garments.

The door burst open.

Everyone froze in a moment of total silence. Standing in the passageway were two huge, swarthy men with long black hair partially wrapped in dirty turbans and full, unkempt black beards. Each held a sword in one hand and a pistol in the other, which they now waved as they screamed something in a language that no one understood. The women shrieked uncontrollably. Aimée slid down the bulkhead to sit upon the floor, still conscious but in shock. The two male passengers backed away from the pirates, spreading their arms protectively in front of the women who huddled behind them. The pirates continued waving their arms and screaming incomprehensible gibberish.

Three more pirates entered the salon.

Quickly assessing the situation, the five brigands conversed amongst themselves. When their private conversation was finished, they forcibly herded the two older and unarmed men from the room, using their swords to slash at them. The women screamed incessantly as they were physically removed leaving Aimée alone amongst the pirates.

Three of them discussed her quietly as they approached where she sat stunned in the corner. They gently lifted her to her feet. She shook uncontrollably, keeping her head down, afraid to look at them, and instinctively covered her bosom with her arms. The pirates exchanged conspiratorial looks as they appraised her — apparently finding her quite desirable. When Aimée found the courage to lift her head and look into their faces, she fainted dead away. However, her direct look gave them a glimpse of her sapphire-blue eyes, which caused a collective gasp.

Aimée remained unconscious as one of the pirates lifted her limp body to carry her above deck. He made his way carefully up the narrow stairs and began crossing towards his waiting ship. When Mr. Braugham saw Aimée's limp body in the pirate's arms, he broke free from the struggle in which he was engaged to leap at the brigand who carried her. In an instant, two other pirates came to their shipmate's aid and beat the young man unconscious with the hilts of their swords. As he crumpled to the deck one of them thrust a sword deep into his body just beneath the ribs. When he pulled out the sword, blood seeped onto the deck forming a large red puddle.

Da Angelique peered over the top of the stairwell as two pirates passed Aimée's unconscious body over the side to waiting hands on the pirate ship. The old woman's weathered black face contorted in a scream as she lunged forward flailing her arms, attempting to stop them. She was too late and quick as lightning, a sword flashed behind her, piercing through her back and silencing her forever.

The male passengers had been tied to the mast, and looked on helplessly as the pirates sacked the ship for valuable goods. They took pistols and swords, jewelry, chests of personal items and barrels of Madeira wine. When their work was complete, they freed the grappling hooks holding them to the Spanish ship, and left as quickly as they had appeared.

As the pirate's ship moved away, the women untied the men and rushed to the rail to watch its departure. When they were certain that it was no longer a threat, they began to tend to the wounded. People staggered around in shock, gathering pieces of their personal possessions that had been cast aside by the thieves.

Madame Leveaux sat on the deck with the lifeless body of young Mr. Braugham gently cradled in her lap. She stroked his handsome face, now streaked with blood, and wept for his terrible fate. The other widow approached her friend. "Is he...?" she gingerly inquired.

"Dead, Madame. Dead before his time."

"And what of the girl, Madame Leveaux? The poor child the pirates abducted. What will become of her?" Knowing the answer, she crumpled to the deck and began to weep uncontrollably into her handkerchief.

Later that day when the vanquished galleon arrived in Palma de Majorca, the ship's first mate wrote a letter to Aimée's uncle telling him of the death of his would-be employee, and of the abduction of his niece by Turkish corsairs. He signed the letter, and shuddered at the thought of the beautiful young woman in the hands of brigands, most likely bound for Al Djazāir, known to Europeans as Algiers, the largest slave market in the world.

Chapter 15

Aimée opened her eyes. She was lying on a narrow bunk in an unfamiliar cabin. Afraid to move, she scanned the small quarters with her eyes, making sure she was alone. She was, indeed. Her hands shook as she ran them over her body to see if her clothing and person were intact. Everything seemed to be in order, except that her heart was pounding madly and she was beginning to panic. She remembered the pirates rushing into the ship's salon, looking into one of their faces and seeing the devil himself. She must have fainted. *How long have I been unconscious—and where am I?*

She sat up slowly, feeling slightly dizzy, and swung her legs over the side of the bunk. Feeling the ship under sail and moving quite fast, she tiptoed quietly to the porthole to look out upon an endless expanse of open sea. Engulfed by the enormity of her situation, she slumped down onto the floor, covered her face with her hands and wept. She did not know where she was, where she was going, or what would happen to her. *And what happened to Mr. Braugham and the other passengers? Why did he not save me?* No answers came to assuage the fear and panic she felt. The prophecy was coming true. She had been stolen by pirates and would surely be powerless against them. Her eyes searched the small cabin for something to use as a weapon to defend herself. *Dear God, what shall I do?*

Aimée dug her fingernails into the palms of her hands in an attempt to make herself stop crying. Lost and alone, with no hope of escape, she began to fear that the men who had abducted her would return soon to rape her. The panic made it difficult for her to take in full breaths. She trembled uncontrollably, as the last of the day's light receded from the small, dirty cabin in which she huddled, alone and more frightened than she had ever been in her life.

In another cabin, the pirate captain, along with his first and second mates, sat on cushions, smoking hookahs and reveling in their good fortune. The young captain released a long stream of smoke.

"What a little jewel she is, an infidel with golden hair and eyes the color of sapphires. Never have I seen such a thing."

The other men agreed, and the second mate moved his hand to his groin.

"I say we take a little taste right now, eh?"

Abruptly the captain slammed his hand on the table top making a loud noise that startled the others. "Do you have four thousand pieces of gold to pay for her, fool? Don't be an idiot. No one goes near her."

"Four thousand?"

"She is a gift worthy of a sultan," the captain added. "When have we ever come upon a treasure that would bring such a price? She wears no ring of marriage and may even be a virgin. That's how I will sell her anyway."

Both of the men silently considered this enticing possibility, then nodded their heads in agreement and settled back to smoke.

"I will sell her to Baba Mohammed," the captain said.

At the mention of the name both men ceased smoking. Baba Mohammed Ben Osman, the Dey of Al Djazāir, was the absolute ruler of all civilians, soldiers and pirates in the infamous port. Appointed by the Sultan to rule for life, he had governed the port autonomously for over thirty years. His reputation for cruelty was legendary, especially amongst Europeans, whose ships he had ravaged for three decades. The kings of Spain, France and Portugal had all placed substantial bounties on his head.

"Baba Mohammed, you say?" asked the first mate. "He will split her in two. They say his *alet* is the size of a full-grown horse's."

"For four thousand pieces of gold, he can split her into as many pieces as he likes," the captain shrugged. "But if he is the wise old goat I know him to be, he will use her very carefully so that she will fetch *him* a good price as well."

Both men laughed and continued to smoke.

A lascivious smile spread across the second mate's face. "If he does not use her for his own sport, he is not the devil I know him to be. I have heard of *how* he enjoys women."

The captain considered this. "It makes no difference to me what he does with her, as long as he pays my price."

"Baba Mohammed," the first mate mused. "I'll wager she'll be dead before the end of her first day with him."

They all continued smoking, each enjoying their own private fantasies of what would happen to the girl in the demon's hands.

The captain imagined what *he'd* like to do to her with his own hands, wishing he could keep her for himself. Unfortunately, he was in no position to throw away so much gold. "While she is on this ship no one goes near her. She is worth much less damaged. Understood?"

The men nodded in agreement, while silently resenting the loss of the exotic little jewel they would never possess.

Up on the ship's deck, the sailors were tearing through the personal belongings they had stolen from the passenger ship. They had opened and finished a keg of Madeira wine, and were drunkenly tossing clothing, linens and small items onto the deck or overboard as their desires dictated. Jewelry, coins and other valuables went into a large trunk that had been previously emptied. Halfway through a leather traveling bag, from which an extravagant feather hat had been pulled and then discarded, a sailor extracted a small portrait in an ornate gold frame. After discerning that the frame was merely gilded wood, he was about to toss it overboard, when he realized that the image was of their young, female captive. He proudly displayed his find to the other sailors, who showed no interest in the worthless keepsake. But for some reason the sailor thought the captain might want it. Holding it to his breast, he took his find below and danced unsteadily into the captain's quarters.

"What?" the captain asked.

Proudly, the sailor held the painting before him at arm's length.

"Ah, the girl." He reached out and took the painting. "I hope this is not the most valuable thing you've found," he added. Then he dismissed the sailor with a wave of his hand, and continued studying the delicate image that looked back at him. *Were I not so greedy I would take you for myself.*

~ ~ ~

Aimée had not moved from where she sat crumpled on the floor beneath the porthole. She had been crying for hours when she noticed that the sky and the cabin were both completely dark. She crawled across the tiny space to the bunk and climbed up, then curled into a fetal position beneath the filthy blanket. The rough, straw mattress smelled of mold and sweat, and she pulled the blanket to her face to muffle her sobs. Exhausted but too afraid to sleep, she held onto the little cross around her neck and prayed for deliverance. *Why is God allowing this to happen to me? Mother Superior was right. This must be His retribution for seeing the old obeah woman. But I made penance and am a good Catholic. How can God abandon me for one sin?*

She lay there and wept until it seemed she had no more tears to cry. Fearing what might happen, she did not allow herself to fall asleep.

As the first light of dawn began to illuminate the room, she cast her sleepless eyes around its meager circumference. It was sparsely furnished with dirty, worn, roughly woven cushions strewn on the floor and one small, low wooden table. She could not identify a blackened object that sat to one side of the low table, and quietly slid down from the bunk to take a closer look. Sitting on the floor next to the table, she gingerly picked up a long hose that extended from a brass vessel that looked rather like a vase. A pungent, burnt odor rose from it, and she noticed charred bits in the brass bowl. Sniffing them, she identified tobacco and concluded that it must be a device for smoking. She turned her attention to the small table, running her hands over the hammered brass tray that held an oddly shaped copper pot with a long, wooden handle and two small, badly chipped china cups.

The sound of her cabin door slowly opening startled her. A swarthy man, garishly dressed in a combination of Arabian and Spanish garb, took a step into the room. She grabbed the small copper pot by its handle, raised it above her head, and shouted, "Do not come closer! Do not!" The room was too dim for her to see him clearly, but he was obviously not European.

The captain, as if comprehending her foreign words, raised his hands, palms towards her to signify that he meant her no harm. He made no move towards her, and spoke soothingly in his unintelligible tongue. The purpose of his little speech seemed to be reassurance, and he continued to speak quietly. When he finished speaking, he bowed and touched his forehead with his fingers, then backed out of the doorway, and gently closed the door.

Fearing his return, Aimée remained frozen in place, still holding the pot over her head. Her heart pounded in her throat, and her head ached. She was thirsty, and her eyes were almost swollen shut from crying.

A few minutes later, the door slowly opened again. This time, another man, even filthier than the first, stood holding a round, brass tray of small bowls filled with food. The leer on his face almost made her heart stop. She inched herself back against the cabin wall to put as much distance between them as possible.

The pirate moved slowly into the cabin, never taking his eyes from hers, and whispering God only knew what in his native tongue. She brandished the pot over her head, which made him laugh softly as he placed the tray onto the little table. Then he backed out of the room, closing the door. She heard a heavy bolt slide into place.

Her stomach growled from hunger, and once she felt certain that he would not return, she inched forward toward the table. The stench of bad fish made her back away again. Soon the odor began to pervade the whole cabin and made her want to retch. She dropped her weary head into her hands and found more tears to cry.

~ ~ ~

The day passed into dusk, and she had never been so thirsty, hungry or tired. The small cabin was stiflingly hot. She climbed off the bunk to examine the contents of the tray more closely. Holding her nose against the rotten smell, she noticed a small glass of light green liquid. She picked it up and brought it to her nose, where the scent of mint almost made her feel relieved. Taking a tiny sip, she found it to be sweet mint tea, and she drained the glass in several gulps. Replacing the empty glass onto the tray, she examined each of the four small bowls of food, finding nothing she was willing to sample.

She was exhausted from lack of sleep and food, with barely the strength to climb onto the bunk and curl up. She fought to keep her eyes open, but lost the battle and was soon fast asleep.

~ ~ ~

The next thing she knew, she felt rough hands running up her legs and probing between her thighs. She screamed before she was even fully awake and screamed a second time before the drunken sailor clamped his hand over her mouth and crushed her beneath him. The stench of his unwashed body filled her nostrils as he grabbed a handful of her hair and jerked her head back to turn her face up to his. He babbled incoherently in his foreign tongue, and with his free hand, lifted her skirts and tore at her underclothes as she struggled uselessly beneath him.

Suddenly, the cabin door flew open and another man moved across the room in one stride. He yanked the besotted man off Aimée and struck him across the jaw with his fist. Even through her screams, Aimée heard the crack of bone as the mate crumpled to the floor. The second man kicked the unconscious body and yelled something out the cabin door that brought two men running to his aid. They dragged the unconscious sailor from the room, while the one who had saved her stood in the doorway catching his breath. He spoke some words quietly to Aimée, who sat upright on the narrow bunk, clutching the filthy blanket to her body.

The pirate backed out of the room still speaking softly, perhaps apologizing, in words that brought her no comfort because she could not comprehend them.

After he had closed and bolted her door, she crumpled into a ball on the bunk. Her head was throbbing and she could only focus on her fear. Her situation was utterly hopeless. She vowed not to sleep again, to fight them off with all her strength. Despite her best efforts to stay awake, exhaustion and hunger soon lulled her back to sleep.

~ ~ ~

She did not stir until the next morning, when there was a soft knock on her door. She scrambled to cover herself as fully as possible as the door slowly opened.

A small boy stood in the doorway. The man who had thwarted her attacker of the previous night stood in the passageway behind him. The boy made a deep bow, then walked over to the table and picked up the untouched tray of food. He bowed again and backed out of the room. The man remained in the open doorway, and a moment later the boy returned with a new tray of food. He gingerly raised the tray towards Aimée to show her its contents, and then slowly inched forward into the room. He knelt to place the tray onto the low table. Straightening up once again, he made an eating motion with his hand, nodding his head yes to indicate that she should eat. He could not have been more than eight or nine years old, and sported a huge grin on his face throughout his entire performance. The man carefully observed the boy's every move, and when his job was done, hurried him out of the cabin, closing and bolting the door.

It seemed apparent to Aimée that the man who had come to her rescue must be in charge, maybe a captain of sorts. She waited several minutes before her empty stomach propelled her forward toward the table that held the tray. Kneeling down before it while keeping her eyes on the door, she picked up the familiar glass of pale green tea and drank the whole thing. She gingerly lifted one of the bowls and gave it a sniff. Wrinkling her nose in disgust at the fishy smell, she set it back down on the tray and picked up a bowl that held what appeared to be some type of grain. Taking a small pinch in her fingers, she sniffed it and found it appealing, surprised by a combination of both sweet and spicy tastes. She identified cinnamon and honey, but there were other unfamiliar tastes as well. Finding the combination to be quite edible and using her fingers—as the barbarians had not thought to include utensils—she quickly finished off the entire contents of the bowl.

Still hungry, she turned her attention to some small, leathery-looking items sitting on a flat wooden plate. Picking one up, she sniffed it and found it fruity. A tiny nibble confirmed her nose's analysis. It was tough on the outside, but soft and seedy on the inside—dried fruit, a fig to be exact, but a type she'd never tasted. She ate all of the little dried bits and climbed up onto the bunk, facing the door with her back to the wall, to take stock of her situation. She was alone and helpless against her captors, but when the man had attacked her, the other one had stopped him. *Why? Did he want her for himself? What if the food is poisoned or drugged to make me compliant?* She hugged her knees in close to her body, determined not to cry. What could she do? She must pray more. She slid off the bunk and knelt beside it, bowing her head, saying penance and begging forgiveness for her transgressions, both known and unknown.

For the remainder of the day, the only time she ceased praying was to use the chamber pot. As darkness descended in the little cabin, she heard a soft knocking on her door. Her heart began to pound, but she made no reply and remained curled up on the bunk as the door slowly opened. The boy who had brought the tray of food stood holding a tray with a lighted oil lamp and another glass of tea. There was also a small bowl of nuts and dried fruit. He bowed slightly, then held up the glass of mint tea and said something in Turkish, which of course Aimée could not understand. What he actually said was, "You like?"

Recognizing the tea, Aimée nodded her head and pointed to the table. The boy understood and entered the room to place the tray there. Then he picked up the tray that held mostly empty dishes, and bowed several times as he backed out of the room.

When he had gone, she got off the bunk and walked to the table to get the glass of tea. On the tray was her portrait, the one that Signore Cavalieri had painted three years earlier, the one that she had carefully packed in her trunk to bring to her aunt and uncle in Martinique. She picked it up and gently ran her fingertips over its smooth, cool surface. Her eyes filled with tears and the sadness that comes with the loss of one's dreams. She held her framed likeness to her heart and wept for everything she had lost: her dreams of a life in Paris, the happiness of her youth on Martinique, her dear cousin Rose, the peacefulness and security of the convent, Da Angelique, and her true love, Mister Braugham. She was so filled with sorrow that, for the first time in her life, she wished to die. She sank down onto the filthy cushions, still clutching the portrait, awash in utter despair, wishing they would kill her and be done with it. Feeling that there was no end to her misery, her despondency was so deep that she could not even bring herself to pray.

Spent and unable to cry anymore, she drank the sweet tea and looked out the porthole at the black expanse of ocean. The moonless sky was filled with stars, but they brought her no solace. Eventually, exhaustion overtook her and she slumped down onto the cushions and fell asleep.

She was sleeping soundly when something brushed across her face. As she opened her eyes and screamed, a large, gray rat ran across her chest. She continued screaming as she climbed up onto the bunk and the cabin door flew open. The captain rushed in, ready to encounter another man, but found it empty of anyone other than the girl. Aimée misunderstood his intent and began shouting at him. "Keep your distance or I will claw out your eyes!"

The captain raised the palms of his hands towards her and spoke quietly until she calmed down. He remained in the doorway and stared at her, unsure of what to do next. By the light of the oil lamp she was able to see his face clearly for the first time. Beneath the black beard and long unkempt hair, his striking handsomeness surprised her. He extended his right hand to her and made a motion for her to come towards him or with him. It did not matter what he meant, as Aimée backed further into the corner of the bunk and shook her head, "no." The captain continued to speak quietly and sweep his arm out the door as if she could leave.

Where does he wish me to go?

When she did not respond, he began moving towards her, and once again, she screamed.

Much taller and stronger than she, he quickly overpowered her and flung her upside down over one shoulder. In this manner, he carried her, kicking, flailing and screaming, up onto the deck, where he dumped her onto the wet planks. Standing over her, he spoke a short command to the few sailors who were on deck and all, except the one who held the wheel, went below. He continued to stare at her creamy, white skin and extraordinary golden hair that cascaded over her shoulders and down her back. Even in the darkness of night, her eyes shone like bright, blue jewels. *Yes, if I did not love gold so much, she would be mine.* His breathing became regular

again, and he slowly turned his back to her and sauntered across the deck to gaze out over the black ocean.

Aimée remained where she had been dropped, until
the captain turned toward her and made a gesture with
his hands, indicating that she was free to walk about. It
was the first time she had been out of the stifling cabin
in three days, and the night air felt cool and refreshing
on her skin. But her heart still pounded with fear and the
uncertainty of his intent. Slowly, she rose to her feet,
backing away to put distance between them, sensing
that he was a man who could be dangerous in ways that
she did not understand.

She kept him in her peripheral vision as she gazed at
the churning sea and wondered if she had the courage to
throw herself in. As if reading her mind he crossed the
deck towards her. She backed away instinctively, then
realized there was no place for her to go except overboard, and she had not found that courage. So, heart
pounding, she resigned herself to her fate and stood her
ground. But she could not look up at him. He stood so
close that she could feel his breath as he gently lifted her
chin to see her face. His large, black eyes held her gaze,
and she shivered as he carefully lifted a handful of her
hair and brought it to his face. Inhaling her scent, he
whispered in Turkish, "If you were mine for a night you
would be mine forever." She did not understand his
words, but the gist of their meaning was somehow
communicated.

Releasing her hair, he sauntered away and lay down
on his back on the deck, folding his arms beneath his
head, not seeming to care about her anymore.

Aimée remained standing at the rail, trying to comprehend the meaning of his gesture and the unexpected feeling it ignited in her. She reached for the rail to steady herself, fearing she might faint. Now she was more confused than ever. She gazed at the churning sea, but kept watch on the pirate out of the corner of her eye, hoping he would not come near her again, and yet, hoping that he would.

When the night air chilled her, she indicated that she wished to return below, and he rose to lead her back to the dingy cabin. As he closed the door behind her, she listened for the bolt sliding closed, but did not hear it. Standing alone in her small, stuffy quarters, she knew that something had changed. She was still apprehensive, but the pirate's actions had given her a sense of her own power. He had seemed apprehensive of *her*. For the first time in several days, she felt safe enough to sleep soundly through the night.

~ ~ ~

The next morning she was awakened by a gentle tapping on her door and once again, the young boy stood with a tray of food and tea. She did not move from her place on the bunk as he entered and set the tray down, picking up the one that had held the lamp and bowl of nuts and fruit.

"You don't like figs and nuts?" he asked in Turkish, which of course she could not understand. But he was very young and sweet and did not appear to have sinister motives. She shrugged her shoulders and smiled at him, causing his smile to broaden as he bowed several times and backed out of the room.

When he had gone, she went to the small table and sipped the warm mint tea. The strange occurrences of the previous night were truly confusing. Why had the pirate acted so and what exactly had she felt? Surely, that excited feeling could not have been the same as she felt in Mr. Braugham's presence. But something about it made her think of Signore Cavalieri. Maybe it was just the headiness of the fresh night air on the open sea. She absently ate some of the grain and nuts and sipped her tea. If the pirates did not mean to ravish her, what *were* they going to do? Certainly they had some plan for her, or they would not have taken her. She sipped the tea and pondered her situation, trying to ascertain their purpose by going over each thing that they had done. The one in charge had protected her from the man who tried to force himself upon her. He spoke to her in a soft, reassuring manner. They served her food and tea, brought her a lamp when it became dark and bowed as they came and went. She found that odd. People only bowed to royalty.

They're treating me like a queen.

All of a sudden, the exact words of Euphemia David's prediction came pouring into her head.

Your ship will be taken by corsairs and you will be placed in a seraglio. The words echoed in her ears. She remembered Mimi squealing, "You gone be a queen!" Then she remembered Rose telling her what a seraglio was. *Why did I not remember until now?* She was going to be sold into a harem. She was to be a concubine to a sultan.

Seized with panic, she stood up and began to pace the tiny room. Being a queen in this manner held no romantic image. For the fiftieth time she looked out of the small porthole at nothing but open sea. *This must not happen.* How could she possibly escape? If only someone knew her plight. *Mr. Braugham and Angelique knew what had happened. They will tell my uncle. He will be enraged and demand that an envoy be sent from King Louis to force the Sultan to return me to my rightful home.*

This thought gave her the hope she had tried so desperately to find. *I can be saved. There is real hope.* It would of course take time, many months at the least, but she would be saved.

She held on to the comfort of this hope, replaying the scenario over in her mind. Of course, there was no way for her to know that both of her imagined saviors had already died trying to aid her.

Chapter 16

By the morning of the sixth day on board the pirate's ship, Aimée no longer shrank into the corner when the door of her cabin opened. Her guard had not been let down, and she still clung to the hope of rescue, but felt familiar with the daily routine. Now that she remembered more of Euphemia David's prophecy, she mulled the words over in her mind, looking for clues to her fate. She did not recall the old woman saying she would come to harm, and even the rough corsairs had not harmed her…yet. So, she sat upon her bunk awaiting the boy's knock on her door.

When he arrived with her morning meal, she found, to her surprise, a large copper bowl of water and a dingy cotton towel. Lest she not comprehend their purpose, the boy pantomimed washing his face and hands.

After he left, grateful for the chance to clean herself, Aimée washed first, then drank her tea. She ate the entire contents of a small bowl of grains mixed with nuts and fruit, then climbed back onto her bunk to further assess her situation. Firstly, she reassured herself, even if all of the prediction *were* to come true, at least she would not be harmed. Then she yawned and tried to think of what came next, but felt too tired. A heavy lethargy fogged her brain, and her thoughts drifted away before she could focus on them. Lying on her side, her hands in prayer beneath her cheek, she thought the shabby little cabin actually looked rather cozy. Warmth enveloped her as her thoughts ceased altogether. She yawned again, smiled broadly for no apparent reason and fell asleep.

The ship was approaching the harbor at Al Djazāir, and the captain wished to transfer his precious package without incident. To facilitate this, he had added opium to her breakfast that morning.

Shortly after Aimée fell into a drugged sleep, the captain and two of his men opened the door to her cabin just wide enough to look in. Seeing that the opium had taken effect, they quietly entered the room. The captain carefully lifted her unconscious body into his arms. He gazed longingly at her sleeping face, and placed a deep, passionate kiss on her mouth.

"Good-bye, little jewel," he whispered.

He knelt to place her gently onto a large Turkish carpet, then carefully unfastened the gold chain and cross from her neck. "You'll have no need of this where you're going," he whispered.

All three men helped to roll Aimée within the carpet like a big cocoon. Once she had been securely wrapped, one of the men slung the package deftly over his shoulder, and made his way up the narrow stairs to the ship's deck. The captain picked up Aimée's portrait and tucked it into his belt.

Outside, the scene was typical of a busy Mediterranean port, with ships loading and unloading cargo and passengers, and sellers hawking spices, food, woven goods, copperware and pots. Had Aimée been able to observe the scene, she would surely have noticed the absence of women. A wild mix of hundreds of men—Berbers, Arabs, Spaniards, Greeks, Black Africans and others—swarmed over the docks and narrow streets leading to the bay, but not one woman. She would have been surprised to learn that Arab women spent most of their time sequestered in their homes and were never actually *seen* in public. All women left their homes beneath the complete cover of a *ferace*, a garment that covered them from head to toe, with a *yasmak*, a veil that covered all of the face except the eyes. Women never shopped or visited friends alone, rather always accompanied by servants or slaves. It would have been even harder for Aimée to imagine that very soon she too would be sequestered in an even stricter fashion.

The group carrying the carpet descended the gangplank into the bustling crowd and wound their way through the narrow, cobbled streets of the *Kasbah*. For the next ten minutes they ascended a hilly street, passing hundreds of whitewashed houses until they finally came to a high walled fortress. A thick wooden door, built into the unadorned stucco wall, held a large iron knocker that one of the men sounded. Moments later the door swung open to reveal a splendid courtyard beautifully overgrown with an abundance of huge, tropical flowers and trees. A tall, colorful ceramic fountain splashed in the center, and a flock of songbirds took flight announcing their arrival. At the far end of the courtyard stood a palatial Moorish house, with white stucco walls, arched doorways and a red barrel-tiled roof. The pirates followed the servant who had opened the door through an ornate archway.

Inside, layers of richly woven carpets covered the floor of the sunken great room. Wide, cushioned banquettes lined two of the walls with low, round brass tray tables before them. A tall, bejeweled brass hookah stood beside one of the tables. The walls and domed ceiling were inlaid with small, vibrantly colored hand-painted tiles in intricate patterns of flowers, birds and ornate curlicues. Richly woven tapestries hung all the way from the high ceiling to the floor on two sides of the room. They had entered a household of enormous wealth and exquisite taste.

The servant motioned the men to sit, and clapped his hands for another servant to bring tea. The men carefully laid down the rolled carpet and made themselves comfortable around one of the low tables. Another servant brought a platter of dried fruits and nuts and poured each a glass of sweet mint tea.

The men were sipping tea and eating dates when Baba Mohammed Ben Osman, the *Dey* of Al Djazāir, captain of all pirates and ruler of the port, entered the room. He was a huge, opulently dressed, imposing figure whose jet-black beard and mustache were waxed into sharply curling points. His almond-shaped black eyes, generously lined with kohl, looked deep and menacing. The men knew that his vaulted position was built on thirty years of ruthless piracy and bloodshed. Despite the mighty price on his head, Ben Osman's ships continued to plunder what they pleased with the blessings of Dey's distant cousin, the Sultan of Turkey.

Baba Mohammed Ben Osman's physical appearance had been carefully designed to support the legend of his persona. His vast silk caftan was heavily embroidered with gold threads, as were his leather slippers that curled up at the toes. Every finger on each hand held rings with precious jewels the size of quail eggs. Ropes of rubies and pearls cascaded from his red silk turban, in the center of which a large diamond-encrusted star held a peacock feather aigrette that shot up three feet above his head. With the turban and feathers, the enormous Turk appeared to be more than eight feet tall.

All three men rose and salaamed as he entered. He and the captain embraced in the familiar manner of men who did business together often.

"Welcome to my humble home, friend. I hope that you are well and prosperous. Sit, please."

With great effort, he lowered himself to join them at the table, his substantial girth covering several large cushions. Glancing at the rolled carpet he asked, "Is it rugs you bring me today?"

"Not rugs, my friend, but treasure," the captain answered with a wink.

"Excellent!" the Turk said, as he reclined back onto the cushions. "Treasure is always welcome. Show us." he commanded imperiously.

The captain's men approached the rug and carefully

unrolled the hidden surprise. Aimée, still unconscious, rolled out and onto her back, her long blonde hair splayed around her head like a halo.

Baba's intake of breath was audible. His eyes grew as large as the jewels on his fingers. Unable to contain his reaction, he whispered "Exquisite." then silently chastised himself. He was a ruthless bargainer, and showing too much enthusiasm this early might cost him dearly.

The Dey immediately turned his attention to the platter of dates, taking his time to choose just the right one. He took a small bite and chewed it slowly, then asked, "Where from?"

"A Spanish ship off the coast of Palma de Majorca," the captain replied.

"Spanish, eh?" He took another bite of the date, and then popped the remainder into his mouth. Sipping his tea, he fixed the captain with a meaningful stare. "Intact?"

"Untouched by *us* for certain, and no ring of marriage."

Baba considered this without comment.

"She was treated like a queen aboard my ship," the captain added proudly.

"Well, well. A queen, no less," Baba mused. He heaved his immense body up and slowly sauntered over to take a closer look. Using the toe of his slipper, he carefully moved aside some of Aimée's hair that covered her face. He saw her flawless white skin, pouty little lips and tiny upturned nose. "A princess, perhaps," he muttered indifferently. He knew instantly what he would do with this magnificent prize, although his face betrayed none of his excitement.

"And eyes like sapphires," the captain added in an obvious attempt to raise her perceived value.

"Better that than rubies," Baba said, feigning indifference and lowering himself down again. "I sincerely appreciate your thinking of me, friend, but I already have more women than one old man can deal with. In fact, I am considering ridding myself of some of *them*."

"But none like this, I'll wager," the captain said. "This one is extraordinary."

"She might prove entertaining," Baba said while carefully choosing another date. "But all things have their price, and between friends even extraordinary things must be properly priced."

He clapped his hands and a servant appeared. "More tea," he ordered, "and raki." Negotiations always yielded better results when one of the parties was debilitated by strong drink and that person would not be Baba Mohammed Ben Osman.

Now the bargaining began in earnest, and continued for almost an hour, during which many plates of cakes and several glasses of raki were consumed by the guests. The young captain was no match for the shrewd Dey of Algiers, member of the royal family of Osmans, who finally agreed to buy the girl for twenty-three hundred pieces of gold.

Baba retrieved the coins and placed them into a small wooden chest, which he set before the captain. Then the deal was sealed with another glass of raki that Baba now also drank.

After he had emptied his glass, Baba's face turned darkly serious, and he glowered at the captain, freezing the younger man with his words. "If I find her not to be the virgin I bought, I will return her body to you for a full refund."

The captain and his men stared blankly at the Dey, seeing the infamous brigand's true nature for the first time. Finally, the captain found words to reply. "I am sure she will delight you, sir, and as always, I stand behind the quality of my merchandise." He hoped that his assessment of her had been correct, for her sake as well as his own.

Baba accompanied the men towards the door and salaamed. "May your next voyage be fruitful."

"And may one thousand blessings be visited upon you and your family," the captain replied. As he salaamed, he remembered the portrait tucked in his belt. He removed it and handed it to Baba. "You might want to give her this. And as you speak her tongue," he added, "tell her that the next time I find such a jewel, I will buy her myself."

"I am sure she will be flattered." He looked at the framed likeness, thinking it did not do her justice.

When they had gone, Baba placed the portrait on a low table and returned to stand over Aimée. She looked like the angels or sirens depicted in European paintings. *What an amazing surprise she is going to be.* He moved away and lowered himself onto the cushions to sip more raki and wait for her to awaken.

Not long afterward, Aimée began to regain consciousness. She lifted one hand to her face and rubbed her eyes, then slowly opened them. Still lying on her back, the first thing she saw was the elaborately tiled dome ceiling floating above her. It took her almost a full minute to focus her gaze, and to realize that she was no longer in the pirate's cabin.

Rolling her head to the left, she saw a bizarre apparition reclining ten feet from where she lay. She instantly rolled to her side and rose to her hands and knees. Seized by dizziness, she could rise no further. Her head dropped forward and she gasped for breath to quell the nausea that rose in her throat.

With her first movement, Baba had begun watching her with great curiosity. He opened both arms towards her and smiled broadly. "*¡Hola, niña! ¿Cómo estás?*"

Aimée did not move, nor did she understand the Spanish greeting.

"*¿Habla español?*" Baba tried. "*¿Español?*"

Aimée weakly shook her head no. She felt sick and was afraid to look directly at the frightful giant who addressed her.

"*¿No español?*" he asked disappointedly.

Still groggy from the opium and with her eyes cast down, she whispered, "*Je suis français.*"

"Ah, French!" Baba exclaimed happily, clapping his bejeweled hands and leaning towards her. "I speak fluent French. What luck. My French is much better than my Spanish. What is your name, child?"

Surprised to hear her native tongue and hoping that he might be impressed by her reply, she lifted her head proudly. "I am Marie-Marthé Aimée Dubucq de Rivery, sir."

"Ah, what pride, Marie-Marthé. Utterly charming. Would you like some tea?"

Aimée violently shook her head no, which made her dizzy again.

"Some raki, perhaps? I assure you that it will cause you no harm. You see, I am drinking it," he said offering her a glass.

Aimée refused once again. "Please, sir," she whispered, "Where am I?"

"My fortunate little flower, you are in my humble home in the city of Al Djazāir, and I am Baba Mohammed Ben Osman, the Dey of Al Djazāir, at your service." He salaamed from his seat.

She digested this for a moment. "Algiers? The Dey?"

"Yes, as you say in France, Algiers. And I—well let me see, in France I believe I would be uh, well, much like, uh, the mayor."

"Please, sir, as you speak my language, take pity on me. Corsairs took me from my ship, against my will. Please help me," she begged, and then burst into tears.

"Dear child, of course I will help you. I am here *only* to help you. But first you must bathe and change into something more becoming." He wrinkled his large nose and indicated her filthy clothes. Then he struggled up from the pillows and graciously extended his hands to help her up. "Come, my child. You have nothing to fear."

Aimée grasped his outstretched hands, and rose to stand eye level with the center of his chest. Her legs were a little shaky, but the strangely attired giant had said he would help her, and she wanted desperately to believe him. What choice did she have? He was the first person with whom she could communicate since her abduction. Despite his forbidding appearance, there was something soothing about his voice, his heavily accented French, and the way he spoke to her as if she were his own little child.

"Ahmet will show you to your quarters and then Zahar will bathe you and help you to change into something very beautiful."

Aimée walked across the great room as if hypnotized, holding one of Baba's enormous hands, and looking up into a face that she found fascinating. Perhaps the opium had not lost its effect entirely, or she simply felt relief at finding someone who was going to help her.

Ahmet, a tall servant, appeared and took instructions from Baba. His eyebrows raised in surprise at Baba's instructions to show the girl to one of the guest rooms reserved for male guests rather than to the women's quarters. This was highly unusual. In fact, it had never occurred during the twenty years in which he had served Baba Mohammed Ben Osman.

Baba turned to look down at Aimée. "Follow Ahmet now," he said, patting her little hand, "and later we will dine together. Then I will explain your extraordinary good luck in being brought to me." He released her hand, salaamed, turned and walked away.

Chapter 17

Aimée followed the servant along long carpeted corridors with arched ceilings and smooth white walls. The house was remarkably cool, despite the heat of the midsummer day. Ahmet ushered her into a large room with a high vaulted ceiling. A low divan, covered with plump silk cushions, stood almost in the center of the room. Large, square cushions surrounded a polished brass tray table, and two ornately carved wooden wardrobes occupied one entire wall. A large turquoise vase, holding dozens of smooth red flowers that Aimée could not identify, sat on a low table next to the divan. Brass wall sconces and several small oil lamps lighted the room. Soft afternoon sunlight filtered through the lattice covering of a small window that opened to an inner courtyard filled with exotic flowers and plants. Unlike the décor of her aunt's opulent house in Paris, this room exuded luxurious warmth, offered comfort in place of style for its own sake and made her want to lie down on the cushioned divan to feel the depth of its comfort. Had she not still felt like a captive, the room might have made her feel welcome.

Behind her, Ahmet clapped his hands, bringing her out of her reverie, and a tall Nubian woman entered.

Ahmet spoke a few sentences to her in an African dialect and then left.

The woman wore a flowing white caftan that contrasted sharply with her ebony skin. The toes of her long bare feet each held a tiny gold ring, and thin gold bracelets graced her elegant arms. Placing her hand on her own chest, she said softly, "Za-har," and bowed her head slightly.

"Za-har," Aimée repeated.

They smiled at each other awkwardly before the slave approached Aimée and began to undress her. The ritual was a familiar one that reminded Aimée of Da Angelique, and her throat tightened.

She closed her eyes and made a silent prayer. *Please reach home soon and tell my uncle of my plight.*

Then she thought of Mr. Braugham, and her eyes filled with tears. How would she bear it until they were reunited? She stood passively, engrossed in her own sadness, as Zahar chatted quietly in a language bearing no resemblance to the one spoken by her family's slaves on Martinique.

When Aimée was naked, Zahar dropped the last of the soiled clothing onto the floor. Aimée glanced at the ruined ensemble that had once been her finest, and thought of her aunt's house in Paris and how unhappy she had become there. But oh, how she had loved those clothes.

She was lost in her reverie when Zahar slipped a thin, white linen dress over her head. Aimée looked down at the garment.

Zahar touched the dress lightly and said, "Caftan."

"Caftan," Aimée repeated.

Zahar took Aimée's hand and led her out of the room like a little girl. They walked hand in hand to the end of a long corridor where Zahar pushed open a low wooden door. They stood in a small, very warm room, empty except for several low divans and small tables. There were carpets on the floor and ornate brass clothes hooks on the walls. Zahar indicated that Aimée recline on one of the divans, said something unintelligible, bowed and then left.

Aimée sat down on the edge of a divan and surveyed the room. *Why is it so hot?*

Intricate patterns of porcelain tiles covered the walls and ceilings. She glanced at the door several times, expecting Zahar to return. When she did not, Aimée got up and walked around the room. *Should I try to escape? If I manage to find my way out of the house, where would I go?* Remembering that she was naked beneath the flimsy gown, she sat back down.

The heat began to overpower her and she lay down on the divan. *What are they going to do to me?* Zahar did not appear to be malicious or have evil intent, but she was just a slave, carrying out the wishes of the giant, Baba, who had promised to help her. She reached for her little gold cross to pray for guidance and found it gone. *They took my cross.* Aunt Lavinia had given it to her after her mother died, and the only time she took it off was while Signore Cavalieri painted her portrait. He said it "takes the eye away from your magnificent skin." Now it was gone forever and she must pray without it.

Mother Mary, full of grace, please guide me in my time of

need. Please deliver me from these walls, from my captors and return me to my family.

She prayed until Zahar reappeared and took her hands to help her stand up. As Zahar tried to slip the caftan over Aimée's head, she met with fierce resistance. Aimée clung to the flimsy shift until Zahar finally let go and heaved a big sigh. The slave put her hands on her hips and cocked her head to the side, perplexed by the girl's resistance. Then she got an idea and smiled, raising one finger to Aimée as if to say, "Wait a minute." She walked across the little room where she pushed an invisible lever that opened a hidden door, so cleverly concealed by the intricate design of the tile that Aimée had not seen it. Zahar beckoned, and Aimée cautiously took a few steps towards the door. The view made Aimée's jaw drop.

She looked into a huge oval-shaped, high-domed room surrounding an indoor lake, large enough to hold several rowboats. At one end, water poured into the lake from two huge pipes and at the other, flowed out like a waterfall. The floor, walls and ceiling were tiled in ornate painted scenes of other rooms that looked like this one — and flowers, and clouds and naked women. Steam rose off the surface of the pool just like mist rising off a lake and wide, tiled steps led down into the water all around. Several tall Nubian women stood against the walls like statues, ready to serve as needed. Long, low banquettes lined the walls and several large, woven baskets held piles of folded fluffy towels. Huge, square pillows covered in soft woven cotton lay on the floor, interspersed with some low divans.

Aimée surveyed the room with abject wonder. Was this a place to bathe? Bathing at the convent was performed in a small copper tub that had been hand-filled with hot water, and the bather wore a long, muslin gown. Everyone in France believed that bathing more than once or twice a year could cause any number of illnesses that eventually led to death. These thoughts flew through her head while Zahar gently removed the caftan, and then disappeared through an open archway into an alcove.

Aimée realized that she was standing naked in a very strange place. She quickly covered her breasts with one arm and her sex with the other. She surveyed the room to find that she was alone except for the statuesque slave women. Cautiously, she walked the perimeter of the pool, peeking behind palm trees and huge potted plants until she ascertained that she was, indeed, alone.

The pool certainly looked inviting. Maybe there was something special about this water that rendered it harmless, but how did they make it hot? Feeling more curious than scared, she approached the pool and gingerly dipped in the toes of her right foot. It felt just a bit warmer than body temperature, so she stepped down onto the first tile step with both feet. Liking the feel of the water around her ankles, she negotiated two more steps, then carefully sat down, submerged to her waist. It was an extraordinary sensation to feel the warmth between her legs and on her belly. The water felt silky smooth and gave off an exotic, sweet fragrance. Dipping both hands in, she cupped the water and brought it to her face to sniff. The fragrance was intoxicating, and she immediately lowered the rest of her body into the pool. The water came to just under her chin, and she stretched out her arms and gently waved them back and forth enjoying the sensual, luxurious feeling. Suddenly, she realized that she was smiling; she covered her mouth to suppress a giggle. The sensations reminded her of bathing in the warm ocean on Martinique as a child, when Da Angelique would let her run naked into the surf. She would splash and play and beg to stay longer when it was time to leave. She hadn't been allowed to play like that since she was ten, and couldn't believe how wonderful it felt now. If this was how the barbarians bathed, she could grow to like it. It seemed to wash all of the sad thoughts from her mind.

Perhaps this is magic water.

A few minutes later, Zahar reappeared, wearing only a length of colorful cotton cloth around her hips. She motioned Aimée to come out of the pool and wrapped her in a big, white towel, then helped her to step onto a pair of very strange wooden sandals. They were made from three pieces of wood, which raised her five inches off the floor. The shoes were cumbersome and almost impossible to walk in, but Zahar indicated that she should wear them. Taking her hand to help her balance, Zahar led her to an alcove off the main room that held five large marble sinks affixed to two of the walls. Silver faucets in the shape of open-mouthed fish poured hot and cold water into the sinks—Aimée had never seen such a sight.

A low marble seat stood before each sink. Zahar led Aimée to one of them, removed the towel, and helped her to sit. The seat was sculpted to hold the roundness of a woman's buttocks, and Aimée sat watching the water pour freely before her, captivated by the wonder and beauty of this extraordinary place.

Zahar ladled bowls of warm water over Aimée's neck and shoulders, then lathered her body with a fragrant soap and scrubbed every inch of her body with a rough loofa, the dried gourd used for centuries in the Middle East. Using copper bowls of warm water, Zahar rinsed off the suds, then tilted Aimée's head back and massaged her hair with a fragrant substance resembling clay. The fragrance reminded Aimée of roses.

Aimée liked the fragrant lather and the feeling of Zahar's fingers on her scalp, and closed her eyes to enjoy the sensation. Zahar tilted Aimée backwards once again and deftly rinsed the soap from her hair.

When she was finished, Aimée's whole body tingled. Taking her by the hand, the slave led her from the sink and wrapped her in a soft white towel. Positioning her on a low cushion, she used a large wooden comb to untangle her long blonde hair, holding the golden strands in her ebony fingers and smiling in wonder. She had never seen such hair before.

When Aimée was combed out and dried off, Zahar helped her to step back onto the wooden clogs, then led her into an alcove with several narrow, waist-high tables. The room had two unusual depressions in its floor, like gutters. Two naked Nubian women, wearing the same type of high wooden clogs as Aimée, led her to one of the tables and motioned for her to lie down on her back. As Aimée tried to discern their intent, another woman appeared, carrying a large wooden bowl with an amber substance resembling honey.

Working quickly as a team, the women lifted one of Aimée's arms over her head and used a flat wooden spatula to spread the warm honey substance onto her armpit. Aimée turned her head to the side to watch, unable to figure out what they might be doing. When she tried to take back her arm, two of the women prevented her from moving it. They continued to hold her arm stretched up over her head while another woman fanned the honey-covered armpit with a large paper fan. After a few minutes the woman stopped fanning and, using her fingers, began to peel up a small corner of the honey, which had now become cold and hard. Suddenly, with the quickest movement, she ripped the substance off Aimée's skin. Aimée yelped loudly as the hardened honey took every one of her golden blonde hairs with it. The pain was intense, but only lasted a few seconds.

Aimée tried in vain to get off the table, but the women held her in place to finish their work. They rinsed under her arm with warm water then applied some fragrant oil to the newly hairless area. Completely mystified by this operation but powerless to resist, Aimée stopped trying.

For the next hour, the two women worked expertly to remove every trace of Aimée's body hair. When they approached her pubic area, it took six slaves to hold her down. But struggle as she might, every hair was ultimately removed. Unlike her legs and underarms, which recovered from the stinging pain rather quickly, her nether region would ache until the next day.

Totally baffled by the hair removal, she wished she could converse with the women to ask its meaning. She could certainly not ask the French-speaking giant, Baba. She wondered if her hair would ever grow back. If her hair did grow back, she wondered if she would be forced to endure this treatment again. Had she understood their language, they could have told her that as proscribed by the Quran, women were forbidden to have body hair. Her hair would grow back within four to five weeks and would be dutifully removed again and again.

When she was smooth and hairless (except for the hair on her head), two slaves slathered her entire body with fragrant oil, expertly massaging it into her skin. This was the first time that Aimée had ever been touched in this way. Strange hands ran over her naked body, kneading her muscles from face to toes. She wanted to resist—*surely it must be sinful*—but these same hands had just performed even stranger ministrations, which she had been powerless to resist. She decided that she should just lie still lest they become angry. But as she lay there pretending to submit, their expert hands and the intoxicating fragrance of the oils lulled her into a state of true relaxation.

When the massage was over and she stepped off the table and onto the clogs, she saw that their purpose was to keep one's feet out of the sticky substance used to remove her hair, which was now all over the floor and running down the gutters.

They wrapped her in a soft cotton blanket and led her to a divan, placing a pillow beneath her head. Motioning her to close her eyes and rest, Aimée immediately fell into a deep sleep, the most restful one she'd had in weeks. When she awoke two hours later, Zahar appeared and helped her don her caftan.

Aimée and Zahar returned to the guest room to find an exquisite assortment of clothing displayed on the divan. With a big smile on her handsome face, Zahar held up one beautiful garment after another for Aimée to see. There were loose silk underdresses like chemises, fashioned in soft pastel colors, with intricate embroidery along the hems. Voluminous silk trousers fastened at the waist and ankles with little pearl buttons. Light linen caftans woven with gold and silver threads had long, flowing sleeves and pearls stitched to their hems. There were a dozen pairs of soft leather slippers embroidered with silver and gold. However, the items that Aimée found most fascinating were the belts made of ropes of jewels. Each was long enough to wrap around her lithe body two or three times.

Zahar showed her how the belts might also be worn as necklaces, wrapped around her neck several times with a long loop that hung past her waist. There were silver ones hung with turquoise, corral and enameled beads, a gold one studded with rubies, sapphires and diamonds, and another of freshwater pearls. Aimée had never seen jewels of this size or variety. They were wondrous but, when she looked down at herself dressed and bejeweled she was seized with panic. *What could be the purpose of all of this extravagance? Am I being arrayed to be ravished?*

The smile disappeared from her face, and despair

took hold. No doubt the price of the giant's help would be her virtue. She sat down on a big silk cushion, put her face in her hands and cried. Zahar brought her a glass of mint tea, but fearing it might be drugged, Aimée would not drink it.

At a loss for what to do, Zahar stood silently until Ahmet arrived. At the sight of the male servant, Aimée wailed louder. As if comprehending the girl's fear, Zahar fussed over her and spoke soothingly but firmly. Even though Aimée could not understand her words, she discerned their meaning—she had no choice. There was no escape. The barbarian was her only hope. Maybe she could appeal to his sense of chivalry, if indeed he had one.

Zahar dried Aimée's tear-streaked face and gently gathered loose strands of her blonde curls to fasten them with a jeweled comb. Then she led her to the waiting Ahmet, whose disapproval of her histrionics was apparent. His haughtiness made her feel like she had during her failure in Paris. Angry and determined that no one should ever make her feel unworthy again, she stamped her little foot and scowled at him. With a raise of his eyebrows, he turned and graciously motioned her to follow.

Chapter 18

Aimée followed Ahmet through three long hallways to a small, oval-shaped room whose ceiling stood miraculously open to the star-filled evening sky. For the second time that day, she had walked into a room unlike any she had ever seen. She stood in the doorway, looking up in amazement. In this house, it seemed that each time her fear arose some wondrous sight obliterated it. The open roof allowed warm night air to fill the space with fragrant scents of night-blooming jasmine and datura, reminding her of Martinique. She stared up at the stars, captivated by the room's exotic beauty.

Baba had been reclining on a mound of plump pillows. When Aimée entered, he heaved himself up to a standing position, clasped his hands together in prayer and gasped at her beautiful transformation.

The rose-colored silk caftan she wore, heavily embroidered with silver threads, matched the silk slippers on her feet perfectly. Thin chains of gold interspersed with rubies graced her ankles and wrists. Zahar had helped her to arrange a sheer golden scarf over her head and shoulders, and ropes of unevenly shaped freshwater pearls, interspersed with rubies, encircled her neck twice, then hung to the top of her thighs. As she removed the headscarf, soft waves of her pale blonde hair cascaded over her shoulders and down her back, almost to her waist.

"*Magnifique, ma petite.* You eclipse the very stars," he said indicating the open ceiling. "Come sit. We will dine and I will tell you a wonderful tale. Come."

Aimée's guard went up, but she did not want to alienate the only person who might help her. Sensing her hesitation, he offered his hand and smiled.

"No one will harm you, *ma petite.* You have nothing to fear, I assure you."

She wanted to believe this exotic giant of a man who spoke French almost perfectly. What choice did she have? She lightly touched his outstretched hand and noticed that the table at which they would sit was inlaid with an unusual bright blue, gold-flecked stone. Its highly polished surface took all of her attention for several seconds as she stood resting her hand in Baba's.

Reading her thoughts he said, "Lapis lazuli. Do you find it pleasing?"

"I have never seen anything like it."

"Yes, it is quite rare. Like you, little flower." He lightly kissed her hand in the French style, unintentionally bringing her back to the reality of her precarious situation.

"Shall we?" he asked, as they sat down at the extraordinary table together.

A servant approached to place a large brass bowl on the table in front of Baba.

"To wash the hands. Like so," he said, extending his hands over the bowl as the servant poured warm water from a pitcher over them. He handed Baba a linen towel for drying.

Aimée mimicked Baba's motions as the servant repeated the procedure with a fresh towel for her. Another servant approached the table and from where he stood, poured a long stream of sweet mint tea into each of their small glasses without spilling a drop.

As Aimée watched both elegant presentations, she thought, *they are so much more civilized than I believed barbarians to be*. The pirates and their ragged ship had given no inkling of such a refined culture. However, Baba's magnificent home was more sumptuous than anything she had ever seen, and his graciousness seemed to indicate good breeding and education, attributes not commonly ascribed to barbarians.

"The color suits you, Marie-Marthé. I hope my selections pleased you."

"They were all so beautiful it made choosing quite difficult. And these pearls," she said, absently running the fingers of her right hand lovingly over them, "they are quite exquisite." Trying to mask the purpose of her inquiry, she innocently asked, "Is this the manner in which *all* guests are welcomed in your home?"

Detecting the meaning beneath her words, Baba laughed heartily. "No, no. Only a guest of your stature, little one, and *that* is rare. Yes, quite unusual. Now I hope that you are hungry, because my cook has prepared one of my favorite dishes in your honor."

He clapped his hands and four servants filed into the room, each carrying a large silver tray. The first approached and knelt to place a platter of sliced, raw vegetables before them. A small bowl in the center of the platter held what appeared to be clotted cream. Baba selected a slice of red pepper and dipped it into the little bowl.

"Yogurt with garlic and mint," he said popping the tidbit into his mouth and selecting a slice of cucumber for his next bite. "Eat, my dear, it is delicious, and you look as though you have not eaten in weeks."

Not finding any utensils on the table, and seeing that Baba had used his fingers, Aimée reached for a slice of cucumber.

Immediately Baba's eyes widened as he put both hands up to stop her. "No, no, *mademoiselle*! Not that hand! Only the right…never the left, never." he exclaimed.

Aimée dropped the cucumber and picked it up again with her right hand.

"That is correct." Baba smiled with relief.

"Why only the right hand?" she asked.

"The left is used for other *personal* things. One never uses that hand for food. It would be unclean."

Aimée did not understand his explanation, but said nothing. She gingerly dipped the cucumber into the yogurt and brought it to her mouth. She was surprised to find it delicious, both tangy and refreshing.

The next servant approached and knelt to place a steaming bowl of grain on the table.

"Couscous with currants and almonds," Baba announced, and Aimée recognized it as the same grain that she had eaten aboard the pirates' ship in a much less elegant presentation.

A third servant lowered a large earthenware platter piled high with fragrant chunks of cooked meat.

"Lamb?" Aimée asked, inhaling its distinct aroma.

"Yes, lamb braised in sweet goat's milk and honey. Delicious."

Finally, the last servant came forward and laid a colorful earthenware platter on the table in front of Baba. It appeared to be some type of pie, covered with powdered sugar. The servant handed Baba a long wooden spoon.

Baba grinned at Aimée. "But *this* is food for the gods...it's called *bistilla*." he exclaimed, plunging the spoon deep into the center of the pie.

Immediately, steam escaped from the hole as Baba continued making the opening larger with the spoon. He inhaled the spicy fragrance of the escaping steam and indicated for Aimée to do the same. She sniffed hungrily and immediately identified cinnamon.

"Ahh, delightful." he said, closing his eyes in contentment. "But we must let it cool a bit."

The servant moved the dish to the other side of the table.

Aimée searched the table again, but could find no utensils. Surely, she was not meant to eat everything with her hands? Before she could ask, a servant scooped a small portion of couscous onto her plate with a large, flat wooden spatula and topped it with a helping of lamb. Baba, who was served first, had already picked up some of the grains with his fingers and brought them neatly to his mouth. He motioned Aimée to do the same.

Careful to use only her right hand, she tried to pick

up the grains as neatly as Baba had, but found it awkward and difficult.

"It is an art that you will learn. Try to use just the tips of three fingers, like this." He demonstrated slowly for her, and again she tried to imitate his motion. "Do not worry. You will learn."

No need, she thought. *I will not be here that long.*

The couscous and lamb were incredibly delicious and she had been very hungry. She wondered if it was permissible to lick ones' fingers but refrained because she did not see Baba do so. When the first course was finished, Baba motioned the servant to serve the *bistilla*. When it was on her plate, Aimée saw that it was actually several layers of paper-thin crust surrounding some unknown ingredients. As politely as she could, she asked what was in it.

Baba thought for a moment. "I believe that you call this pigeon. There are also almonds, pistachios, raisins and sugar."

Aimée's eyes blinked rapidly in astonishment. It looked nothing like pigeon and it smelled strongly of cinnamon. When she picked it up in her fingers, she saw that it contained small bits of meat that indeed looked like fowl. There were also some bits of things that tasted like nuts but were green in color, and some sweet brown things that tasted like fruit. After swallowing her first bite, she decided that it was the best thing she had ever tasted. Her hunger overrode any self-consciousness over her ability to eat neatly with one hand, and she managed to eat two helpings.

Baba watched happily. "I knew you would enjoy the

bistilla. And now we shall have some sweets and rose petal tea while I tell you my wonderful plan."

Until that moment, Aimée had been so engrossed in eating the delicious food that she had forgotten her fear. Now that her hunger was satisfied, her trepidation returned. Her cautiousness rose as the servants cleared the table and brought a platter of sweet cakes, dates, figs and nuts.

"May I ask, sir, how it is that you speak French?"

"Oh, I also speak Spanish, and of course Turkish, and even a little Greek. It is necessary in my business because I deal with so many foreigners."

"And may I ask, respectfully, what business that is?"

He smiled broadly. "Importing and exporting. I own many, many ships and someone somewhere always needs something."

His answers appeased her curiosity and the rose petal tea's sweet perfume lulled her back into a less fearful frame of mind.

When they were reclining comfortably, Baba began. "Marie-Marthé, how can I explain the exquisite turn of fortune in which you have been caught? Perhaps that is not the proper word." He thought for a moment and began again. "As a result of your resplendent beauty, grace and charm, you have been *chosen* for an honor that is dreamt of by thousands of women and bestowed upon only very few." He cleared his throat and took a sip of tea. "Our glorious Empire is ruled by Allah's shadow upon earth, a ruler of the most royal blood and a descendant of Osman kings, the direct line of which has not been broken for seven hundred years. Sultan Abdul

Hamid is beloved by his people and feared by his ene-
mies. His Excellency is also, I might add, a distant cousin
to myself."

Aimée bristled at the mention of the word *sultan* but
did not respond, waiting to hear how this powerful ruler
was going to help her.

Baba continued. "The Sultan lives in the greatest
palace in all the world...a palace so magnificent in its
décor and size that it is unimaginable to a common citi-
zen such as myself. But, I have been to this palace on
many occasions to meet with and pay tribute to our Sultan and the Sultan before him. I can assure you that the
mightiest kings of France, Spain and even Russia are
paupers in comparison."

He paused to let this sink in and sipped more rose
petal tea. Then he continued.

"Marie-Marthé, *you* will be the rarest flower, the
most unique jewel in the whole seraglio."

Aimée heard the word *seraglio* and jumped to her
feet. Unable to catch her breath, she barely whispered
the word, "seraglio?" She stood up clutching her heart
and wailed, "*Seraglio?* But you said you would help
me!"

Baba was perplexed by her reaction. "I *am* helping
you."

The words, "You will be put into a seraglio," rang in
her head, and she sank to her knees in shock. She was to
be a slave after all, a concubine to the Sultan. Fear
gripped her, and a feeling of helplessness brought tears
to her eyes. He had lied to her. Lied!

Baba reached forward and tried to hold her tiny, white hands but she withdrew them. He gazed directly into her frightened eyes and asked, "Do you not understand the meaning of what I have said?"

Trying to hold back her tears she answered, "Yes, sir. I know what a seraglio is but you led me to believe that you would help me, not sell me."

"Sell you? My dear, I would not dream of selling you. I am *giving* you to the Sultan."

"Sir, please, I beg you. Help me to return to my home and my uncle will reward you handsomely. I am betrothed." She sobbed openly, tears running down her cheeks.

Baba rose to his feet and paced back and forth. "Betrothed!" he shouted. "You are a fool. What kind of woman spurns the chance to live in a palace like a queen? Has your beauty blinded me, and in truth you are nothing more than a common chambermaid who is 'betrothed'? And to whom is this betrothal? Eh?"

"To Mr. Angus Braugham," she whispered.

"Mr. Braugham? And who is this Mr. Braugham?" he demanded.

"He is the White Captain, the overseer on my Uncle's plantation on Martinique."

Baba threw his head back and roared with laughter. "A slave master? You are betrothed to a slave master? What kind of barbaric world do you come from?"

Aimée covered her ears against his mockery, but his words had struck their mark. She had never thought of Mr. Braugham in any light other than the dashing young man who had won her heart. She had never thought of him in the lowly position of the man in charge of her uncle's slaves.

Baba clapped his hands twice and Ahmet appeared in the doorway. "Show our guest to her room." He turned to Aimée. "As you remove the silks and jewels you wear tonight, ask yourself how you shall be adorned when you are the wife of the slave master," he said, as he stormed out of the room.

Shaking all over, Aimée followed Ahmet through the halls to her room. Ignoring Zahar, who stood dutifully awaiting her return, she threw herself onto the divan face down, and sobbed into the silk pillows. The only person who could have helped her had just dashed all of her hopes. Hopelessness filled her as she cried harder, gasping for breath and searching her mind for a way out. When Zahar attempted to console her or to help her undress, she roughly pushed her away. "What can I do?" she pleaded.

But of course, Zahar could not understand. Unable to help the distraught girl, the servant retreated to her sleeping alcove and watched as Aimée lay crying.

"What can I do?" Aimée whispered repeatedly as she wept. *If only Mr. Braugham were here. If only someone could help me.*

She cried until she was exhausted. Then she propped herself up among the pillows and tried to calm herself by organizing her thoughts. *If I am brought to the sultan, will Uncle petition the king for my release?* She sniffled and pondered this for a while. *Aunt Sophie has been presented at court. Perhaps she will petition the king.* She absently fingered the ropes of jewels around her neck as she thought. *But how will they know where I am? Perhaps they think me already dead.* This thought brought on another fit of tears. *I must have faith. I must have faith or I will die.* She unfastened a strand of jewels from her neck and used it as a rosary. *Holy Mary, Mother of God, hear my prayers.*

She prayed for as long as she could stay awake and then, just as she had done each night on the pirate's ship, cried herself to sleep. Hope and faith were her only sources of comfort and they seemed to be providing her with less and less.

Reclining on the divan in his private quarters, Baba fumed. The little knowledge he had of women did not help him understand the girl's behavior. He knew enough to know that most women would sell their souls for a place in the sultan's palace. Could women from other countries be so different? Her reluctance angered him because she could be so useful to his plan. By all counts, she appeared to be the piece that had been missing. He puffed thoughtfully on his hookah. Well, he would not allow her to spoil his plans. She was going to the sultan, willing or not. If he had to deliver her in chains, so be it.

Chapter 19

Soft morning light filtered through the latticed window onto the carpeted floor of Aimée's room. She awoke with red swollen eyes, feeling helpless and sad. Her first thought was, *what can I do?* She noticed the pearl and ruby necklace still wound loosely around her left hand, and its delicate beauty made her feel even sadder. She remembered Baba's words—*how shall you be adorned as the wife of the slave master?*—and tears filled her eyes once again. What had she been thinking? What cruel delusion had led her to believe that her uncle might ever allow marriage to a man so beneath her station? She recalled Mr. Braugham's handsome face, his laugh that deepened his dimples, saw him gazing intently into her own eyes. She covered her eyes to make the memory go away. How tortuous would it be to deny his love? And how unhappy might her life have been as a nun after knowing its sweetness? She remembered some of the women in the convent and wondered if they had come to that life as the result of lost love.

Overcome with deep sadness, she sat up slowly and ran her fingers over the chains of gold and rubies wound around her ankles. *They are so beautiful. Are these jewels to take the place of true love?*

Zahar, who had been squatting patiently in the corner, approached the divan as soon as Aimée stirred. Speaking soothingly, she loosened the garments in which Aimée had slept, then left the room and returned a moment later with a tray of food and a glass of sweet mint tea.

Aimée drank the tea, but had no appetite for food.

Slowly and gently, Zahar removed Aimée's remaining clothes and jewelry, then slipped a linen caftan over her head.

Exhausted and despondent, Aimée followed the slave down the long hallway and into the warm room that led to the bathing pool. As soon as Zahar left the room, Aimée began to silently pray. Feeling more weary and defeated than ever before, she could not concentrate on her prayers. Her mind replayed the familiar scenarios of her predicament over and over without revealing any way out. "Dear God," she sighed aloud. "Please show me the way."

Fifteen minutes later, Zahar reappeared to lead her through the hidden doorway and into the pool. However, today she was not alone.

Three large, olive-skinned women sat partially submerged on the steps at the opposite end of the pool. When Aimée entered, their animated conversation abruptly stopped, only to resume at a higher and louder pitch. They immediately began moving through the water like a family of water buffalo, to get a closer look at the strange-looking foreigner. They seemed angry at the presence of an unknown intruder. As they moved closer, Aimée instinctively began to back away. They yelled at her and, getting no response, turned their focus to Zahar.

"Who is she and why is she here?" they demanded in Turkish. "What is the matter with her? Can she not speak?"

Zahar answered in Turkish, explaining that Aimée neither spoke nor understood their language.

Aimée stood frozen as the women ascended the steps and surrounded her. Their fat, naked bodies jiggled with every step, their pendulous breasts swaying heavily back and forth across their bellies, long black hair piled high on their heads, wrists and ankles encircled with gold and jewels. One even had a gold front tooth. They spoke simultaneously as they walked around her, feeling her hair and looking her over as if she were an unpleasant curio.

"Skinny little wretch."

"Must be too poor to buy food, and who would feed her?"

"Her poor husband...she's too skinny to bed!"

"So white, like a plucked pigeon."

"Who would bed such a ghost?"

"Who said you could bathe in our pool?"

Zahar could neither dissuade them nor soothe Aimée's fear, but thought it fortunate that Aimée could not understand their words. Finally, the women backed away a few feet and stood gawking, hands on their bountiful hips, asking questions in a more orderly fashion.

"When did she arrive?" the gold-toothed one asked Zahar.

"Yesterday," Zahar replied.

"From where?"

"I do not know."

"Why is she here?"

"I do not know the purpose of her visit."

"Does her husband have business with our husband?"

"She has no husband here."

"What?" they all screamed simultaneously.

"If she has no husband, where did she sleep?"

"In the guest room off the main hall."

"What?" they screamed again in unison. "In the men's quarters?"

"Yes."

They all spoke at once, gesturing wildly with their hands as Aimée looked nervously from the women to Zahar.

"What is the meaning of this? To whom does she belong? What gives her the right? It is not proper. She is *haram* [forbidden]!"

Finally Zahar said, "She is the guest of the master. It is his wish that she reside in the men's quarters. Do you wish to challenge *his* wish?"

The women fell silent. One did not question Baba Mohammed—not to his face or to anyone who may report to him. The only way to get answers was to have one of their eunuchs question Ahmet. They spat out several more disparaging comments regarding Aimée's small physique and possible ancestry, and then waddled away towards the warm room to begin their investigation as quickly as possible.

Zahar took Aimée's trembling hand and led her to the pool, motioning her to get in.

"You will feel better when you bathe," she said, gently urging the girl down the steps.

Aimée glanced over her shoulder to make sure that the frightening women were gone, and then descended slowly into the pool. Though she could not understand their language, their anger and disdainful manner clearly conveyed their animosity. *What could I have done to anger them so? If only I understood their tongue. If only I knew what to do. Holy Mother.* She submerged her body into the water all the way to her chin and prayed.

When she stood up a few moments later, she opened her eyes and looked down through the water at her naked, hairless body. *Oh, what would Mother Superior think about this?* she wondered. The thought made her giggle. Instinctively, she covered her mouth with both hands and then looked around. *How can I laugh at a time like this?* But there was no one to see or chastise her. *No one is here.* Gratefully, she closed her eyes and submerged herself in the fragrant water again. *There is no one to chastise me or tell me what I may or may not do.* This thought was so new and foreign it took her breath away. She remembered her cousin Rose asking her why she always did as others bade. *Because we must obey our elders and do as the church bids us,* she always replied. *Where were they now? Certainly not here.* She looked around. The room was so beautifully lit and the air so seductively scented, she wished she could somehow ingest it. She closed her eyes and inhaled deeply. Musk and attar of roses filled her with a sense of well-being and happiness. *If only I could always feel like this*. This was how she'd imagined she would feel in Paris—how wrong she had been. In what place might she feel like this forever? She laughed audibly. Certainly not the convent. Not in any home she had ever entered on Martinique or in Paris. This place possessed an opulence and comfort that she could not have ever imagined, and she realized with a start that this was how she wished to live.

Aimée emerged from the water. Taking a big towel from one of the baskets, she wrapped herself in it and lay down on a bed of soft cushions. *There has always been someone to tell me what I must and must not do.* She began to count them off on her fingers: Mother, Da Angelique, Aunt and Uncle, Father Christophe, Mother Superior, Aunt Sophie, and even Rose. Eight different people have continually told me what I must and must not do. *What will it be like without them, and who will tell me what to do now? Was there another way?* She pondered the radical thought. It reminded her of the notions about fate that she'd had on the ride home from Paris—so foreign and yet so familiar. *Could this mean that my fate is now in my own hands?* This was another extraordinary idea that had never before occurred to her. Fate had always been something that others controlled or imposed upon her. Father Christophe and her Aunt continually warned her of the consequence of her sins, hell and damnation and the loss of her soul. Even Aunt Sophie, who turned out to be correct in her admonitions regarding what she must and must not do to be accepted into society.

But I was the one who convinced Uncle to send me to France in the first place. And I was the one who insulted the

Countess and sealed my fate in Paris. I was also the one who chose to visit my family on Martinique one last time. Was it I who set into motion the chain of events that brought me here? And what of Euphemia David's prophesy? It was Rose who insisted I go, but nevertheless, I did go. Have I somehow known of my fate all along?

What if this was indeed a choice that she had made? This thought was so revolutionary she could hardly contain it. *How I wish there was someone I could talk with. I must seek counsel. If only Mother Superior were here.* Then she glanced around at her surroundings. *Heavens no, not Mother Superior.* She thought of the convent. She took in the opulent bathing pool and remembered the convent's stark architecture and simple furnishings. She remembered the emptiness of her daily routine and the boredom and restlessness that surely would have become mainstays of her life had she remained there. She was too afraid to answer the question that now hovered in the forefront of her mind. *Would I choose to go back if I could?*

There was only one person for her to consult now, the only one who understood her language. *If I speak openly with Baba, can I trust him? He has not harmed me in any way. He has actually been very gracious and quite kind, although he does wish to deliver me to the Sultan.* She wrapped herself more tightly in the towel. *But he does not think that a bad thing. To him, it is an honor, not a punishment. He thinks like a barbarian. Perhaps I must also learn to think like a barbarian. What would such a woman do? What would I do, were I such a woman?*

Despite her extremely limited choices, one seemed

absolutely correct. One felt right, suited her and fit like the beautiful silks she had been given to wear. She might enter the Sultan's prison, but she need not be a captive. All her life she had followed the dictates of others. Now, it would be she who would choose her path. She had been found wanting and undesirable in Paris, but was clearly admired here. She would use that to her advantage and choose a new life.

A door of possibility opened in her mind and by the time Zahar came to fetch her, a different young woman rose from the bed of cushions, one who was determined to be in control of her fate, who sensed that a new journey was about to begin, a journey she could never have imagined before this very moment. This new young woman wished to believe that from this day forward, despite the loss of her family, her first love and the only way of life she had ever known, it would be *she* who would determine her fate.

She returned to her room and pantomimed to Zahar that she wished to speak with Baba. Zahar summoned Ahmet, who arranged for Baba to meet Aimée in the quiet, interior garden that adjoined her sleeping room.

For the meeting, Aimée carefully chose a dark blue silk ensemble to offset her eyes. When she observed her image in the large, oval mirror, she deemed herself appropriately attired for what she was about to do. She also thought herself quite changed. She felt older and for the first time in her life, aware of her own power. It was a heady feeling that brought her hope.

She entered the garden before Baba arrived to arrange herself on a divan, propped up on her left elbow so that she might pluck ripe grapes from the silver platter before her with her right hand.

"*Mademoiselle*, I trust you rested well?" he asked as he entered the garden.

She smiled demurely. "Yes, thank you. Quite well, sir."

"And your hunger and thirst have been quenched?"

"Yes, thank you."

He raised his heavily penciled brows and inquired, "No needs unmet? No unhappiness this morning?"

"None, sir, thank you. Yet I do have some questions."

"Ah, well then," he said settling himself on a divan facing her. "I am happy to answer any questions you may have."

"There were three women in the bathing pool this morning and they were quite rude to me. They seemed terribly angry and upset and I can think of nothing I did to incur their wrath."

"My wives," he said with a dismissive wave of his hand. "They are not accustomed to the presence of strange women in their midst. Especially ones that stay in the men's quarter, I am sure."

Three wives? Aimée thought and asked aloud, "In the men's quarter?"

"Yes, my house, in fact all of our houses, are divided into men's and women's quarters. The men may enter the women's but the women may not enter the men's."

"Really? How odd."

"Oh, no, it is proscribed by the Quran. Quite usual here, I assure you."

"Then why am I in the men's quarters?"

"Well," he thought for a moment. "You are neither a member of my family nor of anyone else's family here, neither married nor betrothed. You are also, according to our Quran, an infidel. *You* therefore, do not fall within the rulings of the Quran, and I may house you anywhere I wish." He leaned towards her conspiratorially. "I imagine that my wives would dislike this arrangement intensely as they are spoiled, vicious harpies whose company I rarely seek."

Aimée was surprised to hear him speak of his wives in this manner, but thought it best to let the remark pass. "Then may I assume I will not be discomforted by them again?"

Baba's face broke into a smile and he shrewdly reappraised the young woman. "Well, well. You *are* feeling better today aren't you? Fear not, *Mademoiselle*, they shall not bother you again."

Aimée smiled and nodded. "Thank you. I also have other concerns that I would like to voice, if I may."

"By all means."

"Please hear me out. I have given some thought to your comments of last night and fear that if I am delivered into the Sultan's...palace, where I understand neither the language nor customs, as happened with your wives, I will perish."

"Of course, *Mademoiselle*, I see your point. Language and customs are easily learned. I speak five different languages myself and shall hire an excellent tutor for you while you are here. I promise you shall know enough of both before you arrive. I will also arrange for a person of great importance to guide you in all that you will need to know within the seraglio."

"Within the seraglio," she mused aloud.

"Yes, my dear, you shall never be alone, and living in a state of luxury of which you cannot even conceive. My own meager estates are poor by comparison. You will be pampered and cared for like a queen."

The words of Euphemia David came to her. "Two queens in my house today." She felt excitement like a fluttering in her chest. "And why, sir, do you believe this has been chosen as my fate?"

"*Kismet, Mademoiselle*. It is written that it be so."

"*Kismet?*"

"Absolutely. Fate. Do you not realize that the men who captured you could have used you cruelly then sold you to a brothel or murdered you? Instead, you were given into my hands, and I will give you into the Sultan's...the *Sultan's*, my dear. It is clearly Allah's will," Baba said with an air of finality.

Her eyes filled with tears that escaped and slowly rolled down her cheeks. They dropped onto the bodice of the blue silk caftan, where they left little round stains. The words seemed to seal her fate, confirming that everything that had happened in her life had led her to this moment. This was the fate that had been predicted for her long ago, and somewhere deep inside she must have always known. A feeling of calm came over her, and she lifted her head to look into Baba's eyes.

"It *has* been written, sir. In a very odd manner, I also know that it has."

A smile spread across Baba's face. "You are a precious little flower. My only regret is that once you enter the seraglio I may never again behold your extraordinary beauty."

"Oh, but surely you will when you visit the Sultan," she said.

Baba laughed. "Oh no, my dear. Once you belong to the Sultan, no man may ever lay eyes upon you again. It is 'haram.' Actually, once a Muslim woman is married, no man but her husband may gaze upon her. You see, the very nature of the word for where women live is 'harem,' forbidden. But, there are ways in which we may communicate. You will learn more of this in time. Meanwhile, you will be my special guest until your ship has been made ready."

"My ship?"

"Of course, my pet. How else will you get to Istanbul? It is a very long journey to cross the Mediterranean Sea. We must go past Crete, and then sail for many more weeks up the Aegean to the city. With good wind it should take about fifteen weeks. So it must be a special ship—a ship to take a treasure to her new home. Shall we choose the appointments together? Would you like that?" Baba clapped his hands together like an excited child.

"Appointments? Do you mean, for my cabin?"

Baba laughed. "Your *staterooms*, my sweet. The entire ship will be yours, filled with handmaidens and slaves and tribute," he said, popping a sugar-covered almond into his mouth. Then as if noticing her attire for the first time, he added, "I like the way your eyes match that blue silk—like deep, azure pools. I think that we shall use many lengths of azure-colored silk to cover the walls and divans of your new ship."

Aimée was astounded. She could hardly believe that she sat in this strange place with this very strange man, unafraid and actually filled with eager anticipation of the even stranger life that she would enter. *Wasn't life turning out to be extraordinary for a girl who had had so little adventure or prospects up to now?* Her heart actually seemed to be beating faster and harder, and she felt more alive than she ever had.

They sat this way, facing each other, each smiling with excitement and anticipation.

Aimée smiled because she truly believed that her fate had been met. Why else would she have come to this exotic, wonderful place? Why else would she be filled with excitement? Her destiny had just been shown to her, and seemed to hold more possibilities than she had ever imagined.

Baba smiled because he had secured the final aspect of his plan. It would be so much more pleasant to have her cooperation. In fact, he thought she looked quite different, more assured perhaps. He smiled because he knew the Sultan would be so happy with his new little concubine that Baba would be greatly elevated in his eyes. Should Aimée become a favorite, she would have the ear of the Sultan and her wishes would become his commands. Yes, there were many advantages a Dey could enjoy were he in favor with Sultan Abdul Hamid. Moreover, Baba held one specific desire above all else. When he died, he wished his oldest son, Rahim, to inherit his position as the Dey of Al Djazāir. Baba had been positioning Rahim for many years. What better insurance than a favorite concubine, who could whisper influential pillow talk? The exotic little beauty installed within the harem could provide the most direct route to the ear of the Sultan. But was he investing too much hope in this little girl? He must be certain to make her irresistible. He would need to pay his old friend the Kizlar Agasi [Chief Eunuch] exceptionally well for his influence this time. The Kizlar Agasi was getting on in years and would need plenty of insurance to afford his own retirement.

These thoughts sped through Baba's mind as he gazed into the girl's extraordinary eyes. He smiled at the possibilities they held, and sighed. "Ah, sweet Marie-Marthé."

"Kind sir," the girl replied, "those close to me have always called me Aimée."

Chapter 20

At fifty years old, Baba Mohammed Ben Osman had successfully arranged his life very much to his liking. Being the appointed ruler of Algiers made him its wealthiest inhabitant due to the spoils seized by his pirate fleet, augmented by the tribute paid by local merchants and Pashas. His nine sons each captained a ship belonging to his extensive fleet of sixty-two vessels, a fleet that had served three sultans alongside the Turkish navy in more than eleven wars. He lived in magnificent palatial surroundings, and since all of his wives were well past childbearing years, was no longer expected to provide them with the husbandly duties he found so repugnant. No doubt his rejection and lack of attention accounted for their unpleasant dispositions, but none dared complain, as he was the absolute ruler of his own empire as well as the port of Algiers. His position allowed him to amass great wealth to purchase, build or own anything he so desired, including a small "harem" of exotic young men. He had a particular fondness for Persian dancing boys and when they grew up, those who had found their way into Baba's heart were placed in advantageous positions on his ships. It seemed to work well for all involved. In his twilight years, he derived great pleasure by surrounding himself with beauty of all kinds: artifacts, antiques, jewels and fine rugs. Few things pleased him more than rearranging an entire room just to show off a new acquisition.

Age mellowed the old pirate, although he had been truly terrifying in his youth. He now used deliberate rumors, rather than deeds, to carefully nurture his public persona and inspire terror. This clever ruse discouraged any who might think to challenge his authority or position.

The only item left for him to acquire was the Sultan's appointment for one of his sons, the one who would take his place as Dey of Algiers. He wished to secure this appointment while he was still alive in case the old Sultan, Abdul Hamid, did not live long enough himself to designate the inheritor. If that were the case, the appointment would fall to the heir and new Sultan, Selim. He needed an influential ally with access to the Sultan's ear, and he hoped that would be Aimée. Aimée's influence might need to extend beyond the current regime, and he hoped she would be irresistible enough to bring that about. She would need to tread very carefully to captivate two hearts without incurring the wrath of either, and he believed that to be within her ability.

With this in mind, the next six weeks were filled with preparations to ready the ship that would take Aimée to Istanbul. Merchants called at Baba's house throughout the day, delivering samples of fabrics, furniture and all of the furnishings needed to transform the little ship into a vessel suitable for the Sultan's new concubine. Cabinetmakers arrived with samples of exotic woods, weavers with stacks of carpets and upholsterers with bolts of expensive silk brocades. In accordance with Turkish tradition, Aimée appeared completely covered when meeting with the merchants, and often she chose from the items they delivered without meeting the tradesmen personally.

Aimée required outfitting as well as her ship, so haberdashers, shoe makers and dressmakers brought silks and linens, tassels and trimmings, feathers, leathers and exotic fur pelts. Aimée felt more comfortable in Middle Eastern-style clothes than she ever had in Parisian fashions, gladly trading the confinement of corsets, waist cinchers, bustles and tight shoes for loosely fitting silks and soft kid slippers. Soon, the huge carved wardrobes in Aimée's room overflowed with custom-made items perfectly tailored to her petite frame.

Each night during dinner, Aimée and Baba discussed the choices they had made that day, and each morning they awakened to more purveyors and more choices. All of her fears and reservations quickly vanished amid the sumptuous and festive atmosphere of her new life. How could the staid, austere convent ever compare to the luxurious trappings that now surrounded her? More importantly, she felt accepted and valued exactly as she was. For the first time in her life someone adored her without preaching and teaching her how she must change.

She spent two hours each day bathing and being massaged, and true to Baba's word, the other women of his household never again bothered her. On days when they all shared the bathing pool, the wives remained within their own group. Knowing the purpose she was to serve made them even more jealous, but Baba had warned them well.

In a fortunate stroke of luck, Baba discovered that one of his friends had a French-speaking daughter (the result of a now-deceased French-speaking wife), and arranged for the young woman to instruct Aimée in Turkish.

Each day, pupil and teacher met for three hours of tutoring. Moreover, as well as learning the language, Aimée absorbed information about Turkish culture. The young woman, whose name was Mira, proved helpful in answering many of the questions on Aimée's list. She explained the practice of eating with only the right hand—the left was used exclusively for attending to one's needs in the toilet.

Aimée felt sure that she would continue to adapt to the new culture because thus far, nothing had been repugnant to her. She loved the food, the clothing, the baths, the exotic fragrant oils used on the body and the incense burning in every room. The strange-sounding music intrigued her. Baba often hired musicians to play after dinner, and once he had danced for her, gracefully undulating his immense body and waving a bright silk handkerchief around his turbaned head. The sensuality of the culture appealed to the Creole part of her nature, a part that had never been encouraged or nurtured.

Aimée learned that the Turks were extremely colorful and creative in their art, music, dance, clothing, architecture and food. Although writing was rarely used for anything other than religious purposes, there existed a rich oral tradition of folk tales, history and medicine. Their culture was older and more sophisticated than that of the French, who despite believing otherwise, were barely civilized by the middle of the eighteenth century. Ironically, Aimée grew up believing that cultures such as the Turkish were barbarous when, in fact, Europeans were backward in comparison. The French did not even have indoor plumbing, while the Turks enjoyed flushing toilets, hot and cold running water and heated indoor pools. What's more, all Turkish cities and towns offered communal public baths for those who could not afford their own. While the French covered their dirty bodies and hair with perfume, powders and elaborate wigs, the Turks practiced impeccable cleanliness. French women ruined their skin by covering it with thick, heavy makeup while Turkish women used rich plant oils to enhance healthy complexions, and simply highlighted their eyes with kohl. The practice of removing body hair also served the purpose of eliminating body odor. Over-all, the Turks were a much cleaner society.

Aimée remembered her visits to Paris as an assault on her sense of smell. She had never adjusted to the foul odor that permeated the entire city, polluting even the interiors of fine homes. The fragrant air in Baba's home was perfumed by the flowers cultivated in the interior gardens and by exotic incense, the inside being as fresh as the outside.

However, the Turks did seem backward in some ways. Since multiple wives were the custom, with four allowed by the Quran (along with an unlimited number of concubines), multiple children naturally followed. Since education was considered inappropriate for females, most women could neither read nor write. However, their sophisticated knowledge in medicinal arts and herbal lore was verbally passed from generation to generation.

Some of the cultural contradictions also puzzled Aimée. One evening at dinner, she asked Baba some very personal questions.

"Baba, how many wives do you have?"

"Well, I am a wealthy man and could afford as many women as I choose, but I only have four because, to tell you the truth, I much prefer the company of young men."

Aimée was perplexed. She looked around the room as if an explanation might suddenly appear, and tried to comprehend what Baba had said. The concept of men preferring men was an unfamiliar one. She had not yet learned that Turkish society (and many other old societies) silently accepted men's intimate sexual relationships with one other. Perhaps this stemmed from forbidden premarital relations between men and women, so that young men formed relationships with other young men. It was presumed that young women simply chose to remain chaste.

Baba continued. "Of course, one must have wives to sire children, and mine have given me many. But in the boudoir young men are so much more *visually* appealing, don't you agree?"

She had no idea how to respond. In an attempt to be polite, she replied, "More appealing. I suppose so." She must remember to add this to her list of questions for Mira.

"How many children do you have, exactly?" she asked.

"Nine sons, each the captain of his own ship," he said proudly. *Three with prices on their heads almost equal to mine.* He smiled to himself.

"Goodness. You must be very proud. No daughters?"

"Oh, yes," he said with a dismissive wave of his hand. "Many daughters, all married, and grandchildren. I do not know how many."

Aimée tried to imagine what it must be like to have a family so large that you could not keep track of them all. They continued eating in silence until Aimée began to wonder again about the trip to Istanbul.

"Baba, when my ship is ready, will you be sailing all the way to Istanbul with me?"

"Of course, my pet. My presence will guarantee your safe passage, and I will personally deliver you into the hands of the Kizlar Agasi. A gift as precious as yourself could not be treated with any less dignity."

"Will I live with this Kizlar Agasi as I live here with you? And when will I go to the Sultan?"

"Live with the Kizlar Agasi?" he laughed. "No, no my sweet. You will live in the harem with all of the other *odalisques*—the women belonging to the Sultan. The Kizlar Agasi and his men protect and serve the harem. He is the most important person in the Sultan's employ, and you must make him your ally. He is in charge of the harem, and it is he who will bring you to the Sultan. Remember this dear one, make the Kizlar Agasi your friend and you will need no others."

"But Baba, I thought that only women were allowed in the harem."

"Of course only women, and eunuchs to guard them."

"Eunuchs?" she asked unfamiliar with the term.

"Yes, eunuchs. Do you not know what a eunuch is?"

"No, Baba, I do not."

"Oh, well then." He thought for a moment. "A eunuch is like a gelding. One would not trust a *stallion* to guard the mares, eh?"

Aimée heard this information with incredulity. "Do you mean a *man* who has been gelded?" she asked.

"Yes, dearest, it is a common practice in civilized societies. The Italians cut young boys to preserve their angelic voices," he replied, popping a date into his mouth. "I believe that the black eunuchs also lack the rest of their manly package, or he would not trust them so implicitly. It is a dangerous procedure, but those who survive become quite valuable. The white eunuchs, who guard the rest of the palace, are only gelded."

Aimée took a bite of a fig and thought about this. Having no first-hand experience of a man's anatomy but knowing horses well, the thought of gelding or the other operation to which Baba alluded, made her cringe.

Unaware of her reaction, Baba continued eating and talking. "The Kizlar Agasi is the Sultan's most trusted servant. He has enormous wealth, influence and power, as much or more than any Pasha and because of this, I

am told the odalisques all vie for his favor and friendship. You can see that were he not a eunuch, the women
would be throwing themselves at his feet."

She envisioned a prison with tiny rooms, each occupied by one woman, and in the corridors, uniformed
soldiers with muskets resting on their shoulders, slowly
marching up and down.

"So, there are many of these eunuch guards?" she
asked.

"I do not know exactly how many," he said, placing
a tiny cake into his mouth. "But enough to serve the
needs of four or five hundred women."

"Four or five *hundred*?" Aimée stared at him in
stunned disbelief. "Do you mean to say that the Sultan
has four or five hundred *wives*?"

"Yes, somewhere around that number, but they are
not legally wives as such. The Sultan does not marry."

This information had a strange effect on Aimée. On
one hand, it was appalling to imagine one man with so
many women. How incredibly barbaric! On the other
hand, to be one of four or five hundred women had a
certain quality of safety in it. She imagined that being
one of so many might hold the advantage of her not being quite so obvious. In the event that she disliked the
Sultan's attentions, there were hundreds of other women
from which he could choose. Also, she would not be
alone in a strange, new place. It might even bear sem-
blance to her life at the convent.

With this in mind she asked, "Baba, do the women
weave and sew and embroider throughout the day?"

"Oh, I have no idea how they occupy their time in

the harem. Considering the Sultan's wealth, they could do any number of things—anything they cared to do, I imagine."

"Anything except leave," she mused.

"But sweetness, why would anyone want to leave paradise? You simply cannot imagine the magnificent scope of the seraglio. Everything one could ever want is there or easily obtained."

Baba was right. It was impossible for a girl from a small, unsophisticated island, who had spent the last four years in a convent, to imagine the excessive opulence and unlimited wealth of the Sultan's harem. In fact, it would be impossible for any European to imagine, because none had actually seen it firsthand. Most Europeans imagined the Turkish harem as an exotic, frightening place of depravity, sin, orgies and heartless, absolute rule. Many pictured it as a kind of prison/brothel, as Aimée had when she first heard the word "harem" from her cousin Rose's lips.

Oh, if Rose could only see me now.

"Baba, may I send a letter to my cousin Rose in France?"

"Of course, but it may take quite a while to reach her."

"No matter. I want to let my family know that I am...safe and well."

~ ~ ~

Later that night, Aimée relaxed in the bath, which she had come to thoroughly enjoy. She tried to imagine what her life might have been had she completed the journey home to Martinique. Despite her affection for Mr. Braugham, she felt certain that her uncle would never have consented to their marriage. How had she ever deceived herself into thinking that he would? Consequently, her prospects would have been limited to an older man seeking companionship or a widower needing someone to raise his children. Only a few such men might have resided on Martinique. More than likely, she would not have married at all, but remained the "maiden aunt," living her life in loneliness on her uncle's plantation and caring for her aging relatives. How terribly painful might it have been to live in close proximity to Mr. Braugham? The thought made her shiver beneath the warm water. *No, that would never do.*

She made her way to the opposite end of the pool and ducked beneath the fall of hot water. She could have returned to the convent and taken her vows, she thought. That had been her original plan. She tried to imagine how that might feel.

When she was completely honest with herself, none of the scenarios any longer appealed to her—none offered the possibilities of romance, luxury or excitement that her new life promised to hold. She would have the company of hundreds of other women from countries around the world, *not unlike the convent.* But, the surroundings would be magnificently luxurious: jewels and fine clothing, servants, a tutor for language and people to carry out her every wish. She loved the idea of all of that. Baba had told her that if the Sultan fancied her, she would become rich, important and powerful. Also, the mother of the Sultan was the most important and revered woman in the empire. Hadn't Euphemia David predicted that she would bear a son who would eventually rule?

Clearly, the seraglio held more enticing possibilities than Martinique, Nantes or even Paris. Although Aimée would regret never seeing her aunt, uncle or cousins again, her attachment to them was not as strong as it might have been had they been parents and siblings. Perhaps her practical nature allowed her to accept her fate, or possibly a sense of adventure that had never been given full reign. Whatever the case, Aimée felt more excited by the promise her future held than by anything her former life might offer.

~ ~ ~

October 22, 1781

Dearest Rose,

I hardly know where to begin. Firstly, I am well and residing in the home of a benefactor in the Port of Algiers. He is a kindly elder gentleman named Baba Mohammed Ben Osman, who holds great influence and wealth, and is cousin to the Turkish Sultan. How I came to be here, you will remember, was foretold quite accurately by Euphemia David. However, no harm has come to me, and I believe none will.

I am preparing to enter the seraglio of the Sultan of Turkey, and understand there will be no communication allowed from there. Please do not concern yourself for my well-being, as I have made the decision to do so of my own free will and believe I shall be well cared for, even pampered. From what I have already seen, the Turks are not barbarians as we have been taught. In fact, they appear highly civilized and quite charming.

I wonder how Da Angelique is faring as a free woman and how my fellow traveler Mr. Angus Braugham likes his new position on Martinique. He was very attentive to me on our journey, and I would like you to convey my deepest regards to him when next you write home.

As there is not enough time for you to answer this letter before I depart for Istanbul, I have no way of knowing what your present situation may be, but pray it has improved with the birth of your second child. I also encourage you to take hope in the prophecy (for you), as the most extraordinary part of mine has indeed come to pass.

Please convey the good news of my situation to everyone in our family and know that I will always love you and miss you, my dearest, dearest cousin. If ever I have the opportunity to write again, I shall. Until then, I remain,

Your loving cousin,

Aimée

~ ~ ~

At the end of the sixth week, Baba informed Aimée that the ship would be ready in two more weeks. The last detail that Baba had to attend to was her "dowry."

"Dowry?" Aimée asked. "I am to have a dowry along with all of the beautiful things you have already given me?"

"Of course, my sweet. One may not present oneself

to the richest man in the empire without making him a little richer. It is expected. Have I not told you the story of the famous Turkish pirate Barbarosa?"

"No, I would have remembered a tale of a pirate, I am sure."

They sat in her private garden sipping cups of sweet Turkish coffee.

"Well, uhh, Barbarosa was not really a pirate. He was Lord High Admiral of the Turkish Navy and, as such, was required to pay annual tribute to the Sultan, Suleiman the Magnificent. Each year he tried to impress the Sultan by increasing the tribute of the previous year, until one year towards the end of his life, and this is what a gentlemen in attendance recorded, he presented the Sultan with "two-hundred boys dressed in scarlet, bearing in their hands flasks and goblets of gold and silver. Behind them followed thirty others, each carrying on his shoulders a purse of gold, after these came two hundred men, each carrying a purse of money, and lastly, two hundred infidels wearing collars, each bearing a roll of cloth on his back."

Aimée listened wide-eyed, finding it hard to imagine the ostentatious procession of wealth.

"Impressive, yes?" Baba asked.

"Yes, but my dowry will not resemble *that*, will it?"

"Oh, no, my dear. But it shall be noteworthy nonetheless. I have stores of gold from which to draw, and we must also choose some little treasures for you as well. I would not allow you to arrive amongst those wealthy harem women like a poor relation. You must be appropriately endowed or you will not be given proper respect. We would not want you to begin your new life with less than befits your station." He clapped his hands and a line of servants appeared. "So, I have arranged for some trinkets to be brought to us so that you may choose."

Each servant carried a large strongbox. As the first in line approached, he flipped open the lid to reveal its content—a shining mound of precious gems and jewelry. Aimée gasped, her eyes becoming huge and her smile spreading widely.

Oh, Baba!" she exclaimed. "I have never seen such treasure. May I?" she leaned forward as if to touch it.

Baba laughed. "They are yours to choose, my sweet. Go ahead." He motioned her forward with his hand and the servant knelt, placing the chest before her. She turned to look at Baba, who nodded his head. "Choose, choose."

Gingerly she dipped her right hand into the chest and pulled out a strand of large black pearls with a cabochon-ruby drop the size of her thumb. She let the strand coil into her palm and grinned at Baba.

"A good choice," he said motioning her to dig back into the box.

Placing the pearl and ruby necklace in Baba's lap, she reached in again and brought out a long, delicate gold chain interspersed with small, round diamonds. She immediately wound this around her tiny wrist five times then exclaimed with delight, "Oh Baba, look how they sparkle." She held out her wrist for Baba's inspection.

"Take some loose stones also, my dear. I am told

that the Sultan's jewelers are wildly inventive."

With an impish grin on her face, she dug deeply into the bottom of the chest, and extracted a handful of loose stones. Carefully opening her palm, she gazed at them in wonder as they caught and reflected the light of the sun. They were a rainbow of colors: clear, brilliant diamonds, red and pink rubies, several shades of green emeralds, smoky gray topaz and sky blue aquamarines, in a variety of shapes and sizes from small pebbles to quail eggs. Baba made space in his lap for Aimée to deposit the stones. He signaled the servant to leave, and the next to come forward.

The second chest contained sparkling blue stones that reminded Aimée of the ocean on Martinique at night. She scooped up a handful and turned to Baba.

"Sapphires," he exclaimed. "I like them especially because of the way they complement your beautiful blue eyes. Take another big handful of those." He laughed as she followed his instructions.

The choosing of jewels continued for almost an hour and when complete, Aimée's choices filled two large chests. Baba taught her the names of each precious stone, most of which she had never seen before. He smiled sadly, like a proud father about to send his only daughter into marriage. The bittersweet emotions of letting her go were mixed with hope for her future success. To Baba, Aimée was a rare acquisition as well as a wise long-term investment.

Overwhelmed by his generosity and kindness, part of Aimée wished that she could stay with Baba for the rest of her life. Another part eagerly anticipated her destiny. She ran her hands through the mounds of priceless jewels, which she now owned, never imagining that they were pirate's booty, stolen from plundered ships—just as she had been.

Chapter 21

Istanbul
February 1782

For Aimée, the fifteen-week voyage seemed to take forever. Fortunately, she was able to continue her studies en route as Mira, the young tutor, had been allowed to accompany her. She would sail back with Baba when he returned. Aimée's ability to converse in Turkish improved daily, although she understood more than she was able to speak.

To make the most of her final days with Baba, she asked endless questions about Turkish customs, learning about the Quran's strict dictation of Moslem life. According to Baba, Moslems actually lived their lives by the Quran, unlike most Christians who, it seemed to her, rarely heeded the dictates of their Bible.

On the day before they were to reach their destination, Baba explained the procedure of their disembarkation to Aimée.

"When we arrive at the port, I will send word to the Sultan that a precious gift awaits...a gift requiring the personal escort of the Kizlar Agasi. He will then be dispatched to convey you to the palace."

Aimée nodded.

"On the following day, I will request an audience with the Sultan to present his gifts and your dowry, along with a glowing report of your extraordinary beauty and character."

"I am not to be presented along with the other gifts?"

"No, my dear, because you are not a slave."

"Oh. I had not thought of it in that way. When will I be presented?"

"I do not know the particulars of that. There are proscribed rules for anyone entering the Sultan's presence, and the Kizlar Agasi will prepare you in whatever way is necessary."

~ ~ ~

The next morning, their little ship docked in the port of Istanbul and rocked gently on its moorings as Baba's messenger made his way to the Sultan's palace. Aimée and Baba sat in the salon, sipping rose petal tea as they nervously awaited the arrival of the Sultan's retinue.

"Are you quite sure that we will not be able to visit one another?" she asked with a quaver in her voice. "What if you were my father? Would you be able to see me then?"

"I wish it could be so, my sweet. Truly, I would enjoy watching you blossom." Hoping to lift her spirits, he added, "however, I will be able to get news of you through my friend, the Kizlar Agasi, and to send you greetings through him. But, we will never be in each other's presence like this again." He took hold of her small hands and his expression suddenly brightened into a mischievous smile. "Although...there might be one way."

"What is that?" she asked excitedly.

"Well, when one meets with the Grand Vizier or his council in the Divan, I am told that the Sultan often observes and listens from a hidden position behind a pierced wall, a wall that makes it possible for him to see and hear without being seen. They call this the 'eye of the Sultan.' Were you to become his favorite, which I pray you will, he might allow you to join him in his hidden observations. I could send word of my visits to you through the Kizlar Agasi."

Aimée's face lit up with excitement. "I promise that I shall try my very best to bring this about." She cleared her throat. "Now then, have you any final words for me?" She smiled bravely to lighten the heaviness of their parting.

"Remember to do all that is in your power to befriend the Kizlar Agasi. Make him your strongest ally, because he is responsible for bringing you before the Sultan. You must know that your beauty will be a terrible threat to many of the women in the harem. Like my wives, they will be jealous. The more highly regarded you become in the eyes of the Sultan, the more protected and privileged you will be—the safer from harm. You must do everything in your power to ingratiate yourself to the Sultan, my pet. Everything."

They both looked up as the sound of many feet echoed above them. Aimée's heart beat faster, remembering a similar scene from her recent past.

Baba gently kissed the back of her hand and looked deeply into her eyes once more. *"Adieu, ma petite chérie, bon chance."*

She jumped up, flinging her arms around his neck, and kissing him on both cheeks, wetting his face with her tears. "I shall never forget your kindness to me," she said hugging him. "Never."

Aimée wiped away her tears and pulled the dark-blue silk ferace over her head, fastening the heavily beaded veil across her face. Her heart pounded so loudly in her ears that it almost drowned out the sounds of the Sultan's retinue above her. She stood still, taking deep breaths to calm herself, afraid she might faint from excitement.

Baba rose and motioned her to wait as he went above. He was surprised to see fifty eunuchs mounted on horseback on the dock, twice the number he had expected. Twenty Janissary guards, armed with short swords and daggers, had boarded the ship with the Kizlar Agasi, who salaamed when Baba appeared.

"My old friend, I see that you have prospered and increased in stature since we last met," Baba said.

"And this elegant new ship befits the Dey of Algiers and the greatest pirate in the Sultan's empire," the Kizlar Agasi replied.

"May your wealth and girth increase tenfold," Baba added.

"And your fleet continue to be the scourge of the Mediterranean," the eunuch added with a smile that further distorted his ugly face.

"May the gift I bring you today bring you even

nearer the heart of the Caliph of Islam, Allah's Shadow upon Earth, and make the burden of your road that much lighter to bear," Baba intoned.

"Tell me of this gift, friend," the eunuch replied.

"The rarest, sweetest, most delicate flower to grace the most precious of gardens, my friend. She is a tiny, golden-haired porcelain doll with eyes that shine like the finest sapphires, and the disposition of an angel." He paused for effect. "A daughter of one of the finest noble French families," he embellished, "refined in manner, voice and countenance, she is also clever and astute. Should she be put before the Sultan, I have no doubt she would be embroidered upon his heart forever." He lowered his voice and leaned closer whispering, "She could become your greatest ally, my friend."

"Many have tried," he replied wearily. "Thus far, none have succeeded. The Circassian Kadine is still his only confidant and her son, Selim, the heir."

"Selim," Baba mused. "How old is the boy now?"

"Already twenty and never immured within the Cage," he replied.

"Ah. One year older than my little treasure," Baba said.

A brief silence hung in the air as both men considered possible implications.

The Kizlar Agasi broke the silence. "Hmmm. Well, one never knows what *kismet* may bring. Let us pray that your gift proves worthy of your praise, old friend, and that she kindles the Sultan's desire to the benefit of us all."

Baba handed the eunuch a large leather sack, heavy

with gold. "Care for her well and you care for me," he said.

"I will do my best to protect her and make her ready. Be well and prosperous," he salaamed. "Bring her to me now."

Baba salaamed and went below to fetch Aimée, who had not moved from the spot where she stood.

"Come, my sweet," he whispered. "Follow behind me and keep your hands hidden. It is all arranged." He quickly turned and walked up the stairs as Aimée followed.

Aimée stepped onto the deck and almost swooned at the sight of the Kizlar Agasi towering over the Janissary guards. Even Baba appeared to be of average height next to him. His ugly face was black as night, with distorted features and an angry expression that frightened her witless. He wore a bright red robe, trimmed at the collar, cuffs, and hem with thick, dark sable. Atop his enormous girth, a tall, white conical hat extended two feet, and a jewel-encrusted scimitar hung menacingly at his side. How could she ever make this imposing giant her friend? In a panic, she looked at Baba who made reassuring gestures behind the eunuch's back.

Her heart beating wildly in her breast, Aimée stood still as the guards formed a human wall around her. Instantly swallowed by the mass of guards, she crossed the ship's deck and disembarked.

~ ~ ~

A sprawling array of whitewashed structures dominated the landscape, meandering up the hillside. Curved cupolas and ornate turrets twirled into the sky. Was this city on the hill the palace? Before she could see any more, Aimée was assisted into an ornate carriage drawn by six highly prized "blood bay" Arabian horses. Heavy silk curtains were drawn across the latticed windows, and as the door was fastened shut, twenty guards on foot surrounded the carriage. Fifty white eunuch guards on horseback flanked the party in front and back as they made their way through the streets of Istanbul towards the Topkapi Palace. They were the fiercest men Aimée had ever seen, and the knowledge of their disfigurement made her shudder.

Aimée peered through the curtains, but could not see past her guards. The sounds of the busy market permeated in a cacophony of languages too varied and foreign to identify. The crowd was composed of Turks, Moors, Jews, Arabs, Berbers, Bosnians—all men, and veiled women shopping with their African eunuchs and slaves. She listened to the city and smelled its odor, both foreign and exotic but not unpleasant.

In an attempt to calm her anxiety, she studied the only things she could see, the guard's uniforms. The boots of the Janissaries were yellow, red or black, the feather plumes that swooped down from their turbans past their waists matched the colors of their boots and each turban held what appeared to be a large cooking spoon affixed vertically to its front. *Why a cooking spoon?* she wondered.

Had she been able to observe her surroundings, she would have seen that Istanbul was one of the most beautiful cities in the world, built on seven hills and surrounded on three sides by water: the Sea of Marmara, the Bosporus and The Golden Horn. The first Islamic king had built the Eski Saray, or Old Palace, over three hundred years earlier. Now called the "Palace of Tears," it housed the wives and concubines of former Sultans. The Yeni Saray, or New Palace, which would be Aimée's new home, occupied the first hill, and every Sultan for the last two hundred years had built onto it, adding the buildings of his dreams or needs until it stood like a sprawling metropolis, a city unto itself.

As they approached the Topkapi Palace, the city within a city, the thirty-five-foot-high wall surrounding it stretched almost three miles. The wall contained twenty gates of entry, each manned by fifty palace guards, with Janissaries stationed along the battlements—but, Aimée was unable to see any of this.

The first gate through which Aimée's retinue passed was called Demir Kapi, the gate used by dignitaries arriving by sea. Once inside the outer wall, the retinues of guards left her carriage to join others near the gate. She looked up to see the Janissary guards armed with scimitars, bows and arrows. The carriage continued forward with only two mounted guards and the Kizlar Agasi, riding on an unusually large black Arabian stallion.

Gingerly moving the curtains aside once again, Aimée was now able to see the immense inner courtyard through which they traveled. To her left, a herd of horses grazed behind a low, wooden fence and a row of stables stretched as far as she could see. To her right stood a long one-story building where hundreds of armed guards milled around casually in small groups, barely taking notice of her passage.

Ten minutes elapsed as her entourage crossed the courtyard and approached a gate in another wall. At this point, the two mounted guards turned their horses and trotted back in the direction from whence they had come, and the Kizlar Agasi dismounted to walk his horse beside her carriage.

They were entering the Gate of Salutation, through which only the Sultan could pass on horseback. It was one hundred and fifty feet long and thirty feet thick, with long slits through which bowmen could shoot arrows, and holes large enough for guns. The massive wooden gate was ironclad on the outside, requiring forty guards to push it open. The armed guards who protected this gate also enforced the strict rule of silence for those who entered.

Hundreds of tall, ancient cypress trees lined the courtyard's cobbled pathways, their verdant color reaching straight up into the brilliant, azure sky. Broad covered walkways extended in both directions from the gate, with doorways that led she knew not where. Several odd looking four-legged creatures, slightly larger than common deer, idly grazed on the deep green grass. She stared in wonder at the exotic beasts, with beautiful elongated faces and delicate pointed antlers, and would not discover until almost a year later that they were African gazelles, some of the Sultan's favorite animals, gifts from adventurers. White marble fountains splashed everywhere. The falling water sounded like music. Baba told her that the Sultan who had built the palace three hundred years earlier, had designed it for the sound of running water because he found it to be soothing. She listened to the fountains' melody, hoping it would have the same effect on her.

Another ten minutes passed as the carriage made its way across the courtyard to a third gate, directly opposite the one they had just entered. It was small in comparison, only about thirty feet wide, and topped by a gold-pointed cupola that reflected the sun's rays with blinding brilliance. The Tower of the Divan (where the Sultan's government met), soared sixty feet on one side of the gate, and only those invited by the Sultan passed through its portal. This was the famous Gate of Felicity, through which all new concubines arrived—and rarely ever passed again.

Aimée's carriage stopped as the heavy gates closed behind them, and two eunuch footmen helped her to step down. The rich, green grass felt like a thick carpet beneath her slippered feet, and the heavy scents of jasmine and frangipani permeated her veil. Groves of fruit trees, heavy with figs, pomegranates and other exotic fruits stood everywhere she looked. It appeared to be an exotic, well-manicured park with streams, ponds, shaded lawns and gardens. In fact, it was the innermost courtyard of the Sultan's palace, the most enchanting place she had ever seen.

Momentarily lost in the beautiful surroundings, Aimée inadvertently jumped as the Kizlar Agasi suddenly stood before her. In a shrill, high voice incongruous to his great size, he dismissed the guards and motioned Aimée to follow him. He led the way through an olive grove to a grouping of low marble benches alongside an oval-shaped pond. Water lilies floated on the surface, and four white swans glided by.

The Kizlar Agasi settled his huge body onto one of the benches and signaled Aimée to remove her veil. As the portion covering her face fell aside, he nodded his head in approval. Her nose was unusually small and tilted up at the end, and her perfect little mouth looked like it belonged to a child. No imperfections marred her alabaster skin, and he had never seen such eyes. He motioned her to remove the head cover, which she did, exposing her wavy tresses of palest gold.

The eunuch's face contorted in a smile, and he brought his two enormous hands towards her, palms up, indicating that he wished to see her hands. Slowly she brought them forward, placing them onto his. He stroked one, then the other, turning them over and thinking they looked like they belonged to a porcelain doll. His huge head continued to nod its approval, and his smile spread larger across his face.

"My old friend was correct," he murmured to himself.

Speaking very slowly as to a child, he said, "You shall do very well, I think."

Aimée understood, blushed at his statement and smiled for the first time.

I have not seen sweetness like this in a long while, he thought. *She might well be the elixir that could bring life back to our aging monarch.* He remembered the words of his friend, Baba Mohammed Ben Osman: *Should she be put before the Sultan she would be embroidered on his heart forev-*

er. It would be his job to mold the delicate flower to his will and the will of the Circassian Kadine, the mother of Selim, heir to the throne. He would do everything in his power to protect her and personally oversee her education. She had the looks and charming manner, but he must transform her quickly. Yes, he thought it might be possible. With the proper tutelage, they might rule the Sultan and the empire together.

Chapter 22

The Kizlar Agasi rose, motioning Aimée to follow him towards a group of buildings on the far side of the garden. From behind, his fur-trimmed garments and lumbering gait made him look like a huge clothed animal. Although frightened by his countenance, she thought he had seemed pleased with her appearance, and hoped that her assessment was correct. His displeasure would ruin her chances for success.

Two armed eunuch guards stood quietly talking near a thick wooden door sheltered by a carved cupola. As the Kizlar Agasi approached, he called out an order and the guards opened the door, then stepped aside to let them pass into a small entrance hall with doors leading off from the left, right and center. Beautifully woven tapestries of rich, dark colors adorned the walls, and thick, luxurious carpets covered the floor. In the center of the room an elaborate arrangement of curly willow branches and peacock feathers stood in a tall cloisonné vase. The Kizlar Agasi seemed to grow even taller as he strode purposefully across the low-ceilinged room and held the center door open for Aimée.

They stood at the end of a long, rectangular room with intricately latticed windows set high into the walls.

Aimée looked up and thought, *just like the convent*. Rows of evenly spaced divans, covered in dark grey cashmere and strewn with colorfully embroidered cushions, were neatly arranged along two sides of the room. It looked like a more opulent version of the novices' dormitory at the convent. Although the beds were empty, Aimée felt a strong, feminine presence, warm and sensual rather than austere and pious. She found the similarity comforting, while the disparity of their purposes made her smile. She quickly counted approximately thirty beds, wondered where the rest of the harem slept, and if one of the beds would be hers.

The eunuch led the way through the room saying slowly, "Cariye sleep here."

Aimée did not understand the word "Cariye," but would soon discover it was the word for slave as well as the one used for new harem initiates.

"Your teacher, the Vekil Usta, lives here," the Eunuch explained, indicating a small private bedroom at the far end of the dormitory.

Aimée understood the word "teacher" and surmised the rest. She felt excited by her ability to understand the language and relieved that, thus far, her new surroundings did not resemble a prison in any way.

Immediately beyond the sleeping quarters were servants' quarters and several large dressing rooms piled high with trunks and wardrobes. Beyond these were the kitchens where a dozen cooks were busily preparing food for the noon meal. As they passed through, Aimée recognized the fragrant aromas that began to make her mouth water.

They looked into a small room off the kitchen where several Nubians laundered clothes, then passed into a lovely dining room with low wooden tables surrounded by divans and plump silk cushions on a carpeted floor. Silver trays holding tiny porcelain coffee cups sat on many of the tables.

Mosaic murals of painted tiles covered the walls with a profusion of intricate designs in shades of blue, green, black and white. Several tall water pipes (*nargileh*) stood near the divans, and the Kizlar Agasi pointed to them saying their name. Aimée repeated the familiar word aloud and smiled, enjoying the pleasant way it felt in her mouth. She was wondering where the women who lived here might be, just as the eunuch opened a door into another large room, constructed entirely of white marble with benches lining the walls. Clothes of all colors hung from golden hooks, and dozens of pairs of delicate kid slippers lay scattered beneath the benches. Her nose detected the scents of jasmine, sandalwood and ambergris, and she knew that the bath must be near. She had not bathed in a large pool throughout her long sea voyage, and the thought of submerging her naked body into a hot, fragrant bath made her quiver with anticipation.

The Kizlar Agasi shouted a shrill command that startled Aimée and brought two Nubian girls running into the room from an alcove. They were clearly adolescents, naked from the waist up, wearing multicolored silk loincloths and colorful silk scarves wound around their heads into elaborate headdresses. Thick silver bracelets encircled their wrists and ankles, and multiple beaded necklaces wound around their necks before cascading onto their budding, naked breasts. Smiling broadly, with perfect white teeth, they expertly undressed Aimée in less than a minute. As the girls scurried away, she looked up to meet the level gaze of the Kizlar Agasi, who sat on a bench, leaning forward on the jewel-encrusted head of his heavy walking stick.

The disrobing had happened so swiftly that it caught Aimée completely by surprise. Now she found herself standing stark naked before the fierce-looking giant. She did not know what to do with her hands or how to hide the panic she felt. Realizing that she had been holding her breath, she exhaled all at once, simultaneously remembering that the imposing figure was actually a eunuch. Her nervousness made her giggle. She brought a hand to her mouth to stifle the laughter, and realized how little embarrassment she felt at being naked. Apparently, her time at Baba's had effectively undermined years of imposed modesty, and she now actually enjoyed the sensuous feeling of being naked in a warm room. But she had never stood nude before a man, even though this one lacked the physical accoutrements to threaten her virginity. She was torn between self-consciousness and her wish to present a pleasing image. This was the person whom she must impress and befriend, whose approval was vital to her success. As these thoughts passed through her mind she automatically stood as straight as she could, arched her back slightly to lift her little breasts, and then raised her chin and smiled.

In his wisdom, the Kizlar Agasi read every emotion that passed across Aimée's face and found the whole effect to be quite charming. His eyes evaluated every inch of the front of her petite body—the firm, small breasts, smooth soft shoulders, rounded young belly and shapely thighs. *Too thin, but we can fix that.* He motioned her to turn around.

"Mmmm," he murmured at the sight of her round buttocks. *If the Sultan does not appreciate this, he might as well be dead.* The golden hair and bright blue eyes were novelty enough to peak the jaded old man's interest, but combined with her perfectly proportioned body and innocent manner, she was captivating. *The old pirate was right. If she shows even the slightest aptitude for sensuality, I will be able to fan its flame and train her to fulfill the sultan's every desire.*

"Turn around," he said. When she was again facing him he said, "Your life begins anew, created by me."

She understood only the words "life" and "me" but discerned his meaning, already knowing that her fate rested in his huge, misshapen hands. Their eyes met, recognizing mutual determination. Aimée was going to learn how to become a queen, and this man, who sat before her drinking in her naked beauty, was the one who could make it so.

He clapped his hands and the slave girls appeared, bringing Aimée a pair of *pattens*, the high wooden clogs that she had worn in Baba's bathhouse. The Kizlar Agasi rose from his seat.

"We will meet again after you have bathed and eaten," he said, and left the room.

The slaves helped her to step onto the clogs, then each took one of Aimée's hands and led her through the gracefully arched door, into the *tepidarium*. This was the anteroom attached to all Turkish baths, where bathers acclimated to the warm temperature and steamy air before entering the bath. As soon as Aimée stepped into the room she could hear the muffled sounds of bathers in the next room, and her heart began to beat a little faster.

The slaves led her to a towel-covered divan where she slipped off the wooden clogs and reclined, one elbow propped against soft pillows. They brought her a tiny porcelain cup of dark, sweet coffee, plates of fruits, nuts, toffee and sweet little cakes. She ate some of everything, finding them all to be delicious, and from her cozy perch took in every aspect of the room. She saw marble banquettes lining three of the walls, and counted seventy-two silk pillows lying scattered on the carpeted floor. There were twenty-three low, brass tray tables, each holding a silver coffee service. Two intricately carved wooden doors with ornate silver handles stood in the far wall that she assumed led to the bathing pool. Aimée reclined, feeling sinfully excited by the prospects of bathing, and tried to imagine what would happen after her bath. Would she meet the Sultan tonight?

After about twenty minutes, the young slaves appeared to help her onto her pattens. Leading her to the large wooden doors, each grasped a handle and pulled it open. A wave of perfumed steam immediately engulfed Aimée as the slaves reached out to steady her.

The bathing area was easily twice the size of the one at Baba's house and filled with dozens of young women and servants. The ones Aimée assumed to be the Sultan's concubines, sat on marble stools while slave girls massaged and shampooed their hair, clipped their toenails and rubbed calloused feet with pumice stones. Girls poured perfumed water over each other from long, silver ladles and small golden bowls. Ten women lolled in a small pool of mineral water that bubbled up from a golden spigot in the floor, while dozens of others reclined on the broad steps leading into the larger pool. Some lay prone on raised marble slabs while slaves rubbed their bodies with a rough mixture of ground almonds and honey to remove dead skin and make it soft. Yet, even with all the activity there was a hushed languidness that let one know these women were in no hurry; they had all the time they needed to enjoy their bathing and beauty rituals.

As Aimée entered, all heads turned towards her and conversations came to a halt. Eyes widened and hands flew to cover open mouths. Whispered exclamations were exchanged and breath was held. All activity abruptly stopped. Although accustomed to the entrances of new novices, none of the women had ever before seen one with blonde hair.

Aimée, not understanding their shocked reaction and fearing a repeat of the encounter with Baba's wives, began to back away. A young girl, who looked to be about twelve years old, bravely approached Aimée for a closer look. Her black eyes grew large with wonder as she slowly reached her hand up to touch Aimée's waist-length golden hair. Aimée held her breath as the girl gently rubbed the silky strands between her fingers, then looked up and smiled.

"Soft, like silk," the girl said in Turkish.

Aimée relaxed and smiled at the girl. Then ten other girls cautiously approached to feel Aimée's hair for themselves. They smiled broadly as they ooohed and ahhed and called to the other women to come and touch. In moments, Aimée was surrounded by fifty naked females, odalisques and slaves, gently touching her hair and staring into her sapphire-blue eyes. Relieved that they were merely curious, she thought, *They are all so young.* It was quite a welcome, and she wished that she could understand more of what they were saying, but they all spoke at once in more languages than she could count.

The first brave young girl gently tugged at her hand and asked, in halting Turkish, what she was called.

"Aimée," she replied.

The girl turned to the others and proudly said, "She is called Namay."

She took Aimée's hand and led her to an alabaster seat before a marble sink where hot and cold water ran from gold faucets. The girl filled a bowl with warm water and gently poured it over Aimée's shoulders and back.

Giddy with relief, and enjoying the spirit of playful camaraderie between the naked nymphs, Aimée turned to smile at the young girl and asked, "Your name?"

"I am Perestu. It means 'little swallow.' What means Namay?"

Aimée thought for a moment then replied, "I do not know."

"Oh, then," Perestu replied sagely, "not real name."

Aimée did not understand the girl's comment—it did not make sense to her.

Several young women approached to politely introduce themselves, and Aimée relaxed even more. None of them seemed angry or discomforted by her presence and as she looked around she immediately understood their fascination with her hair and eyes. They were all black-haired, black-eyed beauties, probably Arab, Greek, Georgian and Circassian. They seemed to range in age from about twelve to twenty-five, with the greatest number appearing to be in their late teens. But Aimée had no way of knowing that these were just the new girls destined for the harem, like herself, and that she would not meet the true women of the seraglio or enter its portals for many months.

Entering the baths, Aimée later learned, meant that she was now enrolled in the *Cariye Dairisi*, the school for odalisques through which all novices must pass. The school's lessons included the cultivation of grace, charm and sensuality as well as the artistic pursuits of embroidery, weaving, dancing, singing and playing of musical instruments. All newcomers were also taught to read, write and speak the common tongue of Ottoman Turkish. In this regard, Aimée was far ahead of most of them, including Perestu, who had only been in the school for a few weeks. No girl was ever required to renounce the religion of her birth; however, if one chose to adopt Islam, she simply said aloud, in front of two witnesses, "Allah is great and Mohammed is his prophet."

But the most important aspect of the novice's training was the perfection of the art of love, for pleasuring the Sultan was the true purpose of their existence. Mastering the art of devoting oneself solely to pleasure sometimes took more than a year, and younger odalisques like Perestu might spend two or more years in the school before graduating.

The graduation decision rested solely in the hands of the Circassian Kadine, traditionally the mother of the Sultan, because she knew his preferences, sexual and otherwise, better than anyone else. The current Kadine was in fact, mother of the heir rather than of the reigning Sultan, as he was seventy-one years old and his mother had long since passed. The tests required to graduate from the *Cariye Dairisi* took place over a two day period and included: the preparation and service of coffee (a precise art form), a musical recital, a dance program, dozens of costume changes and the actual performance of fourteen different sexual acts with a eunuch wearing a carved wooden penis and leather scrotum. Of course, Aimée knew nothing of this yet.

Nothing was left to chance, in fear of invoking the Sultan's wrath. It was never prudent to displease an omnipotent demigod who wielded the power of life and death. Historically, disgruntled Sultans often dispatched unworthy concubines by drowning or strangulation, sometimes ridding themselves of hundreds at a time to make room for others who might be more pleasing. Within the world of the harem, one of the few luxuries *not* afforded was that of resting on one's laurels. There were always newcomers to unseat odalisques who had become disgruntled, lazy or petulant.

Aimée hoped to be such a newcomer but, first she had to learn and master those arts not taught at the *Couvent de la Visitation*.

Chapter 23

On the following day, Baba Mohammed Ben Osman, dressed in his most splendid attire, passed through the white marble arches of the Imperial Gate. Above him, fifty armed Janissaries stood guard. He sat astride a bay Arabian stallion, flanked by an impressive retinue of his men, and twelve tribute slaves, stately Nubians dressed in their finest traditional African attire. Each slave wore thick wrist and ankle bracelets of heavy gold. Multiple strands of colorful beaded necklaces stacked up their necks, then fell like a beaded curtain almost to their waists. There were six men, six women, and Zahar, dressed in an opulent Turkish costume. So regal were their dress and bearing that pedestrians paused to watch them pass.

Inside the gate, hundreds of visitors and twice as many Janissary guards milled around in view of the "Blue Mosque," the Hagia Sophia. Two dozen White Eunuchs guarded a long, low infirmary building to the left of the entrance. A bakery, flourmill, treasury, mint, furniture shop, workshop and repair shop all bustled with patrons—a small fraction of the twenty thousand palace workers who lived within its walls.

Baba rode towards the center of the huge courtyard. He was one of thousands who arrived daily to conduct

political, personal or business dealings in the first courtyard of the Palace. Citizens came to register births,
deaths and marriages, and to arrange and celebrate cir-
cumcisions. All petitions to the Sultan were brought
here, as were foreign ministers and visiting dignitaries.

The elaborate protocol required for an audience with
the Sultan began with a ritual bathing. Appropriate
Turkish clothing was provided should the visitor not
already be so attired. The visitor was then carried into
the Divine One's presence by Janissary guards support-
ing him under each arm. Baba was familiar with the procedure, having endured it dozens of times throughout
his associations with four Sultans.

With the hopes of ensuring a positive outcome for
his purpose, each visitor brought the most expensive
gifts he could afford. On this day, the offerings included
a dozen matching Arabian breeding stallions; stacks of
precious, rare furs; two elephants; two golden boxes
filled with large, black pearls; and an emerald cabochon
the size of a duck's egg.

Shortly before sunset, Baba entered the throne room
carried by four strapping guards. One hundred armed
Janissaries lined the silk- covered walls of the throne
room like statues, never moving a muscle. The "throne"
resembled a huge bed made of solid gold, encrusted
with hundreds of large diamonds, rubies, emeralds,
pearls and sapphires. Gold brocade curtains hung down
on three sides from the canopy. The partially raised front
curtain revealed the royal personage who reclined there
on a mound of magnificent cushions.

Baba was pleased to find Sultan Abdul Hamid actually present. To most visitors, the Sultan remained hidden behind his curtains, rarely ever revealing more than a royal finger or hand. However, Baba Mohammed Ben Osman was a distant cousin, former Admiral of the Turkish navy, and captain of all Turkish pirates. His tribute added substantially to the royal coffers, and in times of war, his fleet aided the Turkish navy. Consequently, he was always received personally and with less formality than other visitors.

A cluster of diamonds the size of a man's fist held an aigrette of peacock feathers at the front of the Sultan's tall, white turban. His golden, jewel-encrusted robes, trimmed in ermine, matched the curtains perfectly. Baba was reassured to see the Sultan's vanity still intact, his eyebrows dramatically arched and darkened with China ink, and his long square beard dyed black.

After exchanging several rounds of polite greetings, Baba revealed the purpose of his visit. As Aimée could not be brought before the Sultan in a public place, only her "dowry" would be presented.

"I bring you twelve Nubian slaves today my lord, a humble gift to accompany one of much greater value," he said.

The elegant Nubians were each carried forward for the Sultan to see, and then removed.

The Sultan simply nodded. Everyone brought him valuable gifts.

"My real gift to you is a treasure so rare, so exquisite, so sublime that parting with it tears my heart to pieces." He dramatically pounded his heart with his right fist, and then sighed deeply. "Yet, those gifts which we hold most dear are the most valuable to give, are they not?"

Again, the Sultan merely nodded and stifled a yawn. *It must be difficult indeed, to part with treasure,* he thought, although he had never experienced this himself.

"As always, your sacred imperial majesty, my gratitude is boundless," Baba said, making a deep bow. "I pray that my gift will help to express this *for* me…that she will bring you boundless pleasures and enrich your life with her beauty, grace and adoration. She is of royal blood from the land of the Franks, with hair the color of spun gold and eyes like sapphires."

The Sultan raised his eyebrows ever so slightly. *Hair the color of gold and sapphire eyes?* His curiosity was piqued, and he shifted his position to signify that more attention was now being paid.

Ah, ha. He rises to the bait, Baba thought. *What man can ever resist the exotic?*

"I confess that were I, your humble servant, richer, younger or more virile, I might have felt worthy to keep her myself. But alas, I am an old man, and that would have been a grave injustice."

This brought the barest hint of a smile to the Sultan's face, for not only was Baba fifteen years his junior, he was also well aware of his cousin's sexual proclivities. It was his duty to know the preferences, weaknesses and strengths of the men who wielded power in his empire, and his cousin enjoyed the particular charms of beautiful young men.

Baba continued, "I have personally entrusted her to the Kizlar Agasi who, I am assured, will present her to you as quickly as possible. It is also *her* wish to gift your majesty with her humble dowry. May I now present that to you?" he asked.

The Sultan nodded, and Baba clapped his hands loudly. With his signal, Janissary guards appeared carrying ten chests of gold and jewels. Each open chest was brought forward for the Sultan to view, which he did without moving a muscle. He possessed entire houses filled to their roofs with such treasure and, although he craved more, the acquisitions always left him unmoved.

When all of the chests had been displayed, the Sultan said, "Thank you, Baba Mohammed Ben Osman, you serve me well. I look forward to enjoying your gift." Then he slowly raised the index finger of his left hand to signify that the audience was over, and two guards rushed forward to lower the front curtain completely.

Feeling pleased that the audience had gone well, Baba was carried out of the Royal presence and rejoined his men in the courtyard. They all looked forward to spending the next month in Istanbul before making the long journey home to Algiers. *I shall miss my little golden-haired angel*, he thought, and sighed deeply. *Maybe I will buy a blonde boy to replace her.*

~ ~ ~

The evening call to prayer found Baba in the mosque of the Hagia Sophia, surrounded by a thousand other Moslem men performing their final prayer ritual of the day. He prayed that Allah would grant him a life long enough to reap the benefits of his efforts. He wished to see his son royally appointed, and Aimée at the Sultan's side.

Baba would have been pleased to know how well she was already doing. Aimée's exotic beauty had caused a stir of curiosity and awe among the initiates, who had given her an exceptionally warm welcome. Her uniqueness drew the girls to her like flies to honey. They vied to dress her hair and show her how to apply kohl to her eyes to enhance their brilliance, arguing over who should get to sleep next to her. Despite the language barrier, which they all seemed to share, their attentions had given Aimée a sense of belonging.

Following her bath, Aimée submitted to a thorough physical examination by a palace physician, her teacher and the chief nurse. All were surprised by the intact maidenhead of this rather mature young woman. Fortunately, Aimée could not follow the discussion that ensued, regarding whether or not to break her hymen before the onset of her sexual training, or to leave it intact for the pleasure of the Sultan. They decided upon the latter plan, making their job harder, but (they hoped) ultimately more rewarding.

What name shall we give her? the Vekil Usta wondered, as she summoned the Kizlar Agasi to her quarters.

"Did you find our new student acceptable?" he asked.

"Surprisingly so," she replied. "Still intact."

"Ah, yes, that had been suggested. Apparently, she spent some years in a convent, which may explain her condition," he said.

"Yes, no doubt. She is physically quite perfect and, of course, unique among the others here. Have you any preferences regarding a name?" she asked.

"Yes, actually. Her benefactor said something to me that has stayed in my mind. He said that should she be brought before the Sultan, her beauty would be embroidered upon his heart forever. Quite poetic."

"Yes, it is," she said. "And a lovely old name...Nakshidil, I believe."

"Yes, exactly," he replied. "Nakshidil...embroidered on the heart."

"Well then, that's settled," she said. "Her lessons begin tomorrow."

Chapter 24

Although eager to proceed with her new life, Aimée felt relieved when she learned that she would not
be entering the harem, or meeting the Sultan, any time in
the near future. She had a lot to learn before she would
be on equal footing with the women of the harem and
was still glad to be cloistered from the realities of actual
sex. She had gone from a Catholic convent to Baba's
home which she thought of as a more opulent, Moslem
convent. Now she lived in a seraglio filled with devotees
to sensual pleasure yet forbidden to participate in actual
sex. This served Aimée well, as she was still opposed to
the idea of sexual relations without the sanctity of
church and marriage. How would she ever come to accept it?

After spending her whole life surrounded by French
people, it felt strange to be the only French woman in
the seraglio. As far as she knew, she might be the only
French woman in all of Turkey. She was living in a foreign country without a guide, translator or map, with
other foreign girls, mostly in the same situation. Their
shared circumstance gave rise to kindness and a warm
camaraderie between them.

Her first day in the school began with a meal of yogurt, fruit and sweet mint tea that would prove to be the

lightest meal of the day. Following breakfast, the rest of the morning was spent learning the Ottoman Turkish language, a compilation of Turkish, Arabic and Persian. Aimée was pleased to discover that her lessons with Mira placed her well beyond the level of most of the other girls.

After a long lunch with an enormous amount of food, the remainder of the afternoon was filled by music, singing and dance classes. In the music class, each girl chose one musical instrument to learn and master. Since the harpsichord did not exist in Turkey, Aimée chose the harp.

When I am queen, she fantasized, *I shall have a harpsichord brought to me from Paris.*

As girls became proficient musicians, they were organized into eight-piece orchestras to accompany dancers. These orchestras performed regularly inside the harem for the Sultan, and occasionally for his guests, playing behind pierced, decorative screens allowing them to be heard without being seen. Aimée was surprised to learn that no foreign music of any type had ever been played within the palace walls—another oversight she planned to remedy when she was able. She quickly picked up the traditional dances that would eventually be performed solely for the Sultan, finding familiarity in the strange, sensual movements.

All of the girls practiced the art of embroidery by embellishing their own clothing with brightly colored flowers, birds and geometric designs. Instructions on grace, poise and personal hygiene went on throughout the day. During meals, teachers corrected girls who sat slumped on their cushions or adopted unpleasant postures.

"Grace is an art that must be practiced until it becomes part of your nature, until you are no longer aware of it and have simply become graceful," the teacher explained.

The teachers never raised voices, made threats of damnation or cracked willow branches across hands. Everything was taught gently, quietly and languidly so that learning itself became pleasurable.

The only private classes were those teaching the art of sexual technique. These were tailored to an individual's needs. Aimée's would not begin until she became familiar and more comfortable with the basic theories. However, group classes on the theoretical art of love took place nightly, following the evening meal. These focused on careful indoctrination to the student's purpose of pleasuring the Sultan. It was the same premise that pervaded everything they learned, continual reminders of their true purpose. By the time they entered the harem, their singular devotion would be focused.

Throughout the day the teacher asked, "Why has Allah placed you here?"

To which the girls replied, "To serve our lord and master."

"How will you serve him?" she asked.

"With beauty and pleasure," they replied.

It was a litany of devotion recited by novices dedicating themselves to one lord. Once again, the similarity between the harem and the convent was not lost on Aimée.

She also discovered that admission into the harem did not automatically mean she would meet the Sultan. That decision belonged to the Circassian Kadine, who might *recommend* her to the Sultan. Without her support, a girl could languish unnoticed in the harem for years— or forever. Gossip circulated constantly about others who had left the school months before and still had not met the Sultan. Baba had been right. In order to rise in the ranks of odalisques, Aimée needed to make the Kizlar Agasi her ally. Only he could introduce her to the Circassian Kadine. Without the eunuch's support, the Circassian Kadine might never even know about her.

Fortunately, the Kizlar Agasi seemed to have his own agenda for Aimée. At the end of her first day, he met with her privately in the Vekil Usta's quarters before dinner.

"I am told that the girls are accepting you quite warmly," he said, speaking slowly so that she would understand.

"Yes, sir. They are very kind," she said.

"You have much to learn here and must do so quickly. Do you understand?" he asked.

"I must learn," she replied.

"Quickly," he added.

"Fast?" she asked.

"Yes. The Sultan is old and grows weak. He has only one son and heir. Do you understand?"

He had spoken too quickly for her to grasp the entire meaning. "Forgive me, sir, I understood 'the Sultan is old'—and the rest?"

"Needs sons," he said pantomiming rocking a baby.

"Oh, children." she said.

"Boy children," he said, indicating the male organ.

"A son?" she said.

The eunuch nodded. It was too complicated to try to explain that during the nine years of Sultan Abdul Hamid's reign he had sired only one boy who lived—Mustapha, now a violent and ill-tempered eight-year old. The other royal sons had all met untimely deaths, most likely at the hands of Mustapha's mother, Nuket Seza. She was a shrewish harpy with one goal, to become Mother of the Sultan, the most powerful woman in the empire. Only then could she order the deaths of her detractors, who numbered in the thousands.

The Sultan despised both mother and son, and the thought of the misfit Mustapha one day inheriting his throne was more than he could bear. In fact, it was one of the reasons why he had become so discouraged and uninterested in everything of late. He was almost seventy years old, and the more he felt his mortality, the more he feared his legacy would disappoint rather than enlighten. Also, the prospect of leaving only one appropriate heir was abhorrent to him. How disastrous might it be if his nephew Selim should die, leaving Mustapha to rule? It tore at the very core of his good heart. His failure to provide multiple heirs was a constant source of grief that made the ruler feel impotent and depressed. The more depressed he felt, the less he desired the company of women and if he could not bed women, neither could he produce heirs. It had become a vicious cycle he was helpless to break.

The Kizlar Agasi also wished for multiple heirs,

since he and Nuket Seza did not share the same political aspirations. After the Sultan's death, should Mustapha ascend the throne instead of Selim, the Kizlar Agasi would no doubt be "retired" from his position, and most likely put to death. He had seen the reason for Nuket Seza's viciousness early on, and become the one she blamed for the Sultan's turning against her. Thus, finding a woman able to sire more sons might very well save his own life.

"I understand," she said, although understanding the words did not explain why the Sultan needed *her* to bear him a son when he already had five hundred wives. *Were they all barren?* She did not know that the Sultan had become so despondent he had not summoned a woman to his bed for almost a year. However, she found it extremely interesting that the Kizlar Agasi's hopes for her to produce a royal heir seemed so certain.

He rose to leave. "I will mark your progress daily. Oh yes, and your new name is Nakshidil. It means 'embroidered on the heart.'"

Again, he had spoken too quickly for her to understand, so she asked, "Your name?"

"No, no," he said pointing to her and saying slowly, "*Your* name...Nakshidil."

"My name?" she asked, her voice rising in surprise.

"Yes. Nakshidil," he affirmed.

She regained her composure and tried to repeat the difficult pronunciation asking "Naksadal?"

"No, Nak-she-dil," he said slowly.

"Nak-she-dil," she repeated.

"Yes, very good. It means 'write on the heart,'" and

he pantomimed the words "write" and "heart," thinking that she would understand the word "write" more easily than "embroider."

"Write on the heart?" she asked.

"Yes, good. Study more Turkish," he said, and left her.

Now she understood why Perestu had said that her name was not real. "Nakshidil," Aimée repeated to herself, then ran from the room to find Perestu, who was lying on her divan playing with a small doll.

"Perestu," she said excitedly, sitting next to the girl and taking her hands, "my name is Nakshidil."

"Nakshidil?" the young girl asked. "What means?"

"Write on the heart," she replied proudly.

Perestu's eyebrows knit together in concentration, and then she smiled. "I do not hear this name before. Must be old name. Good name, Namay," and they both giggled. "Good name, Nakshidil," she corrected.

The Vekil Usta called the girls to dinner, and if Aimée thought that lunch had been excessive, the ten courses she would consume over the next two hours would make it look light. Like other meals, it was served as the girls reclined on divans or cushions, leaning on their left elbows so they could eat with their right hands.

The first course of plump little pastries filled with seasoned meat called *borek* was eaten while the girls gossiped about what had transpired throughout the day. The second course of leg of mutton, browned in butter and roasted, was sliced into thick pieces so tender they melted in Aimée's mouth almost without chewing. It came with a compote of musk-flavored, stewed fruits that she ate separately to savor its heady perfume that remained in her mouth long after she swallowed. It was so delicious she licked her lips in delight and made little sounds of ecstasy in her throat as she ate, not realizing she was doing so until Perestu shot her a warning glance.

A cold drink, unlike anything Aimée had ever tasted, was served to clear the palate and cool the mouth.

"What *is* this?" she asked a nearby teacher, who smiled knowingly and replied, "Pomegranate serbet, sugared water and pomegranate juice that has been cooled with snow brought from Mount Olympus, very far away."

She quickly discovered that serbets were a favorite of the girls and the harem women. They were rarely found anywhere else in Turkey because of the ice required to make them.

The next course was a tiny quail, stuffed with figs and pistachio nuts and browned to a crisp. As the bird was cut open Aimée leaned forward to inhale the fragrant aroma of the escaping steam and purred, "Mmmmmm," in response. She did not think that she could eat any more, until she broke off one little leg and took a bite. The crispy skin surrounded succulent meat flavored with fig, and she managed to eat more than half of the little bird and all of the stuffing. This delightful dish was followed by a refreshing cup of cool yogurt mixed with crushed mint and honey, a dish she had tasted for the first time at Baba's. She would have happily ended her meal at that point, but the next dish turned out to be one of her favorites, couscous with raisins and almonds, followed by another icy serbet of sweetened lime. She drank the serbet slowly to savor its flavor and make it last as long as possible.

Perestu, whose little stomach was stuffed, rolled onto her back to rest and was quickly corrected by a teacher. She rolled back onto her side and propped her head up in the palm of her left hand. "Where you come from?" she asked Aimée.

Aimée thought for a moment, and then chose the answer that she believed would be most easily understood. "From Al Djazāir."

"I know this place," Perestu answered proudly. "How you get gold hair and blue eyes?"

"I think from my father but I never knew him. He died right after I was born."

"Lot of gold hair girls in Al Djazāir?"

"Oh, no. Well, I do not think so. I was born far away on a small island—Martinique."

"Far away?" she asked.

"Yes, very far," Aimée answered, feeling a twinge of sadness. Before it could find its way deeper inside her, Perestu asked another question.

"Your mother bring you here to Sultan?"

"Oh, no. My mother died long ago."

"My mother sell me to feed brothers," Perestu said without any rancor. "Boys more good and can work. Girls not so good." She shrugged her shoulders indifferently.

Aimée was shocked to hear such harsh philosophy from such a young child. She had never thought herself to be of less value than a male, but perhaps Perestu was right. She would have to ponder this later. "How many brothers?" she asked.

"Five boy. Two sister marry." She shuddered and made an unpleasant face as though tasting something bitter. "I like here. Better than marry mean old man."

Better than many things, I suppose, Aimée thought.

"How you come here?" Perestu asked.

"I came by ship…a friend," but she could not find the words to describe her situation, so she simply said, "I am a gift."

Perestu's eyes widened in admiration. "A gift girl? She gift girl," she whispered excitedly to the girls closest to them. They in turn, whispered the news to others and passed it around the room. "Oh, very lucky, Nakshidil."

"Is it?" Aimée watched the girls' expressions of surprise and admiration as the news quickly spread. "I had not thought of it that way." In fact, she realized that she knew nothing about how girls came to be in the harem, assuming that everyone was in the same situation as herself.

"Not all gift girls?" she asked.

Perestu who shook her head slowly and pointed at her. "You only."

Aimée shifted her position to make her pose a little more regal, enjoying her new elevated status. *Imagine that. Baba was right again.*

She would quickly learn that there were many ways to enter the harem: as a gift, to pay debts, by choice as a daughter of noble birth, sold for money, for the purpose of political alliances or through the spoils of war.

The last main course of eggplant stuffed with

ground lamb and almonds arrived with another fruit compote flavored with cinnamon and cloves, both spicy and sweet. A final glass of ice-cold serbet made with fragrant flower essences followed, and Aimée closed her eyes as she drank, inhaling the floral sweetness of jasmine and orange blossoms. A broad smile spread across her face. *This is surely the most delicious meal I've ever eaten.*

Another brief respite followed before the desserts arrived. Although, Aimée had been too full to do more than taste the eggplant, she could not resist the incredible-looking sweets. Tiny cakes covered in sticky, sweet syrup, pistachio nugget, and *halvah* were served with the sweet, dark Turkish coffee she had already learned to crave.

She leaned towards Perestu and whispered, "If we keep eating like this we will be big as cows."

"Just so," Perestu replied nodding her head. "They say the Sultan like big, round woman. I too skinny...must eat more. You too," she added.

"More?" Aimée exclaimed grasping her bulging belly and laughing. "I will burst."

Slaves entered, carrying water pipes for the girls who wished to smoke. Aimée enjoyed the fragrance of the sweet-smelling tobacco that Baba had smoked after dinner. She never tried it herself and still found it foreign.

Theoretical instruction in the art of love followed the meal, as the girls reclined, nibbling sweets, drinking coffee and smoking. Sated and full, they struggled to keep their eyes open and to pay attention. But, the wise teachers didn't mind if the girls appeared tired, knowing that this was the perfect time to talk about lovemaking. The opulence of the dining experience, the sensual foods and silk cushions all helped to create a sexually charged atmosphere. Focusing on this particular subject every evening after such a meal eventually became what the girls looked forward to most. By the time they graduated, they would crave the fulfillment of the acts of love. The school nurtured sensuality, and even on this first day, the trained eyes of the teachers could see Aimée's true nature, despite her modest demeanor and obvious innocence in the ways of love.

Later that evening, as Aimée lay on her divan, she thought about the conversation with the Kizlar Agasi. He wanted her to have a son. He could not possibly know about the old woman's prediction of more than five years ago and yet, he seemed to be placing so much hope in her. *Out of all of these women, he believes I can bear the Sultan a son. It must be another sign of Fate pointing towards my true destiny.* She suddenly understood that her purpose was not simply to be a queen; it was to sire a king.

Chapter 25

Realizing and accepting her true purpose made Aimée an excellent student. Her grace, poise and charm blossomed in the openly sensual society, unlike the unnatural strictures of Parisian society, for which she had shown so little aptitude. Turkish social graces were languid and flowing. They focused solely on the physical rather than the intellectual, and wit, to her great relief, played no part.

The Vekil Usta noted the way Aimée held her head, tilted slightly to one side when she listened, giving her complete attention to every word as if she were listening to the most interesting thing she had ever heard. It made the speaker feel like the center of her universe. Her unique walk, gently undulating her hips from side to side, looked more like dancing, and her soft, throaty laugh took everyone by surprise once it was coaxed out and encouraged. Sensuality pervaded every inch of her, every sound she uttered, every gesture she made, as naturally as flowers exude scent.

Sexuality was another matter. Although fascinated by the forthright approach to sexual teachings, she struggled to escape the perspective of her past and at the end of the first week, still felt embarrassed and resistant.

Hoping to dispel this last vestige of Aimée's personal conflict, the Vekil Usta arranged a private chat.

"You are progressing well in all matters except the sexual arts," she began.

Aimée sat silently, biting her lower lip.

"Are you aware of the consequences of failure in this matter?" the teacher asked.

"I think so. I have heard that girls who fail become servants in the harem," she replied quietly.

"Yes, that is true in some cases. You would not be opposed to this?" she asked.

"It would not be my first choice, but I have been unable to surrender myself to the way in which the art of love is practiced here. I do not seem able."

The teacher thought for a moment. "Well, I think you should know that you are much too valuable to throw away as a servant, Nakshidil. A different fate would await you, one you may not wish to choose."

Aimée frowned.

"You possess extraordinary beauty and grace, Nakshidil. The Sultan would never allow such a treasure to be wasted. He would make you a gift to one of his ministers, someone to whom he owed a substantial debt. Someone like Muzrah Kalif, perhaps."

"Who is this man?" she asked timidly.

"Muzrah Kalif is one of the wealthiest men in Turkey and has enriched the Sultan's treasury quite substantially over the years."

This did not sound like a bad alternative to Aimée. "Why might I not choose him if I could?"

"He is only slightly younger than the Sultan, but unlike our sovereign, he is a cruel man. In fact, several of his wives have died under rather suspicious circumstances...and then there are the others. Of course, a man may do whatever he wishes to a wife, but mutilation seems so extreme."

Aimée showed no response.

"Do you understand mutilation?"

"I do not."

"Ah. It involves cutting away part of a woman's body, the part that allows her the greatest sexual pleasure. It is very painful, horribly disfiguring and often fatal. I tell you this not to frighten you but to educate so you will think very carefully about *all* the possibilities available to you and then choose wisely. You may go."

Returning to the bathing chamber, Aimée immersed herself in the fragrant waters of the *hamam*, weighed down by the thought of a fate she had never before entertained. She realized she was pondering the same problems she had at Baba's: marriage, sin, retribution, fate and God's wishes. Only now, if she did not find a way to accept her new circumstances, she would pay an exorbitant price. She shuddered at the thought of mutilation and what if she was beaten like a slave? She enjoyed the pampering of harem life. Never had she lived in such opulent surroundings, eaten such delicious foods and been attended to by dozens of servants solely devoted to her comfort.

All my life I was taught that sex was a sin outside of marriage. But, which God proclaimed that? Apparently not the Moslem God. Do I embrace my new life more than the old one? I certainly do. If Fate means for me to sire a king, surely that must be God's will too.

Submerging herself completely beneath the warm water, a feeling of relief and excitement ran through her body. *I must embrace it all.*

~ ~ ~

In five months' time, Aimée's newly discovered ability to give herself to pleasure was complete and she had made a life-changing discovery: turning her *mind* fully to any task she chose gave her the ability to master it. This newly discovered power made her feel different than she ever had—willful, stronger and more alive. And after the months of feasting and relaxation, her body had begun to fill out nicely, her hips more round, her breasts full and inviting.

The Vekil Usta was proud of the girl and anxious to exhibit her before the Circassian Kadine. With this in mind, she summoned the Kizlar Agasi to her quarters one afternoon in October.

After gently closing the door, she whispered excitedly, "She is ready."

"Truly?" he said.

"She is magnificent. In twenty years as Vekil Usta, I have seen none that could compare to her."

"Well then, let us allow her three days to prepare for the tests, and I will notify the Circassian Kadine. Pray that she fulfills our every wish. Well, done, Zeyneb," he said, using her given name. "You shall be rewarded well."

She bowed to him as he left to arrange for the tests, then summoned Aimée to her quarters and closed the door to insure privacy.

Aimée was shocked and pleased by the news, unable to fathom how much she had changed in so little time.

"I will assist you with preparations," the Vekil Usta said. "We begin tomorrow after the morning meal and have three days to make ready. There is much to do, so eat and rest well tonight."

~ ~ ~

Aimée found it difficult to sleep at all that night. She lay awake on her divan, filled with excitement, her heart pounding in her ears. She had no fear of the tests, knowing without vanity that she was the most talented student in the school. But try as she might, she could not picture herself with the Sultan. She thought of all the lessons she had learned and tried to imagine what her first night of lovemaking would be like *for her*. In theory, she knew everything that would happen, but perhaps a bit of her old girlhood fantasy remained.

From the age of twelve, Aimée had imagined her wedding night and her husband—but *this* was so very different. How would she *feel* without real passion and love? Perhaps passion and love were the true fantasy. *Think of poor Rose.* Doubt entered her mind and for the first time in a long while she thought of Mr. Braugham, then quickly recovered her senses. *That was never meant to be. This is my destiny. The Sultan holds my fate.*

She wiped her cheek with the back of her hand and shifted her position to focus her mind. *I must take control of the situation and remain in control without the Sultan's knowledge.* To do this she must open to him completely. The most enticing seduction was allowing oneself to be seduced.

I may be considered his property, but I will make him mine.

~ ~ ~

It was the last week of October and the palace gardens were still alive and vibrant, the winter fruit trees heavy with apples, pomegranates, pears and persimmons. The last of the summer's flowers blossomed in a rainbow of colors that would wither and die. Throughout the garden, songbirds swooped from branch to branch, and hummingbirds drank themselves giddy with nectar as if they knew it might be their last feast.

The Circassian Kadine received the Kizlar Agasi in her private garden, with its magnificent view of the Bosporus. Swathed in layers of yellow silk, her long, curly black hair was woven with tiny floral blossoms made of gemstones. Several ropes of diamonds loosely wound around her neck and gathered in a shimmering pile in her lap. Reclining on a gilded divan bolstered by silk pillows embroidered with gold and jewels, she was shaded from the sun by a carved, gilded copula. Had the sun's rays been striking her directly, the Kizlar Agasi thought he might have been blinded by the glare.

The Circassian Kadine's position in the harem was an unusual one. She was the favorite wife of the late Sultan, Mustapha the Third, and mother of his son, Selim, heir to the throne.

Had the present Sultan's mother been alive, she would have held the highest position a woman could occupy in the royal household and the Empire: Valide Sultana, Mother of the Sultan. Out of fondness for his nephew Selim, the present Sultan had raised the Circassian Kadine to that position, installing her in a palace apartment second only in size to his own. It did not take her long to ingratiate herself to the Sultan and become his closest confidant.

The Circassian Kadine and Kizlar Agasi secretly belonged to a small group of liberally minded public officials who wanted to open Turkey to the West, nudging it closer toward a more progressive political climate, while also broadening trade. Turkey's dogged adherence to ancient customs had kept it firmly rooted in the past for hundreds of years. Although the country could boast of many "modern" conveniences, barbaric practices still prevailed. The heads of dead criminals were still displayed on pikes along its roadways, and Janissaries were free to go on rampages, raping, looting and killing those who crossed their paths. Recently, another fanatical fundamentalist religious faction had appeared: The "Wahabi," Desert Warriors. If they gained local support they might join with the cruel and unruly Janissaries to make them even more powerful.

Outside the palace walls, the liberal faction was supported by the wealthy and powerful Mufti Velly Zade. With his influence, money and private army, they hoped one day to overthrow the Janissaries, who had become so disproportionately strong during the last few decades. It was becoming increasingly unclear who truly ruled the Empire, they or the Sultan. As the Sultan's melancholy and lack of interest increased, so did the Janissaries' power.

When the Kizlar Agasi entered the private garden, he dismissed all of the royal handmaidens and slaves who waited there. The Circassian Kadine's sensuous mouth curved into a warm smile, the faintest hint of fine lines appearing at the corners of her dark, almond eyes. Her olive skin stretched taught over her prominent cheekbones on an otherwise unlined face, making her look a decade younger than her thirty-nine years.

"Welcome, my friend," she said.

The intimacy of their friendship allowed them to dispense with polite greetings.

"Wonderful news." he said. "She is ready."

The Kadine's perfectly arched brows raised in surprise. "So soon? She must be as extraordinary as you say."

The Kizlar Agasi could barely contain his excitement. "I tell you, Mihrisah, you will not be immune to her charms. I pray that her European perspective will find expression in our purpose. She could become an invaluable ally, the one we have prayed for." he exclaimed.

"Well, your heart has been captivated, and that is a feat that tells me much. You are a harder nut to crack than Abdul. He is simply bored beyond reach."

"Not beyond *her* reach, I'll wager." He paced back and forth nervously. This was the only place where he could speak his mind freely and allow his true feelings to show. "She begins the tests in three days. Then we must both do our parts to bring her to the Sultan immediately. He is already a little interested by my news of her, but as you say, so uninterested in everything, so melancholy." He threw his hands up in a gesture of frustration. "Pray that she will ignite his fires. She may be our last hope. Most certainly mine."

She absently stroked the strands of diamonds gathered in her lap. "Yes, if Mustapha inherits we shall all die. Yet, prayer so rarely yields results that I prefer to take matters into my own hands."

"Yes, my lady," he bowed. "Your very competent hands."

~ ~ ~

Since their plans would not be revealed unless she won the Sultan's favor, Aimée was unaware that so many people wanted her to succeed as fervently as she herself wished to. For the next three days, she practiced under the watchful eyes of the Kizlar Agasi and the Vekil Usta. She had become quite comfortable with the young eunuch with whom she practiced the arts of lovemaking (in a limited fashion), and on occasion, even experienced an inkling of desire which she secretly hoped the Sultan would kindle even more. The eunuch wore prosthetic male sex organs in place of his own, which had been severed, but Aimée believed the boy would have been overwhelmed with pleasure had the organs been real.

Her determination to succeed allowed her to learn

the art of lovemaking in the same way she practiced her harp—repeatedly until perfected. Repetition had made her comfortable and confident, but she had not yet experienced the *benefit* of the sexual act...orgasm was still theoretical.

For her dance performance, Aimée wore a classic costume patterned after those worn for hundreds of years, made with her favorite rose-colored silk. Transparent silk trousers hugged her ankles beneath a full skirt that ended just above her knees. A gold and silver embroidered girdle with dozens of tiny silver bells cinched the blouse just below her belly, which was now quite a bit larger than it had been when she entered the school. Ropes of silver bells encircled her ankles and jangled at every step. Layers of rose-colored silk veils (that would be removed one by one throughout her dance) swathed her shoulders and breasts and tucked into her girdle. The silk turban that wound around her head would also be removed during the performance to allow her blonde tresses to cascade dramatically to her waist.

During her final dance practice, the music began and she twirled around the dance floor, shimmying her hips, stepping quickly, and making the bells on her girdle tinkle loudly. Then the music slowed and she languidly unwound the first veil, undulating her hips in a circle and using the silk to swirl patterns in the perfumed air around her body. As she moved her hips, she hid her face behind the veil, which she then lowered just enough to peek over, and then cleverly tucked it into the silken sash at her waist. As the pace of the music increased, she emitted an ancient cry with one hand over her mouth, her tongue vibrating against her palate, and deftly removed the second veil. She used this to cover her mouth while she ululated and spun in circles around the room.

When the rhythmic drumming came to a sudden halt, she sank to her knees, spreading them wide and arching backwards until the crown of her head rested on the floor atop the veil that she had dropped. In one quick motion, she unfastened her turban, allowing her long, blonde tresses to spill over the floor around her. From this position, she slowly and artfully removed the last of her veils, exposing the hardened nipples of her pert breasts that pushed against her flimsy blouse. She arched her back, higher and higher, thrusting her breasts into the air and moving her upper body as if it were attached to invisible threads from the ceiling. The Kizlar Agasi held his breath.

~ ~ ~

The final day of practice was devoted solely to testing her sexual abilities. She wore a costume that resembled the one she would wear on her first visit to the Sultan. Four chemises of the palest rose-colored gauze were layered over white silk trousers that fastened at the ankle with tiny pearl buttons. Over this, an azure blue velvet caftan, trimmed in sable, trailed behind her with an eight-foot train. Her hands and feet were decorated with intricate hennaed designs, and the pearl-encrusted pillbox hat that would become her signature style perched atop her hair, which hung loosely to her waist. A rope of pearls, interspersed with sapphires Baba had given her, hung in a loop reaching her knees, and a small sapphire butterfly fastened to her hair beside her right eye, complemented her eyes' dark blue beauty.

The young eunuch awaited her, just as the Sultan would, on a huge bed propped up by pillows. He wore a silk caftan opened in front to reveal his smooth, hairless, coffee-colored skin.

Aimée knelt behind the heavy curtain that hung a few feet from the foot of the bed.

At his signal, two slaves parted the curtain. "Stand," he commanded.

Aimée stood with her hands clasped demurely behind her and her head bowed.

"Lift your head," he said and she did as she was told.

"Remove your robe," he said, and the slaves removed her heavy caftan.

"Remove one dress," he said, and the slaves removed it.

"Turn," he said, and she obliged his command by turning slowly in a circle.

"Remove one dress," he said, and the slaves obliged.

"Another," he commanded, and again the slaves obliged, leaving Aimée now clothed in only one of the sheerest dresses.

"Approach," he commanded, and Aimée stepped onto the footstool and climbed onto the bed. She crouched on her knees, her head bowed to the heavy brocade coverlet until he spoke again.

"Come to me," he said.

She began the slow crawl towards his feet. When she was within range of touching them she stopped and waited for the next command, keeping her face bowed to the coverlet.

"You may touch me," he said and, rather than using her hands, she inched her face forward and nuzzled the arch of his right foot with her cheek. Then she slowly took his big toe into her mouth and gently sucked.

The eunuch groaned with pleasure, as she hoped the Sultan would. Taking this as a signal, she ran her hands up the boy's legs, following with soft kisses up one leg then down the other.

For the next hour, she fondled and teased, tickled and sucked before finally kneeling over him to present her sex to his mouth, as she had been taught. She gasped with genuine surprise as the eunuch lightly flicked the moist petals between her thighs with his tongue before rolling her over onto her stomach and placing a large silk pillow beneath her belly.

She barely had time to register the sensation she had just felt, and wondered how she might feel were it prolonged.

Gently stroking her little bottom with one hand, the boy applied a mixture of aloe and sesame oil to the phallus, then slowly eased it into her behind. This was what the Sultan may wish to do, and she must be prepared. However, the Vekil Usta had given strict instructions not to allow the Sultan's seed to spill in this way. Her womb must receive the seed. The seed must beget an heir.

Aimée allowed the thrusting to continue until such time as she felt the real Sultan would be frantic with desire. She grasped the phallus firmly with one hand to guide it towards the entrance to her womb. Hovering over the phallus, she performed the undulating dance of desire expertly while the tip rested at the entrance to her body. She looked up and smiled at the Vekil Usta and Kizlar Agasi, who stood observing a few feet away.

"Yes, yes, that will do," her teacher whispered breathlessly. "The best student I have ever had. Put on your clothes and come directly to my quarters."

~ ~ ~

When Aimée knocked on the door of the Vekil Usta's apartment, her teacher and the Kizlar Agasi were enthusiastically discussing her performance. Both smiled broadly as she entered. The Kizlar Agasi clasped her gently by the shoulders and smiled down at her, nodding his head. "I have no doubt that you will pass your tests quite well."

"I would not be worthy if not for the guidance you have both given me," she said, bowing.

Ah, if only she remains this gracious afterwards, he thought.

That night Aimée felt a greater sense of accomplishment than she ever had. Her strong sense of purpose had allowed her to accept her new goal, and she had even learned to enjoy it. How much more wonderful was it going to be with a real man? She rolled onto her belly and squealed into her pillow. Very soon she would find out.

Chapter 26

August, 1782

On the following morning, Aimée sat on a large silk cushion, her harp poised on her lap. The Kizlar Agasi, the Vekil Usta and several other women whom Aimée had never seen, reclined, facing her on divans set against the room's three walls.

The door opened and a procession of four eunuchs entered, each carrying a large gold tray piled high with dozens of pieces of jewelry: necklaces, bracelets, rings, belts, anklets and hair ornaments. Aimée had heard that some of the harem wives were so rich they possessed more jewelry than they could wear at one time. In order to flaunt their wealth when visiting other wives, slaves carried their excess jewelry before them. Aimée had dismissed this as outrageous rumor, but here it was, literally piles of priceless jewelry.

And then, the infamous Kadine appeared. Aimée gasped at the sight of her (which fortunately in harem culture was a compliment rather than an insult). None of the rumors whispered amongst the novices could have prepared her for the magnificence of the vision before her. The Kadine's fur-trimmed caftan was artfully embroidered with rubies, diamonds and pearls. With each floating step she took, the cloth shimmered so brightly it appeared to be made of liquid light. Her pantaloons, spun from fine golden threads, were cuffed at the ankles with wide bands of diamonds. A ten-inch wide girdle of solid diamonds, for which she was famous, belted a sheer red silk over blouse. Five ropes of diamonds, each stone the size of a grape, wound around her neck, then fell past her knees. Her jet-black hair was caught up on one side by a bouquet of flowers made entirely of precious stones, and a rope of the same jewels encircled her head. Eight magnificent rings adorned her fingers, and elaborate diamond earrings cascaded past her shoulders. At the center of this splendor was the most beautiful face Aimée had ever seen.

As the sun's rays shone through the glass dome of the ceiling and struck the diamonds, a riot of rainbows danced around the walls, floor and ceiling of the room. For a long moment, Aimée was so completely entranced by the opulence and beauty that she forgot her purpose for being there.

When the glorious vision had settled comfortably on a royal divan, the Vekil Usta nodded the signal for Aimée to begin, snapping her out of her trance.

Although the Circassian Kadine did not show more than a polite outward reaction to Aimée's musical performance, she was moved by the girl's depth of feeling and unusual voice. Each song fed her hope that this young woman would capture the Sultan's heart and renew some desire for life. Unfortunately, many young women of promise had disappointed her during the last few years, so she reserved her hope until she could be more certain of success.

At the end of the day, the Vekil Usta visited Aimée in her quarters and praised her performance, assuring her that the Circassian Kadine had also approved.

~ ~ ~

The final day's tests began with dances, and again the Circassian Kadine arrived in extraordinary splendor. Unlike the calm demeanor she had maintained the day before, her response to Aimée's dancing was animated and spontaneous. As she watched, the heat seemed to rise in her own body, and she signaled a servant to remove her heavy caftan. Her shoulders and head swayed to the music and her eyes never left Aimée. She felt encouraged by Aimée's grace and sensuality, believing that a woman who could dance thus would make love with a similar passion.

Eagerly awaiting the final test, she instructed one of her eunuchs to bring her opium pipe. After she had taken a long inhalation she wished that she could witness this exotic creature actually being deflowered, and thought she might ask Abdul if she could observe their first night's tryst. These were the Kadine's thoughts as the young eunuch entered and positioned himself on the bed, opening his robes to reveal his prosthetic manhood. She took another long inhalation of the opium and wished for the girl's sake that Abdul were thus endowed.

The curtains parted to reveal Aimée and the performance that followed proved to be even more exciting than the Kadine had hoped. The Kizlar Agasi was correct. Here was the little miracle that might save them...the next favorite and with some luck, the next Valide Sultana.

The performance left the Circassian Kadine in a highly aroused state. She took several minutes to compose herself, touching her jewelry and her hair and smoothing the layers of gold silk that enveloped her body. When her breathing had returned to normal, she rose and approached Aimée, extending a trembling hand for her to kiss.

"You are a pleasure to watch," she whispered.

Aimée knelt, completely naked, with her head bowed. "Thank you, my lady."

The Kadine lifted Aimée's chin, tilting her face up to look at her. "How old are you, child?"

"Nineteen, my lady."

The Kadine stroked Aimée's cheek. "That is difficult to believe. You don't look more than fifteen."

Aimée grinned broadly, her heart pounding wildly in her chest. "Thank you, my lady." *She likes me, and she is so beautiful. Oh, if only I were as beautiful.*

"You will join my retinue and reside close to my own quarters so that you may attend me personally."

Aimée loved the thought of being close to the Kadine, although she did not grasp the importance of the invitation.

However, the Kizlar Agasi, who stood beside Aimée beaming with pride, comprehended it fully. The invitation was exactly what he had hoped for. This was the highest honor an odalisque might receive, second only to being the Sultan's favorite. It was an honor that could be neither bought nor traded, as only the Kadine could bestow it. He had hoped the older woman would be charmed, would see the same possibilities in the girl that he saw. *Oh, let her be the one,* he silently prayed. He clapped his hands together with glee, then extended them to help Aimée rise.

The Circassian Kadine looked directly into Aimée's eyes, entranced by their beauty. "Sapphires," she said quietly. "Dress her," she instructed Zahar, who stood close by holding the clothes that Aimée had discarded.

Zahar quickly draped Aimée in the sheer dresses and fastened the fur-trimmed cape around her shoulders.

The Kadine graciously extended her hand to Aimée. While Aimée grinned widely, and the Kizlar Agasi followed a few steps behind, they walked together down the long corridor out of the Cariye Dairisi, through the door that led to the harem.

Aimée had spent months imagining the magnificence that waited on the other side of the door, but at first glance, it appeared to be just an ordinary, long corridor. Concealing her disappointment, she walked with the Kadine as they approached several kitchens, one after another. Passing each bustling room, the Kadine leaned confidentially towards Aimée to explain its purpose. Each time she did so, Aimée inhaled the heady fragrance of her perfume, and smiled.

The Kadine said, "This kitchen is used solely to prepare food for the Sultan."

There were too many cooks for Aimée to count without stopping her progress. They came to a second kitchen.

"This one serves *my* needs as well as those of Nuket Seza, the Baskadine [mother of the first-born son], and her son." She disliked the boy so intensely that she could not bring herself to say his name.

Further along the corridor she explained, "This is where meals for the Kizlar Agasi and other black eunuchs are prepared."

Aimée was amazed to learn that these people all had their own kitchens.

The Circassian Kadine stopped at the entrance to the fifth kitchen. "This is where meals for the Grand Master of the Seraglio are prepared, and right next to it," she continued, "is the small kitchen for the chief treasurer and his officials."

A little further down the long corridor she paused at the door to another small kitchen. "This one is for the personal use of the Chief Cup Bearer and this," she said, indicating the wide doorway of a huge room, "is the general kitchen where the rest of the meals are prepared."

To Aimée, it seemed like hundreds of people were rushing about preparing foods of every kind. She did not yet know that the kitchens employed over three thousand people and prepared more than six thousand meals every day.

The Circassian Kadine explained, "All of the storerooms, cold rooms and serbet kitchens are below, where it is cooler."

"Serbets are my very favorite things," Aimée said, smiling.

"Yes, we all love serbets, especially the Sultan. One day I will teach you how to prepare some special serbets...the Sultan's favorites."

She prepares food? Why would she when there are so many cooks?

The corridor turned sharply to the left, where two other corridors leading off in different directions joined it.

"The rooms for cleaning clothes are there," the Kadine said, indicating the corridor on her left, "and the dressmakers' shops, and shoemakers. The herbalists, chemists, tobacconists and nurseries are that way," she said, indicating the right hallway. "We shall proceed forward towards the hamam."

It seemed like a great maze of endless winding hallways that all looked the same to Aimée, who wondered how she would ever learn her way around.

"You will have little need to visit most of these areas again," the Circassian Kadine said, as if reading her mind. "Except for the baths, of course."

The eunuchs walking before them opened a large wooden door leading to the changing room.

It was ten times larger than the changing room in the Cariye Dairisi, and the clothing that had been discarded was splendid. They passed through and entered the enormous tepidarium where a dozen naked women lay on divans, sipping coffee and eating sweets.

As soon as the women saw the Circassian Kadine, they rushed to her, curtseying and smiling, kissing her hand and offering compliments and refreshments. Barely acknowledging them, she continued speaking to Aimée and walking towards the double doors leading to the baths.

The eunuchs pulled open the doors to reveal a warren of several huge rooms with high-domed ceilings made entirely of white marble. The arched doorways of each room opened onto the main bath area, with a pool fed by a splashing, tiered fountain in its center. Water flowed everywhere from waterfalls, marble fountains and gold sinks with gold faucets in shapes of animal heads from whose open mouths it streamed. Steam rose from the pool, and the unmistakable scents of jasmine, musk and ambergris permeated the hot, humid air. The heady fragrance made Aimée want to strip naked and submerge herself in the pool. Hundreds of women were being scrubbed, polished, shampooed, manicured, massaged, oiled and hennaed by hundreds of slaves.

Aimée had never seen anything like it. It looked like a bustling subterranean city, populated solely by naked women.

As women noticed the royal presence in their midst, they stopped whatever they were doing, hoping the Kadine might notice them. One woman even prostrated herself in a clumsy attempt to kiss her moving feet.

With nothing more than a nod of her regal head to acknowledge any of the women who greeted her, the Kadine said to Aimée, "My private bath is adjacent to my apartments, and I rarely enter here. You are welcome to use that as well, should you desire more privacy. I always find these baths so very busy," she said with undisguised disdain.

Aimée's presence also caused a flurry of whispers, speculating on who she might be. "Look at her hair." one pointed out. "She is a graduate or she would not be permitted here. But why would the Circassian Kadine accompany her when she rarely even speaks to us?"

Speculations flew through the air. By the time the party had departed, a dozen explanations had been born: the young woman was a foreign princess whose father had given her as a gift to the Sultan, she was a distant cousin (of royal blood) of the Circassian Kadine, she was a queen who had deserted her husband and country, etcetera, etcetera, etcetera. Curiously, almost all of the rumors included something about royalty. None came close to the truth of the little French convent girl abducted by pirates, possibly because the elegant young woman bore no resemblance to that little girl.

Before Aimée had completed her traverse of the hamam, two women hurriedly left to report to Nuket Seza. While the Baskadine rarely used the communal harem bath herself, having one of her own, her spies kept her informed of any important news or events that transpired there. Although she did not yet know who the new odalisque might be, she knew of her presence before the hamam door had closed behind Aimée's back. The description of her exotic beauty sent Nuket Seza into a fury. Within minutes, she assembled a dozen women, and instructed them to bring her details, "or else."

The Kadine's party exited the hamam and walked down another corridor that ended at an ornate, copper-clad door. When the eunuchs opened it, Aimée thought that they were about to step outside because the ceiling suddenly climbed to four stories high. Before her was a large, square courtyard surrounded by a three-story building. Wide verandas ran along the front, with hundreds of doors opening onto them. Many of the doors stood open, allowing Aimée a glimpse of luxuriously decorated bedrooms.

"The sleeping quarters," the Circassian Kadine explained as they crossed the courtyard.

Now Aimée understood that they were walking through the living quarters of the harem, and a little chill passed up her spine. *This is where I shall live.* It bore no resemblance to the harem she had imagined, the long, narrow hallway patrolled by armed guards.

They crossed the courtyard, and entered another copper-clad door that lead to yet another corridor.

The Kadine indicated an imposing looking iron door on her right and said, "The eunuchs' quarters. This door is locked each night and opened each morning by the Kizlar Agasi."

Aimée had heard gossip of women carrying on affairs with eunuchs. She had questioned the validity, but now wondered why else the harem guards might need a locked door.

As they continued forward, soft daylight filtered into the corridor through windows that opened to the outside, which were covered with intricately carved wooden lattice, gilded with gold. The lattice allowed light to filter in while preventing passersby any view of the interior.

The Kadine explained that the only men allowed here, other than eunuchs, were the Tressed Halberdiers, who delivered firewood to the harem. They wore two locks of false hair, extending from both sides of their turbans to their shoulders, like curtains, to prevent sideways glances that might reveal an odalisque to their eyes.

"Of course," she added, "any woman encountering one of these men, will make herself quite visible. The false hair does not impede a straightforward glance, and odalisques are starved for attention. Imagine spending all of your time in preparation for the act of love and rarely even *seeing* a man."

A pang of fear made a small knot in Aimée's stomach. She had been so focused upon her goal that she had never considered failure a possibility. Now the Kadine was telling her how common failure was...hundreds of women never even seeing a man. *What if the Sultan does not favor me?* She looked out through the pierced lattice. *This paradise would indeed become my prison.*

The exterior courtyards on either side of the hundred-yard passage were carpeted with thick, green grass and landscaped with exotic foliage, fountains and streams. As they walked, the soothing sounds of splashing water accompanied them. The corridor ended at an ornate bronze double door, guarded by two black eunuchs.

As the party approached, the guards pulled the doors open to reveal a large, round room with cushioned banquettes along its walls and small ornate tables scattered throughout. Sunlight poured through a glass dome in the ceiling, illuminating the smooth white plaster walls. The room was warm and bright, filled with the scent of frankincense. Colorful arrangements of fragrant pink and yellow roses overflowed from large cloisonné vases on elaborate gold stands. Thick Persian carpets cushioned their steps as they crossed the room and passed through an archway into another larger room. These were the private apartments of the Circassian Kadine.

The Kadine dismissed the eunuchs and turned to the Kizlar Agasi. "Shall we dine together this evening?"

"Certainly," he replied. Turning to Aimée he said, "I will see you very soon."

"Please," the Circassian Kadine said, indicating an ornate divan to Aimée. "Before you are shown to your room there is something we must discuss."

The Kadine settled herself onto another divan and clapped her hands. Three slaves appeared immediately, each carrying a silver tray. The first tray held two tiny, gold porcelain coffee cups that the girl carefully set down on the table between the divans. A second slave, whose tray held an ornate *jezve* (coffee pot) inlaid with silver and gold, poured thick dark coffee into their cups. When she was finished, the third servant placed a yellow silk napkin next to each cup and then departed.

Aimée's eyes darted around the room in an attempt to take in the opulent furnishings—richly woven tapestries, gilded furniture, priceless Venetian glass vases and jewel-encrusted boxes. The beautiful face of the Circassian Kadine was more exquisite than anything else in the room.

The Kadine sipped her coffee, then carefully re-placed the delicate cup onto its saucer, and smiled. "You are surely a gift from whichever God one may choose to believe in."

Stunned by the flattering remark, Aimée blushed, and then smiled. "Thank you, my lady."

"You have talents beyond most women in this har-em, my dear, and I want you to know that I am going to bring you to the Sultan as quickly as possible. How much has the Kizlar Agasi told you?"

"Told me about what, exactly, my lady?"

"About the Sultan."

"Oh, I have learned much about our sovereign. I know of his kind nature and his love of wild animals, his enjoyment of music and dance and his fondness for the sensual pleasures of..."

The Circassian Kadine stopped her with a wave of her hand. "Do you know that the Sultan is deeply mel-ancholy and has lost interest in all of these things?"

Genuinely surprised, Aimée replied, "No, my lady, I did not know this." Teachings on the Sultan had not in-cluded weakness or failings of any kind.

"He has no favorites, and only one son," she added. "It is very important that he take an active interest in things again. There are *political* reasons of which I will not yet speak. However, we believe that you may be able to rekindle his interest in private pleasures and through this perhaps renew his interest in other things as well. Do I make myself clear?"

Aimée wondered who the "we" referred to, and re-membered Baba saying that a favorite would have the

Sultan's ear. "Yes, my lady. I believe that I begin to understand."

The Kadine smiled. "Intelligent as well as beautiful," she whispered. She finished her coffee then carefully replaced the cup. "Good. Now let us bathe while your room is being prepared. I think I know exactly what you will like. Come," she said, then clapped her hands for the slaves to attend them.

Aimée did not know whether the latter comment referred to her room or the bath, and did not care. It was obvious the Kadine's taste greatly exceeded her own. She followed behind watching light reflect off the older woman's sparkling robe. Was she walking through a dream? It was just as Baba had said: magnificently beautiful rooms, objects, gardens, clothing, women and jewels. The most important woman in the harem was taking her under her wing, and she might play a different part than she had ever imagined. Filled with expectation, Aimée began to visualize her new role. Not only could she be a favorite and mother, she might become a confidant and ally to the Valide Sultana.

The Circassian Kadine gave instructions to a eunuch, who bowed and then left. The two women entered a small changing room, where four slaves expertly removed their clothing and covered them with sheer linen caftans. Entering the tepidarium, they reclined on divans, sipping coffee and nibbling on almonds with a thin, crunchy coating of sweetened gold.

The Kadine asked Aimée to talk about her life before she entered the harem, and was happy to learn that she had been well educated. She already knew that Baba

Mohammed Ben Osman had been the young woman's benefactor. As a former captain in the Sultan's Navy, along with his fleet of fast ships, Ben Osman could be a powerful ally. Her instincts had been right in believing the girl to be more than just another sensual beauty. She was also clever and well connected. Perhaps she might even prove to be trustworthy. Of all the women who had entered the harem in the last ten years, she was the first to grasp the possibilities of her role beyond its obvious personal gains. *She might be the one.*

By the time they submerged themselves in the fragrant water of her private bath, the Circassian Kadine believed that she had found the key to her success. Although the temptation was strong to seduce her and take her as her own without the Sultan ever knowing of her existence, she chose instead to use her for a higher purpose. She had waited ten years for a woman like this, and another might never come. There would be time enough to satisfy her personal needs. For now, she would enjoy her new protégé from afar while grooming her to blissfully enslave the Sultan. They had precious little time, and so much to secure before he died.

~ ~ ~

After three hours of ministrations in the baths, the Circassian Kadine instructed one of her eunuchs to escort Aimée to her new room.

"I am sure that you will find it satisfactory, but I think you will not be there very long. The favorites have their own apartments, you know."

Aimée curtsied and kissed the Kadine's hand. "Thank you, my lady. I fear that I cannot adequately express my gratitude."

"Oh, we shall find a way in due time, dear one," she said, kissing her lightly on the cheek.

Aimée followed the eunuch down the corridor that led from the Circassian Kadine's quarters to a small, splendidly decorated room. The walls were draped with yards of heavy embroidered silk in shades of blue, and a small cloisonné bowl filled with golden almonds sat on one of the tables. A large wardrobe and carved cedar chest, already filled with her belongings, stood against one wall next to a tall, ornately framed Venetian glass mirror. Egyptian musk smoldered in an incense burner, and a vase of bright red tulips from the Kadine's own greenhouse sat on one of the tables.

Aimée touched one of the petals and remembered the first ones she had ever seen at Baba's. *It seems so long ago.* Her eyes misted with tears as she tried to understand her feelings. Everything was so wonderful...better than she had imagined. But, fear seemed to hover just beneath the beauty and tranquility. She gazed at her reflection in the tall mirror, and tried to glimpse herself in the future. Would she ever be as powerful and assured as the Kadine?

Zahar appeared in the doorway. "Dress your hair?" she asked in Turkish.

"Yes, and lay out my clothes for dinner, please," Aimée replied.

Her thoughts shifted to the present. Tonight she would dine with the women of the harem for the first time. She must dress well enough to impress, but not so resplendently as to incur jealously. She had learned a lot in the last six months, but she had the feeling that her real education was about to begin.

~ ~ ~

Dinner lasted over two hours and consisted of fourteen courses that began with lamb kebabs and ended with coffee serbet flavored with cloves. Many women greeted her and fussed over her hair, as the students had done when she first arrived, but the innocent excitement of the *Cariye Dairisi* was absent. In the harem, competition and jealousy prevented easy acceptance of a newcomer. There was too much at stake to form fast friendships, and women remained reserved until they could learn how much of a threat a new girl might be to their own success.

They asked Aimée many questions while offering little information themselves, and seemed unnerved by most of her answers. The more she revealed the more of a threat she became in their eyes. Had they any idea how much of a threat she really was, they might have banned together and poisoned her on the spot. Nuket Seza's informants asked the most questions and, as they hurried off to make their report, wagered as to whether or not the young woman would live to celebrate another birthday.

Following dessert, many of the women smoked tobacco from bejeweled nargileh, while others grouped together to smoke opium.

"Elixir of the night?" one of them offered, extending the pipe in Aimée's direction.

She politely declined, and joined a group who had gathered to play music for others who danced. Conversation was minimal, and Aimée realized that the language barrier must prove too great for some to master Ottoman Turkish. Many of those women clung together in groups where they could speak a familiar language such as Russian, Greek or Circassian.

Aimée missed little Perestu, and wished that she were there with her. She wondered how long it might be before she would join her in the harem, and hoped it would not be very long. She felt lonely in the unfamiliar crowd, even while playing music. It seemed that once again, her life had undergone a drastic change.

Suddenly feeling exhausted, she laid down her harp and went to her room, where she tossed about fitfully on her divan, unable to drive one niggling thought from her mind. *What if the sultan does not favor me?*

Chapter 27

Sultan Abdul Hamid looked lost among the silk-brocade pillows piled on the oversized bed upon which he reclined. The contrast between his sallow skin and dyed black beard made him appear to be ill, which in a sense, he was. The mounds of sumptuous bedding that surrounded him, embroidered with brightly colored peacocks and tulips, represented two things that had formerly brought him joy to behold.

His dispassionate gaze wandered around the room, coming to rest upon a small vase of dead tulips in a niche in the opposite wall. *How long have they been dead?* he wondered, without taking the next logical step of asking what incompetent servant had allowed them to remain so. Just a few months earlier, that servant would have paid dearly for allowing dead flowers to remain within the Sultan's sight.

The Sultan sighed deeply. *Maybe if I close my eyes sleep will come.* He rolled his head back further onto the mound of pillows, but did not fall asleep. After a few minutes he opened his eyes and began surveying the room as if he had not just done so moments before. This time, he noticed the serving trays holding bowls of dried fruits and nuts that had not been touched. His appetite for food had left him, along with most of his other appetites. He sighed again. *Maybe if I close my eyes, sleep will come.*

The huge bronze door that led to his sleeping room opened, and his chamberlain, the Bas Musahib, stood in the doorway and bowed deeply. He was a short, stout man in his mid-sixties stooped beneath the weight of his responsibilities and one of the only people permitted to address the sovereign directly.

The Sultan did not notice him until he spoke.

"Sire," the chamberlain said, clearing his throat nervously.

"What is it? I'm resting."

"I pray that your majesty is well and that one thousand blessings be bestowed upon you and the illustrious family of Osman."

"You may dispense with further formalities. What nonsense causes you to disturb my rest?"

"Sire, the Divan is in session and would like to know if you will be honoring them with your royal presence today."

"Today is not Friday, is it?" the Sultan asked.

The chamberlain cleared his throat nervously again, and thought in frustration, *the Divan does not even meet on Fridays.* "No, sire, today is Tuesday, and the Grand Vizier has brought new demands of the Janissaries before the Divan once again, but without your council, he cannot approve or disapprove..." his voice trailed off. He had made this same speech to the Sultan for the past five weeks, every Saturday through Tuesday, when the Divan was in session.

The Sultan did not seem to comprehend the chamberlain's words, although he answered with annoyance. "The Janissaries keep their own council, do they not?"

Since this question made no sense whatsoever to the chamberlain, he tactfully replied, "Ah, yes, often they do in fact keep their own council, but in this case, sire, the decision lies with you."

"Not today," he said, with a dismissive wave of his hand that indicated the meeting to be over.

The chamberlain could do nothing but make his exit. He bowed and backed out of the room, shaking his head in disbelief at the problem he faced. What would he tell the Divan? How long could he continue to make excuses for the Sultan's refusal to partake in matters of state? Week after week, he had been lying and fabricating, and he did not know what would happen when they finally called him to account. Meanwhile, the Janissaries had become adamant about getting a resolution, and to show their displeasure, had once again begun the incessant and unnerving pounding on their kettledrums. In the last week they had piled more than thirty severed heads next to the Gate of Salutation. How many more would fall before the Sultan would act? He shuffled back to the Hall of the Divan, entering through the private entrance used only by himself and the Sultan, and wondered what excuse he would make this time. *How will this end?* he asked himself, pursing his lips and shaking his head sadly from side to side. *To whom can I turn for help?*

~ ~ ~

Shortly after noon, as the officials of the government's Sublime Porte were leaving the Hall of the Divan, the Kizlar Agasi entered the apartments of the Circassian Kadine as she sat at her loom, weaving.

"Terrible news," he said. "Once again, the Sultan did not attend the Divan, and the Bas Musahib is pleading with *me* to do something. It has been three weeks since the Janissaries have presented their demands, and the council is unable to respond without the Sultan's approval. Three weeks. Those heathens are murdering people in their beds!"

The Circassian Kadine stopped her weaving, and sighed. "Well," she said, and then sat in quiet thought for a few moments. "If he becomes any more despondent I fear the Janissaries may openly revolt. Let us move our plan forward immediately. Arrange for her to dance for him tonight."

The Kizlar Agasi nodded his head enthusiastically. "Yes, Mihrisah," he said. "Yes. We must do *something*."

"Bring her to me at once."

The Kizlar Agasi rushed from the room and within minutes reappeared with Aimée.

"May we dispense with formalities?" the Kadine asked.

"By all means, my lady."

"You are going to dance for the Sultan tonight," she said.

Aimée drew a sharp breath. "Tonight?" She had only been in the harem for two days and thought she would be given ample time to prepare for this occasion.

"I realize that this is sudden," the Kadine said. "But certain events bring great urgency to our situation. I assure you that you will be furnished with all you require, and I will personally insure cooperation of the royal presence. Are you prepared, child?"

"I shall be, my lady," she replied. Inside, her heart was pounding. *Tonight?*

"Good. I would like the dance of the seven veils. The costume that you wore for your test will do nicely, and I will add some jewelry."

Aimée's heart and mind were both racing. *I must calm myself. Consider only what is necessary to make my performance perfect.* "May I ask if I will be required to perform any other entertainments?"

"That is our hope. Pray that his majesty wishes it. I will do what I can to encourage this. With that as our intent, you will perform in his majesty's bedchamber rather than in the Hall of the Sultan." She turned to the eunuch and said, "Bring my Kutuchu Usta [herbalist] to me at once."

As the Kizlar Agasi left the apartments to fetch the most senior harem herbalist, the Circassian Kadine began pacing back and forth, speaking aloud to herself.

"We must be sure that he is awake enough to see you dance and to respond, but he must be relaxed enough to not resist. A euphoric, that is what is needed...a euphoric aphrodisiac...rhinoceros horn—but with what? The Kutuchu Usta will know. Now, my dear," she said to Aimée. "You must prepare yourself. Use my private bath, and I will send my hairdresser and beauticians to you. When you are attired, come to me and I will give you final instructions. You will begin as the sun sets."

~ ~ ~

Aimée spent the remainder of the day in preparation for the night she had been awaiting for six months. She was bathed, shampooed, manicured and waxed. Her skin was scrubbed with a mixture of ground almonds, honey and yogurt until it felt like alabaster. Her entire body was coated in a mixture of rice flour, sesame oil and fragrant oils. The paste was allowed to dry, then washed off with bowls of warm floral water. Perfumed oils were massaged into her skin as she lay on a heated marble slab.

Throughout the ministrations, Aimée focused her attention on her goal, and rehearsed her dance in her mind. She was not afraid of failing in her performance, and hoped that it would elicit the desired response. She must do everything she had been taught to arouse his desire. Everything.

After being scrubbed and polished, her hair was dressed, her nails and toenails dyed with henna, and the intricate henna designs drawn on her hands and feet were renewed with a fresh application. Kohl was used to darken and extend the shape of her eyes and, finally, she stood over a smoldering brazier of fragrant ambergris and musk to scent her entire body.

One hour before sunset, Aimée arrived at the Circassian Kadine's apartments.

"You are splendid," the Circassian Kadine pronounced, reaching out her hands to hold Aimée's. "An angelic vision. Come, I wish to give you a special adornment."

They walked to a dressing table that held a small, sandalwood box inlaid with mother of pearl and gold. The Kadine opened the box, and withdrew a long rope of the thinnest gold interspersed with dozens of diamonds.

Letting the piece of jewelry dangle from her fingertips, she said, "Take off all of your clothes."

Aimée did not understand why she should need to undress to put on a necklace, but did as she was told. When she was naked, the Circassian Kadine stepped forward so that their bodies touched and reached around her waist to fasten the diamond chain behind her back. The string of diamonds encircled Aimée just below the waist and slipped down to rest on her hips. The Circassian Kadine knelt down and carefully turned the belt so that the clasp fell just above the nether lips, trailing a string of six large stones that lay between them.

"Oh," Aimée exclaimed looking down at her body, "I thought it was a necklace. It tickles."

The Circassian Kadine held Aimée's hips and looked up from where she knelt. "Yes, that is its purpose. As you dance, the stones bring on your arousal so that your desire may match the Sultan's. It is also quite enticing when it is finally revealed. May it bring you luck and the adoration of the Sultan," she said, her voice heavy with desire.

Aimée was either too naïve or so entranced by the

delicate beauty of the belt that she did not notice the Kadine's heightened state of emotion. "Thank you, my lady."

The Kadine remained on her knees, staring at the object of her desire. It was so close; she had only to move her face forward a few inches to kiss the virgin lips. She abruptly rose and adopted an officious tone to chase the wanton thoughts from her mind. *I must focus on the higher purpose.*

"You may dress," she said without looking again at Aimée's naked body. "I have prepared a potion for the Sultan, which I will bring to him shortly. It will take effect by the time you are halfway through your dance. He should be quite aroused by the time you finish, but may appear to be sleepy or tired. He may even mumble his words or speak unintelligibly, but do not let this dissuade you. Even if he does not command it, you must display yourself to him fully. Do you understand?"

"Yes, my lady."

"If he merely gestures, without speaking a command, go to him anyway, crawl to his feet and proceed as you have been taught. Do not let his tiredness dissuade you from your purpose. And this is most important...should he not be firm enough to penetrate your maidenhead, use this yourself," she said reaching into the pocket of her jeweled girdle and extracting a small marble penis. "Allow your blood to drop onto his manhood, and he will never know."

Attempting not to show her surprise, Aimée took the small replica and tucked it into a pocket in her girdle. A feeling of fear and revulsion began to grow in the pit of her stomach. *Break my maidenhead myself?*

Unaware of Aimée's thoughts, the Kadine continued. "When you remove your girdle hide it in your hand, and then secrete it in the folds of his bedclothes. I know you will succeed," she said, grasping Aimée's shoulders and kissing her lightly on the lips. "Report to me immediately afterwards. The Kizlar Agasi will escort you up the Golden Path."

The "Golden Path" to which the Circassian Kadine referred was nothing more than a long corridor leading from the private apartments of the favorites directly to the Sultan's bedroom. It was the path taken by all odalisques and favorites to liaison with their master.

The Kizlar Agasi walked before Aimée, turning around several times to deliver last minute instructions. "Pay no attention to his tiredness, should he seem so, and do not let protocol keep you from your goal." He appeared more nervous than Aimée. "He will remember very few details tomorrow, but let us pray that he remembers you."

Two heavily armed eunuchs guarded the massive bronze doors that led to the Sultan's sleeping chamber. As they approached, the Kizlar Agasi spoke one brief command and they pulled the doors open.

At the far end of the room, the Sultan lay among his pillows, wearing a dark green robe trimmed in ermine. He had been propped up enough to appear to be sitting, but his head drooped lazily to one side and hung over his shoulder. The Kizlar Agasi backed out of the room and closed the doors. The harem musicians, who had preceded Aimée into the room, began to play. The Sultan straightened his head with some effort and opened his eyes wide to see what was going on.

Aimée took a deep breath, releasing her hold on the marble phallus hidden within her girdle. There was no time for thought now, no time for sinking into the sorrows of her past, no time for regret. She had made her choice, and there was no other.

Lifting her head high, she spun effortlessly around the room and, purely for effect, pulled off the dark purple veil that covered her hair, allowing the long, blonde tresses to fall free. This elicited the desired response, as the Sultan leaned forward slightly to get a better look. He followed the hypnotic swaying of her mane, then signaled for her to remove the veil that covered her face. When the veil was discarded, she beamed a smile directly to him, hoping he would notice her blue eyes. He squinted to see her more clearly, then leaned back against his pillows.

The dance was long and complicated, designed to titillate and arouse. At the halfway point, Aimée noticed the Sultan's shoulders swaying slightly and his head tilting from side to side. Whatever potion the Circassian Kadine had administered seemed to have taken effect.

Aimée shimmied her hips as she spun around the room faster and faster, shaking the little bells on her girdle and gracefully unwrapping the second-to-last veil from her body. Then the music stopped as she sank to her knees and spread them wide. At this the Sultan leaned forward and opened his robe. She arched her back and brought her hips forward, bringing her pelvis down towards the floor. The Sultan seemed entranced.

He had seen the same dance performed many times, but not by one such as this.

The slow rhythmic drumming became a heartbeat to which Aimée's hips moved independently from the rest of her body. Still on her back, the crown of her head resting on the floor, she arched her back higher as she shimmied her belly and breasts. The pace of the music increased, and the musicians cried out their ancient call, vibrating their tongues against the roofs of their mouths.

Aimée slowly twisted up to a standing position, arranging herself for the Sultan to see her profile. Then she rolled her body back and forth in a wave that began at her knees and reached all the way up to the top of her head. She moved so fluidly it looked as if she did not have a backbone. The music played faster and faster, and she began to spin wildly, ululating shrilly. When the music stopped abruptly, she sank to her knees again, spreading them even wider than before. She slowly peeled the last veil from her body, sliding it away, then teasingly holding it between her parted thighs, like a curtain, raising and then lowering it, exposing and then hiding herself. By bringing her knees together then apart, she allowed the Sultan intermittent glimpses of her sex, adorned with the glittering diamonds, through the transparent trousers.

The Sultan reached between his legs and stroked himself, whispering something that she could not hear.

She removed her girdle and secreted the small penis in her hand. Then she unfastened the flimsy trousers, which fell away from her body, exposing her open sex fully to his view.

"Come now," he whispered hoarsely, making a beckoning motion with his right hand. Her advisors had been right. The old man did not stand on protocol when he was aroused. Seeing her climb onto the bed, the harem musicians quietly made their exit.

Aimée began the slow crawl to the Sultan's feet, and could see the tip of his withered sex poking through the folds of his open robe. His eyes looked glazed and he mumbled things that she could not understand, but she did not stop her forward progress until she had taken one of his feet in her hand and nuzzled it to her face. She ran her tongue along its arch, then took the big toe between her lips and circled it with her tongue. The Sultan moaned and reached down to grasp her hair with his hands. He allowed the flaxen curls to fall through his fingers, looking on in wonder. He slid down onto his back, and pulled her on top of him, bringing her sex to his mouth to lick her.

Despite the old man's unappealing appearance and intoxicated state, her body responded. She knelt over him, holding his head in her hands to thrust her hips against his mouth. She had never felt anything like this, and fought not to lose herself in passion's grip. Reaching back to feel him, she was pleased to find that he was hard. She turned around and took his member in both of her hands, to bring it to her mouth.

The Sultan drove a finger deep into her bottom and moaned loudly.

When she thought that he was ready to spill his seed, she straddled him and guided him into her body. A searing pain shot up her spine, but she bit her lower lip and continued to press her hips down onto him. She looked down to see her blood trickling onto his testicles, and gasped in pain as he began thrusting into her harder and faster, controlling the movement of her hips with his hands, until his entire body shook with pleasure and he screamed, "Ahhhhhyy yaaaaaa."

The old man collapsed onto his pillows, his member immediately becoming flaccid and slipping from Aimée's body. For several minutes he lay on his back with his eyes closed and his mouth open wide, breathing hard. As his breath began to return to normal, he opened his eyes and noticed Aimée, who had carefully dismounted and was kneeling beside him. He touched the blood on the inside of her thigh, fascinated by the dark, scarlet streak against her milky white skin. Then he slowly raised his eyes to meet hers. Surprised by their deep sapphire color, he smiled wanly.

"Blue eyes? Hmmmm." He closed his eyes and drifted off for several moments.

Aimée was not sure if he had fallen asleep. Her throbbing pain took all of her attention, as she waited for a sign of consciousness from him.

A moment later, he opened his eyes sleepily and whispered, "What is your name?"

"I am called Nakshidil, sire."

"Nakshidil?"

"Yes, sire," she affirmed.

"You have given me pleasure, Nakshidil. You may go now," he said, closing his eyes.

Aimée bowed her head, retrieved the marble phallus from its hiding place, climbed off the bed, and gathered her clothing into her arms. She put on her robe and gingerly began to open the door. As soon as the guards saw the door move, they pulled it open all the way and looked in on the Sultan, who appeared to be sleeping soundly.

Aimée wiped the tears from her face and bit her lower lip to keep from crying more. She walked as quickly as she could to the apartment of the Circassian Kadine and found her reclining on a divan, smoking a nargileh that filled the room with the pungent smell of opium.

"My sweet child," she whispered, smiling as if she had just awakened from a lovely dream.

"It is done, my lady," Aimée managed to say, as her legs gave out beneath her and she sank to the floor. Having been so focused on preparations for the evening, she had not allowed herself to feel any of the fear or anxiety that would normally have accompanied the monumental act of losing her virginity. Now that it was over, a wave of sadness rocked her body as she realized her girlhood was gone. She was now a woman. She covered her face with her hands and sobbed as confusing emotions assaulted her—thinking of her Aunt Lavinia, Mother Superior, and Father Christophe, a lifetime ago. *I am unwed. No priest has given the Lord's blessing. I have entered into an unholy union. I do not love him, and he does not even know who I am. I am ruined.* Feeling utter despair, she sobbed harder. *I am alone and, surely, God has also forsaken me.*

As she collapsed, the Circassian Kadine clapped her hands and shouted, which brought three slaves and two eunuchs running into the room. "Tend to her," she commanded, frightened that something terrible had happened. What had that foolish old man done to the girl to cause such upset?

One of the eunuchs picked Aimée up in his arms and laid her down on a divan, where she curled into a ball and cried into the silk pillows.

The slave girls brought coffee and a nargileh filled with opium. They fanned her with large peacock-feather fans as she cried harder than she had in many months. All of her strength left her as she gave in to the unexpressed emotions she had secretly harbored since entering the seraglio. Her release was so powerful that after several minutes, her sobs began to subside. When she was once again in control of herself, she propped herself up onto her left elbow and took a sip of coffee. She had chased away the old demons by reminding herself that she was no longer a child.

Wiping her tears away with the back of her hand, she smiled wanly at the Kadine. "I am all right. It was just a shock, I suppose."

"Of course. I understand. Would you like to smoke? I find it very soothing."

"No, thank you," she declined.

"What did he do to you, child?"

"Nothing more than was expected. He was quite aroused, and I did not need to use this," she said, handing her the marble phallus. "Afterwards, he asked my name."

"Asked your name? Really? That is very good. He must have been pleased."

"Yes, my lady. He said I had given him pleasure, and then fell asleep."

"He said that to you?"

"Yes, my lady."

"Excellent, child, excellent. You are the first in many months. Would you like some?" she asked again, offering the long pipe.

"No thank you, my lady. I would like very much to bathe and then sleep."

"By all means. Use my bath and we will speak in the morning. Come to me after the morning meal," she said drowsily, and closed her eyes.

~ ~ ~

Aimée sat beneath a steaming hot waterfall in the Kadine's bath, allowing the water to cascade over her head and shoulders. She must never allow sad thoughts about her past to intrude again. It would do her no good, she told herself, to long for the impossible. She was truly a woman now, and life was going to be different. She must remain focused on the future and hope that her efforts to please the Sultan had been successful. *Mother Mary, uphold my purpose.* She immediately blushed at the blasphemous prayer. *How can Mary still be mother to me?* The tears returned despite her resolve. The Holy Virgin had always brought her comfort. Well, she would find other sources of comfort now.

A little while later, curled up on her bed, she used a little trick she had invented to help her sleep. She imagined herself in the future, bedecked in the finest clothes and jewels, sitting upon a golden throne with an infant son in her arms. The vision always filled her with joy—sometimes it even brought tears of happiness to her eyes. She smiled contentedly, and then slept soundly, neither stirring nor dreaming.

When she awoke in the morning she noticed a small bloodstain on her gown and as she rose from her bed, felt a slight trickle run down the inside of her left thigh. She smiled to herself and fixed the cotton cloths that she used during her moon times. Then she ate a small breakfast and went to see the Circassian Kadine.

Chapter 28

When she entered the Kadine's apartment that morning, a very different woman greeted Aimée. The Kadine was gracious as usual, although businesslike, firing a stream of questions. She wanted to know every detail of the previous night: *Was the Sultan awake? Did he smile? Had he become hard? Had he penetrated her maidenhead himself? Did he cry out?*

Aimée's answers appeared to relieve the Kadine's anxiety, and she began to relax. "You are the first in a long time to elicit such responses," she said.

The Kadine clapped her hands and a slave appeared with a tray of coffee. She poured two servings into tiny gold porcelain cups, and handed one to each woman.

"Well," the Kadine said with a smile, "we shall see what gift he sends. That will tell us much."

"Does his majesty always send a gift following a night of pleasure?"

"Only if he is pleased. The more pleased, the greater the gift." She raised her eyebrows and sipped her coffee, realizing that she was as nervous as if she herself was awaiting word from the Sultan.

"Let's bathe together this morning, and I will leave word to notify us immediately should a gift arrive for you."

Aimée hoped to receive a splendid gift, and wondered what might happen in the event that she did not. "Should I not receive a gift, my lady, will I be called upon again?"

"That is difficult to predict," the Kadine lied. "But it is far too early to become concerned. The Kalif is not even awake at this hour. Come. Let's bathe."

The two women spent the entire morning in the baths, speaking very little while enjoying the pampering ministrations of the well-trained servants. Afterwards they ate their mid-day meal together in the Kadine's apartment and made light conversation to pass the time and cover their nervousness. However, by then, both had begun to doubt the eminent arrival of a gift.

They had just finished their final serbet of pears and roses, when Zahar burst into the room unannounced, carrying a small, beautifully wrapped package. "My lady," she said breathlessly, handing it to Aimée, "For you...from the Sultan."

It was a small package wrapped in fuchsia silk, and tied with thin, shimmering ropes of silver. Aimée unwrapped the silk to reveal a small sandalwood box set with mother-of-pearl. She admired the intricate carving and design, examining it carefully on all sides then holding it up for the Circassian Kadine to see. "Isn't it lovely?"

Almost bursting with anticipation, the Kadine said, "The box is not the gift, I hope. Open it, dearest."

Aimée slowly lifted the top off the box and gasped. It was filled with sapphires. There must have been fifty stones of every shape and size. Her mouth dropped open as she held the box for the Kadine to see.

Instantly, the Kadine's face transformed with the magnitude of her smile, as her hand flew to cover her heart. "Oh, my dear. My dearest dear, you have done it. You have won him. He has never given such a gift. Never."

Aimée gazed at the gems, filled with excitement. "They are so beautiful. What does this mean, my lady?"

"It means that he will send for you again and…" her voice trailed off because her thoughts were coming faster than she could speak. "Summon the Kizlar Agasi at once," she said to Zahar. Then she turned back to Aimée. "I have much to tell you, my dear."

While they awaited the arrival of the Kizlar Agasi, the Circassian Kadine began a new phase of Aimée's education by explaining the Sultan's descent into lethargy.

It seemed that until a few months earlier the Sultan had been active in affairs of state and interested in all aspects of the Empire. Although, following the Ottoman tradition of the last two hundred years, he did not physically participate in any military enterprise; his wisdom guided the Empire's continual wars on many fronts. But a crushing darkness had descended upon him of late, and every attempt to spark his interest had failed—until the previous night.

Aimée bit into a fig. "Maybe he is just tired of women with black hair."

"Or perhaps he is simply tired of being Sultan," the Circassian Kadine replied.

"Well, if that is so, what can one do? Does our government make provisions for such a thing?" Aimée asked.

The Circassian Kadine tilted her head to one side and studied the girl. "What a fine mind you have to even think to ask such a question."

Aimée was flattered, but did not understand why a simple and logical question should elicit such a response.

The Kadine took a deep breath and considered whether it was time for her to say what she was thinking. Deciding in the affirmative, she let out a long sigh. "I will speak freely because it seems you have won the Sultan's favor. I believe that you can play an important role in the future of the Empire." She paused to sip her coffee and let her statement take effect and then continued.

"I came to the seraglio when I was nineteen years old—a gift from my father, who was governor of Nalchik province in Circassia. As the eldest of four girls and with no brothers, I stood to inherit all that belonged to my family when I married. For this reason, my father had educated me well. I understood the machinations of governments, ours as well as others that were different from our own. Had I been a man I would have followed my father as the next governor. Because I was not a man, I chose to do the next best thing. Circassia had been under Turkish rule for a hundred years without any representation in that government. The Turks did not care that Russia threatened us continually. I gave myself in an attempt to protect my country."

Aimée was fascinated. "And was it so?" she asked.

"Yes, Circassia was protected while Mustapha Sultan lived, and for the first six years of Abdul's reign. But he has become weak with age, and the Janissaries have become stronger. Circassia will prevail. It is Turkey that concerns me now."

"Please, my lady. Tell me about the Janissaries. I know very little."

"The Janissaries are taken as young boys of seven or eight from Christian families. They are converted to Islam and trained for many years to make them fearless warriors. They believe themselves to be the keepers of the Faith, and call themselves the 'Soldiers of Allah.' They go into battle with war banners displaying inspirational quotes from the Quran. Their allegiance is to Allah first, and then to the Sultan. Within the palace, they function as guards, and in the city as police. The Sultan's army is made up of Janissaries. They are not castrated, like eunuchs, but until recently were required to be celibate and to live apart from everyone else. Even though they may now marry and have children, they still choose to live apart and sleep, eat and converse solely with each other. Their exclusivity and separation causes them to form unusually strong relationships with one another. In many ways, the lives of the Janissaries are much like those of the women in the harem." She paused for a moment to allow the last bit of information to sink in.

"Over the last few decades the Janissaries have become increasingly more powerful, influencing the decisions of the Divan and going so far as to make war without the consent of the Sultan."

"What might happen if the Sultan's own army turned against him?" Aimée asked.

"In the past, they have deposed Sultans whose policies displeased them. Now they number slightly more than forty thousand. When they are angered, they show their displeasure by beating their huge copper cooking pots. They turn them over and empty out the food, to signify that they reject the Sultan's rations, then beat on them like drums. You can hear them from some parts of the seraglio. They ride into the city at night and slaughter infidels, Christians and Jews mostly, but often anyone who crosses their path. They sever the heads and stack them outside the Gate of Salutation to remind the rest of us of their power."

Aimée covered her mouth with one hand. The violence was shocking and seemed incongruous in the place that she had come to think of as "paradise." This might explain why the French called the Turks "barbarians."

"At the moment, the Janissaries have a list of demands that were brought before the Divan five weeks ago. Due to the Sultan's lack of interest, he has not attended that assembly in almost two months and the council is unable to vote on the demands without the Sultan. If he does not act, the Janissaries will simply do as they please, so you see why it is vital that we find a way to rouse him from his lethargy and take command."

Aimée nodded, but could not shake the gruesome picture of a pile of severed heads.

"In the past, Janissary revolts have taken the lives of thousands of people as well as Sultans," she added.

"And in answer to your question, there is no *government* provision for a Sultan who simply loses interest. However, there is a long tradition of Sultan's being 'retired' permanently, either by ambitious members of their own families or members of the government. In this case, there are two factions who would like to do exactly that, one being the Janissaries and the other being Nuket Seza.

"Nuket Seza, the Baskadine?" Aimée asked.

"Yes, unfortunately, the Baskadine. Her son, Mustapha, is only eight years old, but she has already fashioned him into a contemptible little monster. This is another unfortunate harem tradition for women seeking power. She would like nothing better than to rule through him, and should something happen to my son, Selim, little Mustapha would become Sultan. Nuket has managed to eliminate all other potential heirs; ten of the Sultan's newborn sons and two favorite Kadines."

Aimée's eyes widened in disbelief. "How could she?"

"Poison or suffocation. She made several attempts to poison Selim, and almost succeeded once. That is why I employ my own food taster, you know. She has also aligned herself with the Janissaries, who have the power to eliminate both the Sultan and Selim. If a child sultan were on the throne, the Janissaries would have total power to rule, you see. Nuket Seza knows nothing about politics, but a great deal about treachery and self-interest. The Janissaries would snap her like a twig, but she's too stupid and power hungry to see this, and thinks she can rule them." She sighed deeply. "Were I more like her I would have had her removed long ago. I certainly should have. But I care more for politics than treachery. Unfortunately, they often go hand in hand."

"I had no idea," Aimée murmured, shocked by the violent turbulence that simmered beneath the utopian ambiance of the seraglio.

"Of course not," the Kadine said sarcastically. "Women of the harem are not concerned with such things. Ha!"

"She murdered ten children and still lives? It does not seem possible."

"Almost the same number of girls were killed as well, my dear, but probably by their own mother's hands."

"But why? I cannot imagine taking the life of an innocent child, any child...and my own? I have never heard of such a terrible thing."

"Girls have no value here, except to give birth to boys. Infanticide is an unfortunate tradition used to insure the ascendance of one's own child. Try to imagine how it might feel to be one of hundreds of insignificant bees in a hive suddenly given

the chance to become queen. This is what happens when a harem woman gives birth to a son."

Aimée was amazed she'd not had the slightest inkling of this other world within the seraglio. Apparently, her education up to this point had been carefully designed to paint only a partial picture of luxurious, sensual bliss and days spent enriching oneself in the arts and preparing one's body for pleasure. The Circassian

Kadine exposed a ruthless underside—power-hungry women who stopped at nothing to achieve their own ambitions. If the Sultan chose to favor her, she would need to be a great deal more than a pampered wife and mother, idling away her days in luxury. Her role would be infinitely more complicated than she ever imagined. It might also be a lot more interesting—and a lot more dangerous. *What was it the old witch said about my son's throne and the blood of his predecessor?* She was trying to remember the words when the Kizlar Agasi entered.

"Did the gift arrive?" he asked.

"Behold," the Circassian Kadine said indicating the ornate little box.

The Kizlar Agasi closely examined the contents of the box, then squealed in his high-pitched voice, "I knew it, I knew it!" Then he did something that he had never done. He knelt before Aimée and gathered her into his arms, bestowing kisses all over her head. "My little angel," he whispered. He took her face in his huge hands and brought his own very close to look into her eyes. "Now our real work begins," he said, and touched his forehead to hers.

"I have already begun to explain," the Kadine said.

"Good, good," he said, rising to his feet. "I will call on the Sultan and discover what I can. Stay here, Nakshidil. I shall return shortly."

"He is very fond of you," the Kadine said with a smile, as the Kizlar Agasi left the room.

"He has been extremely kind for one who frightened me so in the beginning."

"You must understand that we have had many disappointments. Girls arrive for the Sultan almost every week, more than five hundred in ten years, and *none* has been favored. Without a favorite we have no ally, and what is worse, with a Baskadine like Nuket Seza we have an enemy."

"My lady, may I ask how you believe I may be of help in influencing His Majesty?"

"The Divan meets on Saturday. Your role is to ask that he allow you to accompany him there."

"To the Divan?"

"Yes. You must convince him that your greatest desire is to see him in his role as leader of the Empire, wielding power over the council. We hope that he is still vain enough to welcome the chance to exhibit himself so. He will secrete you in the 'Eye of the Sultan,' behind a pierced wall where you may see without being seen."

Aimée remembered Baba telling her about this private place in the Hall of the Divan as a way they might make contact.

The Circassian Kadine continued. "The Kizlar Agasi, who is an important member of the council, will initiate the vote on the matter of the Janissaries petition. It will pass in the presence of the Sultan, which is all that is required."

"Do you mean that the Sultan does not actually need to vote on the matter?" she asked.

"That is correct. The council has already made their decision. It is only necessary for the Sultan *to be present* when they declare their decision."

"The Sultan is merely a figurehead?" she asked in astonishment.

"Not always, but fortunately, in this case, yes."

"Then who truly rules?"

"That is an excellent question," the Kadine replied with a cryptic smile, and said no more.

The Kizlar Agasi came loping into the room, breathless from his haste. "Tomorrow night!" he exclaimed. "He wants to see you again tomorrow night. I have not seen him so excited in years. He would see you tonight, but fears that it is too soon to be able to perform properly. He has already begun to prepare himself as we speak. Oh, what good fortune. Allah be praised."

Chapter 29

In preparation for Aimée's second visit to his bed-chamber, Sultan Abdul Hamid did not intend to imbibe a potion containing opium, as he wanted to be wide-awake to enjoy his luscious new odalisque. However, following the advice of his personal Kutuchu Usta, two aphrodisiacs would be added to his favorite ambergris serbet. He remembered the young girl's golden hair, sapphire eyes, and little pink blossom between her legs. Just thinking of her sparked the fire in his loins, a fire whose coals had been cold as ice for far too long. He felt alive.

He called for his chamberlain, who appeared almost instantly.

"Sire?" he said, bowing.

"Have my stallion saddled. I wish to ride out to the sea."

"Immediately, Sire, it is done," he said, running from the chamber. As he fled, he grabbed the arm of one of the eunuchs and shouted excitedly, "Alert the Kizlar Agasi. The Sultan rides to the sea!"

By the time word of the Sultan's wish had reached the royal stables, the entire palace knew the old monarch had been brought back to life by the new odalisque.

Nuket Seza's spies brought the news to her in her private bath, where she was being massaged. In response, she shoved her masseuse out of the way and heaved her corpulent body to an upright position where she sat clenching her teeth, her face distorted in deep concentration. Despite the seven years she had been in the harem, Nuket still struggled to speak the Turkish language. She haltingly asked, "Old sultan leaves bed to ride?"

"Yes, my lady. They say he appears to be recovered and quite well."

"Miserable little bitch whore," she screamed to no one in particular.

Such behavior had prevented Nuket Seza from gaining favor seven years earlier. Initially, the Sultan had assumed her ranting and raving to be a result of her pregnancy. He supposed that some women did not handle pregnancy all that well but after her second outburst in his presence, he simply stopped sending for her.

When she bore his first son, the Sultan was elated. He immediately decreed that Nuket Seza should have private apartments and all of the things befitting her new position of Baskadine, mother of the first-born son.

When the baby was three months old, the Sultan sent for her once more, and was dismayed to discover that the post-partum Nuket Seza was even worse. She seemed to be in a permanent state of agitated dissatisfaction that caused her to rage, abusing her servants and wreaking havoc everywhere she went. Fearing infanticide, she forbade everyone contact with her child, excepting his Sutnine [milk mother]. During visits to his father, the boy screamed and flailed his tiny arms when being held, quickly alienating the disappointed Sultan.

The only thing worse than the way Nuket Seza treated servants was the way she treated her child. When he cried, she beat him until his Sutnine could take him from her, out of earshot, where she tried to comfort and quiet him. By the time he had become a toddler, he cringed like an abused dog at the sight of his mother and hid from her whenever he could. This only enraged her more so that when she found him she beat him even harder.

At the age of three the boy began to hit back and Nuket Seza found this behavior enormously entertaining as well as admirable. She brought the two-year-old son of one of her servants into her household so that Mustapha would have someone smaller than himself to abuse. When the servant saw the bruises on her son's body she brought him to the Kizlar Agasi, who removed the child and his mother from Nuket Seza's household, sending them away from the seraglio with a generous pension.

From that time forward, the Kizlar Agasi systematically removed Nuket Seza's abused servants and replaced them with ones dismissed by others for misdeeds and bad behavior. Being in service to Nuket Seza became a threat that hung over the heads of servants should they misbehave.

As Mustapha grew up, his behavior became so appalling that the Sultan had not laid eyes on him for four years. Nightmares disturbed Mustapha's sleep, unless he swallowed an opium pill before retiring, and by the

time he was eight years old, he had come to depend upon and look forward to his brief, nightly respite from the
hell in which he lived.

After receiving the news of Aimée's success, Nuket
Seza emerged in a rage from her bath. Mustapha
dropped the toy soldiers with which he had been playing and ran to hide in an old, unused ventilation pipe
that had not yet been discovered by his mother.

Nuket Seza saw the pile of soldiers on the floor, with
heads and limbs torn from their bodies, but could not
locate her son. After searching in all of his known hiding
places, she collapsed onto a divan that groaned beneath
her weight.

"Bring me Arak, you useless, lazy whelp!" she
screamed at one of her young serving girls.

Arak was an anise-flavored liquor that was, like all
forms of alcohol, forbidden by Islamic law. Despite its
prohibition, many odalisques enjoyed an occasional
dram. Nuket Seza was the only one who drank until she
became incoherently drunk.

She flung a half-empty bowl of almonds against the
wall, where it smashed into dozens of pieces. "I want
food, you stupid curs! Now. Bring me pilaf and mutton
and fish. I want fresh fish, not stinking garbage like you
give me last night. Fresh, you hear me?" she screamed,
as her frightened servants ran from her rooms to the
kitchen.

She ate and drank gluttonously, muttering to herself
and trying to choose the best way to eliminate her new
competitor from a menu of imagined scenarios. Fortunately for Aimée, Nuket Seza did not possess the intelli-

gence required to concoct a sophisticated plot. However, her lack of intelligence was replaced by hatred and determination.

~ ~ ~

Oblivious to the plot against her, Aimée prepared for her second visit to the Sultan. She summoned one of the harem jewelers, recommended by the Circassian Kadine, and together they designed an extraordinary use for the Sultan's gift. The sapphires would be strung onto long chains of gold so fine as to be invisible. These strands would be woven into her loose, blonde hair to look like they had been showered upon her, which indeed they had been. The jeweler and his assistants worked all day and all night to complete the order, and when the strands were fixed in place the effect was spectacular. As her hair caught the light, the stones moved and sparkled. To complement their beauty, Aimée instructed the harem dressmakers to design an ensemble of sapphire blue silk embroidered with golden threads. Next to her skin she wore a transparent gold silk chemise through which her rouged nipples pressed like little rubies.

The Circassian Kadine had insisted that she wear the diamond belt, since it had brought her such good luck, and once again, fastened it around her naked body. If she could not possess the girl, she could at least devour her loveliness with her eyes.

Delighted by Aimée's unique design for the sapphires, the Kadine said, "Clever girl. The effect is quite extraordinary."

She reached her hand out to touch one of the jewels, and Aimée tilted her head so that it would shift away from her grasp. The Kadine laughed as the sapphire dropped away from her fingers but did not fall.

"I am sure that His Majesty will approve. Now, this evening you must try to engage him in conversation and direct it towards the council meeting on Saturday. It is vital that he attend."

"Yes, my lady."

"Oh, yes, I forgot to ask. Where are you in your moon cycle?"

Aimée thought for a moment and calculated in her mind. "I will bleed in another two weeks," she said.

The Kadine's eyes widened with delight. "Excellent, my dear, excellent. You must pay close attention to your cycle from now on." She held the girl's shoulders and placed a kiss on her forehead. "Go now, and report to me before you retire."

As Aimée made her way up the Golden Path, the Saray Usta, charged with recording all odalisques' visits to the sultan, wrote the name "Nakshidil" and the date of her visit in the register reserved for that purpose. She had entered it for the first time on the morning following Aimée's first visit, as it had been a spontaneous copulation, rather than a scheduled one. Should a pregnancy occur the book would either prove or refute royal paternity.

This time, in order to prolong his pleasure of her, the Sultan closely followed the protocol that Aimée had been taught. He had her undress very slowly, discarding one piece of clothing at a time, telling her to turn her body this way and that, and to strike various seductive poses. The sapphires fascinated him and his delight in their beauty seemed to animate his face more than Aimée had seen on their first night. *Or perhaps he is not so drowsy*, she thought.

When she mounted him, he told her to face him as he reclined upon his pillows. She wrapped her legs around his waist, and leaned forward to place kiss after kiss on his face and head, allowing her hair to spill over him like a golden waterfall. She reached behind herself, encircling her thumb and middle finger around the base of his member where it entered her, and gently squeezed to increase his pleasure. He moaned and she squeezed harder as his thrusts became faster. His hands held her hips, pulling her down harder onto him as he drove himself deeper into her.

Aimée responded with honest enthusiasm, and suddenly lost herself in a sensation that began in her toes and seared through her body until it burst into a million stars that poured from one small point between her legs. Unable to control herself, her whole body vibrated as she cried out in unison with the Sultan, who continued thrusting his hips against the very spot from whence the stars had burst.

They collapsed simultaneously, Aimée's body going limp and slumping down onto him as his flaccid member slipped from her and the warm fluid slowly trickled out.

Totally unprepared for what she had just experienced, she struggled to regain her composure. Fearful that she may have offended him, she whispered, "Forgive me, Sire. I was overcome."

He tenderly moved her hair aside and looked into her eyes. "Forgive you?" He was so out of breath he could hardly speak. "Nakshidil, you fill my heart with joy." He took one of her hands and placed it over his pounding heart. "For this, I will thank you, not forgive you."

The fact that he had given her pleasure, had made her shriek with ecstasy, gave him a sense of manhood he had never felt before. The wonderment of shared pleasure filled him with excitement.

She laid her cheek against his chest, her body still tingling from the orgasm, and smiled to herself. *He may not be young and handsome, but I love the way he makes me feel.*

The Sultan sighed. "You shall be rewarded well."

She straightened herself and remained sitting astride him. "My reward, Sire, is to be with you."

The old man's face softened into one of the sweetest smiles she had ever seen, and for a moment she thought that he might cry.

"Well, then, you shall have an apartment next to mine, and we shall both have our fondest wish."

Aimée hugged him and planted kisses on both cheeks, both eyelids, his nose and his forehead. "Thank you, Sire. That would please me greatly." She rested her forehead against his and smiled broadly. "There is one thing that I would ask of you, if I may," she added.

"Ask anything, little one."

"I would enjoy seeing you as you are in the Divan, dressed in your finest attire and leading the men of the government."

The Sultan laughed. "What an odd request. To see me in the Divan?"

She nodded her head.

"Well, that is easy enough to grant. You may accompany me to the Divan when we meet next. Let me see…on Saturday."

"Thank you, Sire."

"You may not speak or make your presence known," he cautioned.

"Of course, Sire."

"The Kizlar Agasi will explain the procedures and escort you." He stroked her hair and smiled at her curiously. "The Divan, of all things."

A short while later, as Aimée returned to the Circassian Kadine's apartments to make her report, she thought, *why, he is just a sweet old man.*

The Circassian Kadine and Kizlar Agasi were thrilled. In just four days the extraordinary young woman had breathed new life into the Sultan and restored their hope for the Empire. It seemed the ally they'd been hoping for had finally arrived. In two nocturnal visits, she had attained the stature of Haseki Sultana [favorite], with her own apartment, bath and retinue of servants. It was a meteoric rise, the likes of which had not been seen since 1541 when the Ukrainian odalisque Roxelana wed Sultan Suleiman the Magnificent, making him the first Ottoman Sultan to ever legally marry. More than two hundred years later, Roxelana's legend was still discussed with reverence among the harem women.

~ ~ ~

Later that evening, Aimée returned to her little room in the harem where she would sleep for the fifth and last time. She lay awake on her bed, excited by having experienced the "wave of love" as the girls in the *Cariye Dairisi* called it. Mutual satisfaction was a concept that had been whispered about, but never taught in the school. Before tonight, Aimée had found lovemaking enjoyable in the same way as dancing or singing, both of which allowed her to express herself from a deep emotional place. But regardless of how good her performance might be, neither singing nor dancing ever produced the exquisite sensation she'd experienced in the Sultan's bed. Now she understood why women risked their lives for pleasure. She squeezed her legs together and giggled at the memory of the intense sensations, remembering the way his member felt inside her body. Oh, she wanted to feel that again and again. She wished she could go to him right now. How would she ever be able to wait until he sent for her again?

Her body was so aroused and excited that she had a hard time falling asleep. She stretched out sensually on her back and replayed the scene of her recent lovemaking over in her mind, loving every moment, without the slightest fear it might not continue. How could she know how truly lucky she was to be leaving the room in which she slept, for the safety of her own apartment? Nuket

Seza's minions were already reaching out to the harem guards they knew to be bribable. The Kadine and Kizlar Agasi hoped that in her new apartment, the Sultan's personal guards would be above the *bahis*, the bribes that Nuket Seza would offer. If they were not, all would be lost.

Thank you for reading *The Stolen Girl*. If you enjoyed the book, please consider leaving a review on the site where you purchased the title.

Only the Best,
Zia Wesley

Coming soon, Book II in The Veil and the Crown series
The French Sultana

(Excerpt follows)

The Veil and the Crown
Book II

Chapter 1

Following a short period of drunken and confused
deliberation about how to best eliminate the new favor-

ite, Nuket Seza settled upon the plan she always chose. She would poison the girl's food. Her personal Kutuchu Usta (herbalist) reminded her that serbets were the easiest food to alter since they were not cooked. One simply added the poison to the glass before it was served. Nuket remembered using a poison serbet in her attempt to rid herself of the Sultan's annoying nephew, Selim, and would have succeeded had the Circassian Kadine's meddling Kutuchu Usta not administered an antidote so quickly. She smiled to herself and thought, *the new little whore does not have a Kutuchu Usta who can interfere, does she?*

"Poison her in the hamam," she told her herbalist.

As the woman left to do her bidding, Nuket Seza congratulated herself, confident that her problem would be solved and the new girl would soon be dead. But shortly before the noon meal, her spies reported that Nakshidil had not returned to the baths.

"She bathes privately with the Circassian Kadine," they said, cowering away from her reach lest she strike them.

"Old Kadine," she growled. "Meddling whore."

She considered this information carefully. If the girl couldn't be poisoned in the baths, she would have to die during one of the meals.

The Baskadine lolled in her private pool, trying to decide at which meal she should eliminate the girl, when another of her spies burst in with even more disturbing news. Nakshidil had been summoned to visit the Sultan for a second time.

"Second visit?" she exclaimed. He had not summoned any girl for a second visit in many years. Her mind began to spin wildly out of control. She hauled her substantial girth out of the water and stomped angrily back and forth along the pool's edge. "Arak!" she screamed.

Within minutes a servant arrived bearing a bottle and a small crystal glass. Without interrupting her frantic pacing, Nuket Seza knocked the glass from the servant's hand and grabbed the bottle, tipping it to her lips to drink deeply. "Must kill the little whore fast," she muttered aloud.

Swallowing another gulp, she made her decision. Since serbets were not served at breakfast, the first opportunity would be the following day's noon meal. She summoned her Kutuchu Usta, and instructed her to poison Nakshidil's first serbet on the following day. Feeling pleased with her own cleverness, she flopped down onto a divan and finished off the remaining Arak then passed out, to her servants' great relief.

Had she known Nakshidil would leave the harem for her own apartments, she would certainly have poisoned her morning yogurt instead. But Nakshidil's promotion occurred so quickly that by the time Nuket Seza rose from her inebriated slumber the following morning, the new favorite was already gone.

The Baskadine fumed. It would now be much harder to slip poison into *anything* she ate because her food would come from her private kitchen, served by her own servants. It was going to cost her a fortune to bribe the people she needed to do the job now.

Her blood pressure rose quickly along with her anger. Her face turned crimson and her head began to throb. The foiling of her plans was bringing on one of her horrendous headaches, and she shrieked in response, sweeping all of her glass unguent bottles from their shelves with one huge arm, sending them smashing onto the floor.

Upon hearing the breaking glass, Mustapha ran to his special hiding place. His mother searched frantically. When she could not find her son, she flogged one of her servants instead, and then forced her to drink the poison intended for Nakshidil. Within minutes, the servant's contorted body writhed on the floor in agony. Watching the woman's painful death seemed to be the only thing that finally enabled the Baskadine to calm down. When the death throes ceased, she summoned her eunuchs to remove the body.

The suspicious eunuchs asked politely how the woman had died.

Nuket Seza casually shrugged and replied "Must have eat something bad."

No one in her service who knew the truth would ever dare to tell although others would no doubt suspect.

~ ~ ~

Had Abdul Hamid been more like his predecessors, he would have had his gardeners strangle Nuket Seza and Mustapha long ago. That was the method preferred by Sultans for hundreds of years to rid themselves of treasonous officials, unpleasant wives, and relatives who might one day pose a threat to the throne. But Abdul

Hamid thought the practice barbaric, and had never employed it himself. He disliked murder almost as much as the *Kafes* [cage] in which he had resided for fifteen years before assuming the sultancy.

The Cage had originally been designed as a way to protect heirs from the traditional practices of fratricide and infanticide. It was a tall, narrow, three-story brick building, void of windows on the ground floor. Once incarcerated within its walls, all contact with the outside world was forbidden. Deaf mutes served as guards, cooks and servants. If an heir came of age while residing there, a few odalisques were admitted—and remained imprisoned. No education, culture or entertainment was allowed and the heir was kept ignorant of political and current events. No human contact or nurturing was provided. As a result, a boy might be incarcerated at the age of seven and released at the age of forty to assume the sultanship—most often, as a deranged lunatic. Ottoman history was filled with the horrifying deeds of such men.

When Abdul Hamid was incarcerated, he was fortunate to have been thirty-five-years old, well-educated and quite cultured. Still, fifteen years of deprivation left its mark, mostly in that it prevented him from incarcerating Mustapha. However, had he known of Nuket Seza's intentions to kill Nakshidil, he would surely have made an exception for her, as well as her son.

Ignorant of the brewing storm, the Sultan happily installed Nakshidil in the third largest apartment in the palace, conveniently connected to his own by a secret passageway directly behind his massive bed. He ordered the Kizlar Agasi to oversee the furnishing of her apartment, and notified the Chief Treasurer to begin paying Nakshidil a generous monthly stipend. The Kizlar Agasi would advise the new favorite on how to best invest her fortune. He would also manage her properties and those of any children she might bear. Through the coming years, although she knew nothing of it yet, Nakshidil would amass a large fortune in her own right.

After the Sultan finished giving orders regarding Nakshidil, he notified his chamberlain of his intention to ride out to pray in the Hagia Sophia mosque that evening. It was a time honored custom for the Sultan to pray in one of the city's public mosques on Fridays. Abdul Hamid had not done so for six months.

On such an occasion, a large retinue of ministers, important women of the harem, and the Grand Vizier accompanied him. The Sultan's horse was covered in jeweled cloths for all to see, unlike other public appearances when the tall-feathered turbans of the eunuch guards blocked him from view. Quite often, as many as ten thousand citizens and foreign visitors crowded into the First Court to watch the procession.

Given their first opportunity to leave the harem in six months, the women rushed to prepare themselves. They primped and preened, bathed and scrubbed, hennaed and coiffed, then donned their finest clothes and jewels, despite the fact that they would be completely covered.

Nakshidil and the Circassian Kadine would not attend the march to prayer, preferring instead to organize the new apartments. However, Nuket Seza took advantage of the occasion to be "seen" in the Sultan's presence. Everyone knew that the woman who walked in the most honored place, directly behind the Sultan's horse, was the Baskadine, mother of the first heir. Consequently, she spent the entire day in preparation, devoted two full hours to the choice of her ensemble, and finally settled on her gaudiest purple ferace. The unfortunate result was startling. She looked like a huge, glittering eggplant.

As the procession passed through the Gate of Felicity towards the mosque, Nuket Seza followed closely behind the Sultan's horse to insure her vaulted position. Out of breath, and trotting to keep up, she strained her neck in a futile attempt to see over the horse's rump. She huffed and puffed, grateful when the Sultan's horse stopped a few yards from the steps of the mosque. Bracing her hands on her chubby knees, she bent forward to catch her breath, as the stallion lifted his tail to drop a steaming pile of dung at her feet.

The Sultan understood instantly, maintained his composure, smiled broadly and nodded at the gathered crowd.

Her bejeweled kid slippers now splattered with manure, The Baskadine summoned her eunuchs with one shrill command. They quickly surrounded her to shield her from the snickering crowds, and made their way back to the seraglio.

~ ~ ~

Knowing that Nuket Seza would be infuriated by Nakshidil's new appointment, the Circassian Kadine mobilized her loyal spies within the harem to learn of any factions aligning themselves against the new favorite. Certainly, there would be other women resentful of a girl who had captured the Sultan's heart in just five days, when they had spent years being overlooked. Nuket Seza might easily enlist these disgruntled women to support her in some act of jealous retribution. To safeguard against this, the Kadine carefully instructed Nakshidil's new eunuch guards, and chose a trustworthy Kutuchu Usta to serve her personally.

The Circassian Kadine then summoned a small army of palace artisans—upholsterers, furniture makers, glass blowers, carpet sellers, and drapers—to Nakshidil's new apartment. The men were led through the harem blindfolded, and received by women who were completely covered. Eunuchs, outnumbering the craftsmen three to one, stood guard as the new occupant chose suitable furnishings.

At one point, Nakshidil entered into a discussion with a furniture maker who did not seem to understand her request.

"A chair," she repeated for the third time.

Turning to the Circassian Kadine for help, she asked, "How do I say 'chair' in Turkish?"

"There is no word for chair because we do not have such a thing. Of course we had chairs in Circassia." She stopped to think for a moment. "Perhaps we might draw a picture of one to illustrate."

Together they drew a chair resembling the Rococo style that had been fashionable in Paris during Aimée's visit. It was square, with a high backrest, ornately carved and gilded in gold leaf, with a plump, down-cushioned seat. She wished it to be upholstered in deep magenta velvet.

The furniture maker looked at the sketch and asked, "And the purpose of this piece is?"

"To sit upon," Nakshidil replied.

Mystified, the man simply agreed. It was not his place to question the Sultan's women, and he had fashioned stranger objects for other odalisques. He would be well paid whether or not the things he made were useful or comfortable.

"I would like two chairs," Nakshidil said to the artisan.

"So that you may sit with me when you come to visit," she added to the Kadine.

~ ~ ~

That evening the Kadine instructed Nakshidil in the protocol and attire required for her visit to the Hall of the Divan on the following day. She must wear a plain black ferace and yasmak so as not to be visible through the pierced wall. The Kizlar Agasi would escort Nakshidil and secrete her within the "Eye of the Sultan," before leaving her to join the council. In order that her presence remain unknown, she would enter through the private door used only by the Sultan and his chamberlain, prior to the council's arrival.

Due to her early admittance, she would not observe the elaborate processional entrance made by the Divan members and the Sultan. Therefore, the Kadine described the procedure that had been followed for three hundred years. Just after daybreak, the council members of the Sublime Porte, as the government was called, gathered in the First Court with their retinues of clerks and guards. According to Ottoman law, each man was attired in the robe, turban and boots specified by his rank. Uniforms comprised a rainbow of colors, with feathers, furs, turbans, conical hats and a wide variety of swords, knives and weaponry. Group by group, the members slowly marched five hundred yards across the courtyard to the Gate of Salutation. When the entire group had assembled at the gate, they proceeded into the Second Court, where as many as ten thousand Janissaries, gardeners and gatekeepers stood to watch them walk by. Passing into the Second Court, the officials formed two long lines, making a pathway for the Grand Vizier and the Sultan into the Hall of the Divan. As a sign of reverence, the men stood with their arms crossed over their chests and downcast eyes that never looked directly upon their sovereign.

Once inside the Hall of the Divan, visitors were always overwhelmed by its opulent splendor (which was its purpose). The floor and walls were gilded in pure gold, and set with hundreds of precious jewels that glittered and sparkled in the sunlight that poured through the glass-domed roof.

~ ~ ~ ~ ~ ~

Journey to the End

In 1972 a woman I barely knew gave me a book she said I must read. It was written by an English woman and published in Great Britain in 1954. The book was a compilation of four separate stories, each a biographical essay of one woman. The common thread was the fact that they had all lived extraordinary lives in different parts of the Middle East during the eighteenth and nineteenth centuries. Two of the women had actually lived disguised as men. Each story captivated me but one had an unusual effect. As I read, I felt as if I were watching a movie, remembering rather than learning of it for the first time.

That particular story was about a young woman named Aimée Dubucq de Rivery. It was only 31 pages long, but I never forgot it. In fact, over the years, I fully expected someone to make it into a movie. Eventually, I loaned the book to someone who never returned it and because of its age (and no internet), I didn't find it again until 1987.

I was in London on vacation and on my way to the Victoria and Albert Museum. I was walking alone, on a narrow cobbled street, when I stopped suddenly without knowing why. I looked around and noticed a tiny old bookshop across the street and immediately crossed and went in. "Do you have a copy of *The Wilder Shores of Love?*" I asked, "I believe I do," the elderly gentleman replied, and within less than a minute, I was holding it in my hands.

Upon rereading it, almost twenty years later, I experienced the same strange effect. Once again, I tucked it away when I got home and went on with my life.

Another ten years passed and in 1997, my life took an unexpected turn. Following a devastating dispute with my long-time business partner, I walked away from the company I had founded and made successful. I was unprepared for life without a sixty-hour workweek and retired to my very remote little farmhouse in Crestone, Colorado. For the first couple of years, I did all of the things I'd never had time to do: created huge vegetable gardens and grew all my own veggies, learned how to can and pickle, refinished and repurposed old pieces of furniture, painted, landscaped, opened a tiny antique business in a local co-op, read voraciously, meditated, and did lots and lots of Yoga. I was busy, creative, happy and feeling quite pleased with my life when one morning I awoke as if someone had shaken me and yelled in my ear, "Get up! You need to write."

I made myself a cup of coffee, sat down at my computer and began to write. I was watching a scene like a movie and simply wrote what I saw. "The sun was just starting to set on the island of Martinique, when two young girls crept silently out of their room at Trois Islets plantation. Wearing only their sheer cotton night gowns, they made their way across the expanse of manicured lawn and into the foreboding jungle." The girls were Aimée and her cousin Rose and the story of their lives had just begun to unfold.

From that moment, for the next two years, I wrote an average of ten hours a day. I wrote as fast as my fingers could type without hesitation. At the end of each day I would excitedly relate what had happened (what I had discovered) in the story. I had never written a novel, and had no training in that area although I had written six non-fiction books between 1981 and 1995. Throughout the two years of writing Aimee's story, whenever I became unsure of what happened next or who a new character might be, I would close my eyes and sit quietly until the images and information came to me. In this manner, I believed I was imagining events and characters that made the story work. It was not until a year later, in my third year of writing the book, that I discovered these imagined characters and events to be true. For the first two years, I did no research what so ever on the story. When I began investigating, I was shocked to find the very things I had "imagined."

While sharing this information with my daughter, we began to consider the possibility that Aimée wanted her story told and might somehow be providing the information. Her life had been spent within the walls of the Harem of the Sultan of Turkey from the age of nineteen to the day she died. Despite the enormous contributions she made to Turkey and the world, very few people ever knew her name...even in Turkey. Due to the influence of this one woman, the Ottoman Empire was saved from Napoleon and adopted Western methods of warfare that allowed them to defeat Russian invasion. Through her and her progeny, the Empire opened to Western culture, music, dress, furniture, art and food and began its emergence into the modern world. Some would say she might have caused its downfall by these very acts.

In 2008 after completion of what I considered to be the first book, life got in the way of art and I put it away. I did not open it for four years when I'd decided to see if I thought it was worth resurrecting. After working diligently for the past year, it is finally finished.

Last month, while researching background on some of the Sultans, it occurred to me that I did not know the exact date the Ottoman Empire ended. When I looked it up, it happened to be my exact birthday, March third of an earlier year, 1924. Wow, I thought, that's a funny co-incidence. I wondered who the last Sultan was. In another minute I'd found him and when I saw his photo, my eyes filled with tears. That's odd, I thought, why am I crying? When I looked at his dates of birth and death, all the tiny hairs on my arms stood up. He died in August of 1944, exactly nine months before I was born. I sat there, staring at his face and crying, feeling sad, grateful, excited and incredulous. I believe this is the person who wanted the story told because when he died, Aimée's story died with him. He was the last Sultan of the Ottoman Empire, Abdul-Majid Kahn II, the blue-eyed great, great, great, great, great, great, great, grandson of Aimée Dubucq de Rivery, Nakshidil Sultana.

About the Author

Zia Wesley (Hosford) is the best-selling author of six non-fiction books on natural beauty and cosmetics.

Her latest books in this genre include: *Zia's M.A.P. (Master Anti-aging Plan) to Basic Skin Care, Zia's M.A.P. to Growing Young* and *Zia's M.A.P. to Men's Skin Care.* They are currently available online through all of your favorite e book sites.

The Stolen Girl is Zia's first historical novel.

You can follow Zia on her website and social media for updates and more information about the Veil and the Crown Series.

Website
www.ziawesleynovelist.com

Facebook
www.facebook.com/zia.wesley.1

Twitter
twitter.com/ZiaWesleyNovels

Pinterest
www.pinterest.com/ziawesleynovels/

And email Zia to sign up for all her social media outlets
zia@ziawesleynovelist.com

65919602R10213

Made in the USA
Middletown, DE
06 March 2018